Hot Stepmom Summer
A Lesbian Novella Collection
I-V

Hot Stepmom Summer Series: The Collection
M. L. Sexton
Copyright© 2023 M. L. Sexton

M. L. SEXTON

I Wanna Give You Your Flowers

3

Prologue

Bzzz! Bzzz!

Lakyta groaned as her phone vibrated on her nightstand. Looking at the bedside clock, it was only 6:30 in the morning. She could hear the rustling downstairs of her teen son, Cason. Her phone vibrates again as she rubs her eyes and tries to sit up. She rolls her eyes when she sees it's her best friend, Kayla. Kayla has never called her this early. As she's about to answer, she hears something crash on the floor downstairs as her son screams for her.

"Mom!"

Lakyta drops her phone and bursts out the door and flies down the stairs. She makes it into the living room as Cason turns to look at her, tears streaming down his face. She looks at the television to see Kayla reporting breaking news of the war going on in Iraq. Then the doorbell rings. She slowly turns to look at the door and can see through the frosted glass two officers standing on the other side. Her heart begins to race, threatening to burst through her chest. On shaky legs, she takes one step at a time to the front door as the doorbell rings again.

Cason sniffles behind her and begins to sob as she turns to look at him. Her cheeks are wet, having not noticed that she was crying, too. Then all sound was drowned out by her heartbeat as she opened the door to see two familiar faces, and she knew what

4

they were going to say. Their mouths moved as they spoke words that didn't reach her ears. They rushed forward as she crumbled to the ground, and everything went black.

When she came to, one officer was sitting beside her as the other was consoling her son. Lakyta tried to sit up but quickly went back down from the dizziness.

"Ma'am, please take it easy. I know how hard this is. Lieutenant Barnes was a good man and an even better soldier."

"What happened?" Lakyta asked. The soldiers looked at one another, deciding on how much they should tell her in front of her son.

"Ma'am, I think this would be best to discuss in private,"said the woman officer who was sitting next to Cason.

"I'm sixteen! What the hell happened to my dad?" Cason screamed.

"Cason, come here sweetie," Lakyta beckoned. He stood up and stalked over to her. She was now sitting up and he sat beside her laying his head on her shoulder.

"Well," the male officer hesitated, "he was close to successfully finishing a mission. He and his team were on their way back when they hit a landmine. There was nothing left of the humvee." Lakyta couldn't breathe as Cason stilled next to her. Mike never would've even made it to the infirmary.

Even though they had been divorced for ten years, Mike was still a huge part of her life, and she still had love for him. He was a hands-on father, even from across the ocean.

A few hours after the officers left, many of the neighbors came by to give their condolences and food for her and Cason. Cason had stayed in his room and refused to come out. She didn't know how they were going to get through this. Mike was scheduled to come back for at least a year before deploying again. He and Cason had a trip planned over the summer after football camp to travel through as much of Asia as they could.

She heard the lock to her front door turn as it was swung open. She knew who it was before they called for her.

"Lakyta?" Kayla shouted.

"In the kitchen."

Kayla came into the kitchen with red puffy eyes and wrapped both arms around her best friend.

"Babe, I'm so sorry. I tried to call and tell you beforehand. I didn't want you to find out before the officers came and told you, which by the looks of all this food, they already did." There was food that covered the island, the counters and the kitchen table. "Where's Cason?"

"In his room. I've left plates of food for him outside his door. He's eating, but he won't come out. Kayla, he's really gone." Lakyta sobbed as Kayla squeezed her tighter.

"Auntie Kayla," came a low voice behind them. They both turned to see Cason standing there, eyes bloodshot and red undertones to his mahogany skin.

"Oh, come here baby," Kayla said as she and Lakyta opened their arms and cocooned him. "We will get through this."

1

Lakyta

Three months later…

"Cason, let's go! You're going to be late for school." Lakyta shook her head as it sounded like a stampede above her head as Cason got himself together. This was their routine every morning now that he was back in school after being virtual for three months due to his father's death.

He bounded down the stairs and kissed her cheek as he grabbed his lunch.

"I'll be home a little late today mom," he said. "We have a new trainer coming in to work with us who will be helping out during summer camp." It was the last week of school before football camp started.

"Okay, well make sure you text me when practice is over. Do you work today?"

"No, ma'am. I'm off. See you later!" He was out the door before she could say anything. The start of his car and the sound of his engine becoming more faint meant he was out of the driveway. She still wondered if getting him a car with some of his father's life insurance money was such a good idea. The school was only five miles away, but he was only 16 and could sometimes be irresponsible.

She packed up her breakfast and lunch, then grabbed her coffee cup and keys off the counter to head out the door for work. Her job was only a 15 minute drive from her house, but it usually took close to 30 with traffic. That was Houston for you. When she arrived, the parking lot was empty. Her employees didn't come in for another couple of hours. She opened the nursery and put her things away before she filled a watering can and went around to water all the plants.

The nursery was close to 2500 sq ft, and it was the second largest in Houston, but the most popular in the state. She sold flowers that were rare to the state, being the only botanist who knew how to care for such rare plants.

After watering them, she sat in the sunroom on her yoga mat and meditated for 30 minutes. It was something that the grief counselor had suggested after Mike passed. She and Cason saw the counselor a few times a month, depending on their needs. Cason saw the counselor more often.

When she had rolled her mat up and went to the front, she began looking through orders that had come in overnight. There were 35 local, and 41 that needed to be shipped. Thankfully, according to the schedule, there were seven people scheduled to come in today. She spent the next hour or so on a few orders before her employees came in and took over as she went to the greenhouse where she spent most of her time.

Around lunchtime, she met Kayla at Kindred Stories for some coffee and book shopping. She loved books almost as much as she loved plants. Recently, she had gotten into reading sapphic romances. She'd never been with a woman before, but she had a few encounters that left her feeling wanton.

"Hey, boo," Kayla greeted as Lakyta walked in. "How you doing?"

"I'm good. Feeling better each day. You?"

"Girl, let me tell you…" That was cue for when Kayla was about to gossip. Lakyta listened as Kayla talked about the mess going on at her job. One of the new news anchors was sleeping with a producer who was married to her cohost. News got out and there was a cat fight, Kayla's words, on the newsroom floor right before they were to go on air.

"I'm shocked no one decided to broadcast it live," Lakyta responded.

"Oh, a couple of the producers thought about it. Anyway, why are you looking at weight loss books?"

"I want to shed a few pounds. Ever since Mike passed, and really it started before, I've put on quite a few pounds, plus my grief counselor thinks it would be good for me."

"Why don't you get a personal trainer? I heard there is a very popular one here in town who works with celebrities."

"Sounds expensive."

"It's not like you don't have the money. Ever since you became a botanist, you have been securing the bag. I get that smelling flowers is therapeutic, but so is sweating and moving your body."

"I don't know, Kayla. I feel like with a personal trainer, I have to commit, and we both know how I am with commitment."

"How about this? Since you're off tomorrow, I'll set something up. They make house calls as well and I know how you feel about gyms. I'll even pay for the first month, which is eight sessions. What do you think?"

"I think that you have an ulterior motive, and that I'm going to regret this, but I'll do it. Set it up. No earlier than nine. I have to get back to work."

"Yes!" Kayla celebrated. They hugged and said "goodbyes" as they headed to their respective cars.

The rest of the day was busy which made it go by quickly. When she got home, Cason had texted her that he was going to stay at his teammate Bryan's house. She texted Bryan's mom and asked if it was okay and she assured that she and her husband would be there. Since he wasn't coming home, she decided to order takeout.

After eating, she took a nice, long, hot bath. She stayed in until she was pruned and then moisturized with her new oil she made from some of the plants at the nursery. She grabbed one of her books that she had bought during her lunch break and curled up in bed. It wasn't long before her eyelids got too heavy, and she dozed off.

The next morning, she woke up to a text from Kayla that Anndee, her new personal trainer, would be there at 9:45. It was currently 8:30, so she had time to get herself together. She grabbed her yoga mat and put it out on the floor of her sunroom to do her morning meditation before she made a cup of coffee and checked on the nursery.

Her doorbell rang at 9:44, which she was impressed that this man was early. When she opened the door, an audible gasp slipped from her lips before she slammed it shut. Her hands were shaking and her heart was racing. Her clit was throbbing and it

10

hadn't done that in response to anyone in a long while. The doorbell rang again and she slowly opened it.

"I've had many people be shocked that I'm a woman, but this has to be the first of someone slamming a door in my face," the woman laughed. "I'm Anndee, by the way."

2

Anndee

"Are you going to let me in?" Anndee asked.

"Yes, yes, sorry, I was expecting…nevermind, come in." From the client questionnaire, and photos, they did not do justice for the woman who stood in front of Anndee. This woman was about two inches shorter than her 5'11 frame, and the sports bra showed her full, round breasts that Anndee was sure were heavenly without a bra. The yoga pants made her ass sit tight and her thighs still jiggled.

Around her midsection was a little fluffy, but that was how Anndee usually liked them. She watched as the woman led her through the beautiful house and to the kitchen.

"Would you like water before we get started?" Lakyta asked, not daring to look at Anndee. She could tell the woman was flustered, her amber skin flushing with a red tint.

"Naw, I'm good. Where is it that you wanted to workout at?"

"Um, the sunroom? It's where I usually meditate and practice yoga." Anndee raised an eyebrow. A woman who did yoga was her weakness. *Wait, why am I thinking about this,* she asked herself. This woman is a client.

Anndee followed the woman to the sunroom right off the back left side of the house. It was full of plants hanging from the ceiling and lining the windows. In the center was a yoga mat, a towel, and a water bottle.

"So," Lakyta began as she finally decided to look at Anndee. "I've never had a personal trainer before, and I'm not sure how this works."

"Well, let's start with getting to know one another. I read your questionnaire and it was very vague in the responses."

"What was vague about it?"

"Well, for starters, under goals, it said, and I quote, "I want to be able to pop my pussy without my fupa slapping against my thighs."" The sheer mortified expression on Lakyta's face confused Anndee.

"I can't believe that bitch put that on there," Lakyta muttered.

"I'm sorry?"

"My friend Kayla filled out the questionnaire for me. She was the one who set this up. What else did she put on there?"

"That you were single and ready to get snatched so you can have a hot girl summer."

"I'm going to fucking maim her." Anndee chuckled as Lakyta tried to hide her blush.

"It's all good. But now that I'm here, I want to hear from you what it is that you want from this."

"Well, my grief counselor says that working out will help with my anxiety."

"I'm sorry for your loss."

"Yes, thank you. My ex husband died doing his duty to this country a few months ago. I got a grief counselor for my son, but I also seemed to need it. She also says that meditating and yoga will help. I just want to feel good and increase my endurance and stamina."

"You have a race planned or something?" Anndee asked, raising an eyebrow.

"No, I just want to…to…to be able to walk up a flight of stairs and not get winded." Anndee knew she was lying but decided to not press the issue.

"Okay, so to start, let's take a nice jog around the block and back and see where we are."

"I can do that." After locking up the house, Anndee jogged alongside Lakyta around the block, and since it didn't seem to wind her, they did it a couple more times.

Once back in the sunroom, Anndee watched with great pleasure as Lakyta did 20 jumping jacks. She had on a nice high impact bra, but they still bounced a little. Now Anndee never looked at her clients the way she was looking at Lakyta. In fact, she wholeheartedly believed in keeping her personal and professional life separate. But it was something about Lakyta that made her want to risk it all.

Once she finished her jumping jacks, Anndee told her to take a one minute break for some water. It seemed that Lakyta's endurance was fine, so she figured that they would just focus on cardio today, doing some burpees, inchworms, and HIIT drills, finishing it off with a little ab and leg work.

"Have you done squats before?" she asked. Lakyta nodded. "Okay, let me see your form." Lakyta did what she thought was a squat, but her back was hunched over, and her hips were tucked in. Anndee laughed as Lakyta straightened.

"What's so funny?" she frowned.

"I'm sorry, I didn't mean to laugh," Anndee swears as she wipes the tears from her eyes. "It's just, your form can get you really hurt. Let me help you." She stood behind Lakyta and placed a hand on each of her hips. She felt the woman stiffen from her touch.

"When doing squats, you want to sit back with your hips like you would if you were going to sit in a chair. I'm going to hold your hips and guide them back." Anndee gripped Lakyta's hips and pulled them back, pressing Lakyta's ass into her pussy. It throbbed at the softness of it as they sat back. "Okay, don't arch your back, try to keep your back straight. It helps to clasp your hands in front of you." She placed a hand on Lakyta's lower abdomen and told her to tighten her core. She placed a hand on either side of the woman's rib cage, right below her breasts and pulled her up gently so she could straighten her back.

"Now, we're going to pulse."

"Pulse?" Lakyta questioned.

"Yes, it's kind of like a bounce. I'll guide you." Anndee pressed firmly against Lakyta's back and gripped her hips as she herself pulsed and Lakyta followed along. With her legs open like this, Lakyta's ass was rubbing against her clit. She quickly jumped back and told Lakyta to keep going as she stayed behind her for a moment to gather herself, and then moved to the side.

"Alright, give me thirty more seconds."

When they were done, Lakyta walked Anndee to the front door. Anndee watched the sweat trickle between the woman's breasts and then lifted her eyes to the woman's face.

"Same time on Wednesday?" Lakyta asked, interrupting Anndee's thoughts.

"Ugh, yeah, right, same time." She turned to leave and get in her car. This woman was going to be the death of her professionalism.

Later that day, Anndee went to the high school to talk to the head football coach, her cousin, and meet the team. She would be helping them train over the summer as a highly paid gig.

"Hey Anndee," Jarren said. They gave each other dap and headed to the football field. She and Jarren had grown up together and oftentimes would workout together. When her father died in battle, and her mother committed suicide a couple months later because she couldn't take the loss of her husband, Anndee stayed with her aunt and uncle, Jarren's parents. They grew up as sister and brother.

"What's going on man?" she asked.

"Shit, glad as fuck that you agreed to do this. These boys need to be whipped into shape come fall. One of the players just came back a few weeks ago from being out of school since his pops passed."

"Hold on," she said as she pulled his arm to stop him from walking. "That player's last name wouldn't happen to be Barnes, would it?"

"Yeah, how you know?"

"I think I trained his mom this morning?"

"Trained trained, or *trained trained*?"

"Nigga trained, as this was our first session. Says her grief counselor said it may help." She rubbed her chin and looked off in the distance.

"Ah shit, I know that look. Listen, don't let whatever you and Ms. Barnes have going on mess with Cason's head. He's my star player and it was tough to get his head back in the game once he came back to school. Yeah, it's the off season, but we keep them conditioning year round."

"Man, ain't nothing going on with her. You know how I like to keep shit professional."

"I know, but by the look on your face, and I've seen Ms. Barnes, it won't be professional for long."

They made their way out to the field house where the boys were already working out. Since it was a predominantly Black school in a predominantly upper class Black area, their equipment was state of the art.

"Man, we didn't have anything nearly as nice as this back in the day," she whistled.

"Yeah, well, they have the funds, and I mean the funds, so money is no object. I remember asking the principal for some of the machines. A week later, this is what it looked like. I didn't ask any questions."

Anndee looked around and was impressed at the equipment, but for her, she rarely used equipment when training. Even though she mostly did house calls, there were times that she went to the gym, and even then, she barely let her clients touch any equipment.

"Alright gentlemen, hustle up." Weights could be heard dropping as sneakers scuffled against the floor. The boys crowded around and Anndee was glad there was no funk to smell.

"This is Anndee, the new trainer working with us this summer, and she is my cousin. If things go well in the summer, she may stay on for football, basketball, soccer, and baseball season for both the boys' and girls' teams."

"Whoot! Whoot! Whoot! Whoot! Whoot!" The boys cheered.

"So, let's listen to what she has to say."

"Thank you, coach. I'm glad to be here and work with you all. Some of you may or may not know me, which is fine, because once we start working, your thoughts of me will change, I can guarantee that. For our first day, so I can get a feel for you all and your work ethic, let's head to the field and give me six laps around the track." The boys frowned and looked at one another. "I said, six laps. Move!" The boys scrambled over each other to get out of the door.

"They just don't know what they're in for,"Jarren chuckled.

After practice, one of the boys jogged over to Anndee. She could tell he was Lakyta's son. He didn't have her complexion, but he did have her eyes and nose.

"Hey, Ms. Anndee," he said.

"Please, call me Anndee."

"Oh, okay, well, Anndee. Coach said that your dad died in the service when you were young. My dad died, too, a few months ago in Iraq."

"How are you holding up?" she asked as she sat on the bottom bleacher. He sat about a foot over to her right.

"At first, I was angry at him. I hated him because I felt like he lied. We had a trip planned to go to Asia over the summer after football camp. He was going to be home for a year and would get to see me play on the varsity team for the first time in person. I gave my mom a hard time in the beginning. I didn't blame her. She was just pushing too hard. Then, a grief counselor started coming to the house and she helped a lot. I was wondering, if it's okay, I mean we just met and all, but if after practice some time, I can talk to you."

Anndee thought about it for a moment. This was unchartered territory, and she didn't want to overstep any boundaries. But she also didn't want to say no. She could tell from the look in his eyes how much he needed and wanted this.

"I tell you what, if your mom says yes, then sure, I'll be happy to."

"Shit really?"

"Language."

"Sorry. I'll be sure to ask her tonight."

"And I need it in writing."

"Is it cool if I can have your number?"

"I don't see why not." Cason gave Anndee his phone so she could plug her number in.

"Thanks, Anndee." He jumped up and ran off to the field house. She hoped she didn't make the wrong decision.

3

Lakyta

"You sneaky ass bitch," Lakyta feigned deceit. "Why didn't you tell me Anndee was a woman and fine as hell?" She rolled her eyes as cackling came through the phone. It was around seven that same evening and she had been busy the rest of the day to get her mind off of Anndee. The woman showed up at her door in a black fitted tank top, black basketball shorts, a black cap to the back, and her hair in a low bun.

All Lakyta could think about was the woman's full, smooth lips sucking on her clit as she ran her hands through her hair. *Focus,* Lakyta scolded herself.

"I'm not even sorry because I know you're not really mad. I figured you could use some eye candy while you worked out."

"How do you even know I like women?"

"Bitch, I'm your best friend. I know everything about you." Lakyta plopped on the couch and curled her feet up, sipping a glass of wine.

"Yeah, well, a warning would've been nice so I wouldn't slam the door in her face."

"You what?" Kayla screamed, succumbing to a fit of laughter.

"I'm so glad you think this shit is funny. I'm glad she didn't take offense. She thought it was funny as well."

"I wish I could've been a fly on the way for that session."

"Nothing happened, well, until she was showing me how to do squats and my ass was rubbing against her pussy while her hands were all over my damn body."

"Oh?" She could hear both of Kayla's eyebrows rising.

"Pipe down. It was just a lot. I mean I haven't had anyone touch me since Mike and I divorced."

"Okay, so after work tomorrow, since you have a half day, we are going to the spa and we are getting you primped and primed. I forgot it had been that long."

"Primped and primed for what? She's just training me."

"That's what you say now until y'all are hot and heavy and naked in your sunroom. Your pussy does not need to look like it can fit in with the plants that are hanging from your ceiling." Lakyta choked on her sip of wine and went into a coughing fit as Kayla mimicked a hyena on the other end of the phone.

"I hate you. I'm hanging up now." She was certain Kayla didn't hear her over her laughing as she hit the red button to end the call.

She went to the kitchen to check on her lasagna and saw that it was ready. The front door opened and she went around, frowning.

"Hey, Cason. I thought you were staying at Bryan's."

"His mom made white chicken with raisin potato salad and baked sweet potatoes." He scrunched up his face and she tried to hold in her laughter, but they both wound up in a fit of giggles.

"Well, the lasagna is done. I was just about to pull it out of the oven."

"I'll set the table."

Once they were seated, she said grace and they ate as he told her about the new trainer and how practice went.

"The new trainer worked us hard. I know I'm going to be sore tomorrow."

"Sounds like he is trying to get y'all into shape."

"*She* really is."

"She?"

"Yeah. Coach had already told me about her before she came. He said she lost her dad in the line of duty when she was a kid. He figured I could talk to her. I asked her and she said yes only if you say yes. Please say yes." Lakyta chuckled.

"I don't see why that wouldn't be okay."

"Yes. Also, she said she needed it in writing, but I think maybe if you call her and tell her, it would be better." He picked up his phone and tapped away, then her phone dinged. "That's her number, and please don't embarrass me."

"Why would I embarrass you?" He tilted his head to the side and turned up his lips to the right. "Okay, I won't embarrass you." He got up to clear the table and kissed her on the head.

"I'll be in my room doing some homework."

"Okay." She poured another glass of wine as she packed up the food to put it away. When she crawled into bed, she hit the number to call. It was only nine at night, so hopefully, it wasn't too late.

"Hello?" a familiar voice answered on the second ring. Lakyta gulped to keep from choking.

"Anndee?"

"Hello to you, too, Lakyta."

"Sorry, hi. Um, your son gave you my number."

"Huh?"

"I mean, my son gave me your number." Lakyta was swearing off all alcohol. "You're the new trainer?"

"I am. I see he asked about me talking to him. I hope that's okay."

"It's fine," she said, a little too hurriedly. "It's fine. The more people he has in his corner and can talk to, the better."

"Cool. Is it okay if I take him to get pizza after practice tomorrow and get a little acquainted?"

"Well, I made lasagna tonight. How about you come here?"

"I don't think that's appropriate, Lakyta. You're my client and that is the only reason I should be at your house."

"Okay, I'll tell you what. How about on Wednesday, after my session, since you'll already be here, you can talk to him then? It's just I really don't know you and I'm not comfortable with you taking him somewhere."

"I completely understand, and Wednesday will work."

"Great. See you then."

"See you then."

That next afternoon when Lakyta got off work, she met Kayla at some spa she had been dying to go to for months. It was located in River Oaks, and immediately she knew she was about to spend a coin.

Walking inside was like walking into nirvana. There was a large stone waterfall straight ahead behind the receptionist desk.

To the left and right was a waiting area with gold upholstered chairs that had cherry oak trim around the back, and the legs.

The floor was granite marble squares with clear squares in between that had fish swimming in them. The windows gave a feel of being inside a cathedral, though Black Jesus would not be in a place like this.

When her eyes landed on Kayla who was looking down at her phone, she hustled over and sat beside her.

"Bitch, what is this place? Am I going to have to give up my first born? A blood offering? My left kidney?" Kayla chuckled and shook her head.

"I admit it is a bit much, but…"

"A bit much?" Lakyta gasped. "How much is this place?"

"Does it matter? The station gave me two free reservations to check the place out so that I can report on it as part of the new business segment. So, they paid for the most expensive package. Be prepared to have your kitty wowed."

When they were called back, they went through a set of stained wooden doors into a hallway. Each side of the hallway was lined with doors, and at the end of the hall was another set of double doors.

"You can change in here," the woman they were following said, pointing to two doors right next to each other. "I will wait out here."

Five minutes later, they were in long silk robes and headed through the next set of double doors. There was a large pool in the middle of the room that was steaming, giving the vibes of a hot spring. There were massage tables that lined around the pool.

What Lakyta immediately noticed was that the place was open. There were no private rooms for massages. So there were naked men and women in the pool and on the tables.

"Where are the private rooms?" she asked Kayla. Their guide overheard her and turned around.

"There are no private rooms except for waxes."

"Can we do that first?" she begged.

"We do massage first so you can feel relaxed when it is time to get waxed. It helps your nerves. This way." She led them to two tables to the left side of the pool where two women were waiting.

"Please, take off your robes and lie down," one of the women said. Kayla took hers off first and laid on one of the tables.

"Come on girl," Kayla beckoned. "Take the robe off." Lakyta slowly untied her robe and when it fell open, one of the women gasped, her hand flying to her mouth. "What the fuck is that?" Kayla's eyes were huge as she looked at the huge bush between Lakyta's legs.

"What? It's been a while. That's why we're here." As the robe slipped off, both women gasped as Kayla's mouth fell open.

"Now I see why you don't want to go to the gym. You have matching bushes under your arms. The bush triplets."

Lakyta groaned as she went to lie on the table. The massage lasted almost two hours and included deep tissue and hot rocks. When they were done, they had the option of waxes or the pool first. Lakyta quickly opted for waxes.

They were fortunately put into separate rooms. Each room had a corner waterfall, essential oils in a diffuser, and soft music playing. The lights were dim and almost had a romantic vibe.

"Take off your robe and lie on the table," the woman said. She did as instructed. The woman pushed both legs up, back, and spread them, making Lakyta feel exposed. She hadn't had her legs up like this since Mike, and it was making her feel some type of way.

"I am going to apply the wax. It is rather warm." As soon as the wax touched her, she jumped. As the woman spread it on the outside of her pussy lips, she knew the woman could smell her arousal, and she was ready to run out of there, sticky pussy and all.

"I will now apply the strips." The pressure from the woman's hands pushing the stripes against her, went straight to her clit. She pressed one hand down and told Lakyta she was going to count to three and rip it off.

"One…two…three.." The woman ripped the strip off and then applied pressure, but that didn't stop the scream that felt like it came from the depths of a volcano and erupted out of her mouth. It was a mix between pleasure and pain.

The woman told her she was going to repeat the process. Lakyta could feel her juices running down the crack of her ass, and she knew the woman had to have seen it. She did the other side and she screamed but not as loud. Her clit was bulging at this point and she wasn't sure why when this was not a sensual or sexual experience. The woman applied wax right above the slit that she was sure was not covering her clit.

When the woman applied the wax, heat flooded to her core, and as she applied pressure right above her clit, the woman ripped the strip off and her hand slipped. Lakyta cried out as an orgasm set every nerve in her body on fire. The woman never moved her hand and Lakyta squirted, as if she wasn't already embarrassed enough.

The woman cleaned her up and continued her wax as if nothing happened. Lakyta knew that if she was several shades lighter, her entire body would be red from shame. She couldn't believe that because it had been that long, a massage and wax would detonate her like a bomb.

Pussy bare and armpits smooth, she couldn't wait to get dressed and leave. As soon as they stepped outside, Kayla bent over with laughter.

"I assume you heard?" Lakyta muttered, folding her arms across her chest.

"I couldn't help but to hear. You legit orgasmed from a waxing. This is fucking gold. I can't wait to use this in my segment."

"You wouldn't dare?"

"Oh, I would. I'll be sure to leave your name out though. Let's get some lunch and you can tell me all about your experience."

4

Anndee

Wednesday was a busy day for Anndee, full of clients and then late training with the football players at the high school. She couldn't help but to think about her next session with Lakyta. She had spent Tuesday night researching Lakyta and going through her social accounts to get a better feel of her. It was borderline stalking, but it was something about this woman. Her only hang ups were that Lakyta was a client and her son wanted her to be a mentor/counselor.

After work, she headed to a bar to meet Jarren for drinks. Even though it was a school night for him, he was still down to get a little lit.

"So, I hear you're going to mentor Cason," Jarren said as soon as she sat down.

"Hey, Jarren, How are you? How was your day?"

"Fuck the formalities. I just saw you a couple hours ago."

"Whatever. Yeah, his mom said it was cool, only problem is, she prefers I do it at her house or at the school, and at the school is not looking likely."

"I fail to see the problem."

"She's a client, man. I can't just be up in her house if we aren't working out."

"Well, why don't you just make y'all sessions later and then you can talk with Cason?"

"That's what she suggested, so we start tomorrow." She took a swig of her beer that Jarren already had waiting for her.

"I would say you got it pretty easy. I mean her kid already likes you."

"But don't it seem weird, like I'm trying to get to her through her kid?"

"No, because you met her first. Why are you trying to talk yourself out of this?"

"I just don't want word to get out that I sleep with clients like all these other personal trainers out here."

"But you aren't sleeping with her and I've known her for quite a while. I don't think she's that kind of person."

"Yeah, well, if shit goes left, I'm blaming you."

The next morning, Anndee got a notification of a cancellation from Lakyta. There was no reason in the optional reason box, but it still didn't make sense. She looked at the time and knew that the nursery was open. She hoped that Lakyta was the only one there. At this hour.

After dressing in some knee length linen shorts, a t-shirt, some sneakers and putting her hair into a high bun, she made her way to the nursery which wasn't too far from where she lived, only a ten minute drive. She only saw one car and remembered it was the same car in Lakyta's driveway, which meant she was here.

The bells chimed as she walked inside. There were plants everywhere. It was a large place and she wasn't sure how she'd be able to find Lakyta.

"Just a minute," she called from the back. Anndee stood at the counter and waited as she heard footsteps quickly coming closer. Lakyta stopped when she saw Anndee. Anndee smiled at the flustered expression on her face.

"What are you doing here?"

"Wondering why you canceled our session."

"Do you do this to all your clients? Just show up at their place of work and wonder why they canceled?"

"Actually, I came to get some flowers to put on my parents' graves. Today is their anniversary." It wasn't a lie, but it was only part of the reason for her being there.

"Sure, what kind of arrangement would you like?"

"My mom liked tulips, and anything you have that's in various shades of blue will be fine for my dad." Lakyta nodded and moved around the plants. Anndee watched in amazement and awe the way her hips swished.

Ten minutes later, Lakyta was ringing her up. She still hadn't answered Anndee's question, and after she paid, she lingered a moment.

"Anything else I can help you with?" Lakyta inquired, her eyes looking everywhere but at Anndee.

"Look at me, Lakyta." Lakyta looked up. Anndee eyed her lips and how smooth they looked. She was sure they tasted sweet. "Why'd you cancel?"

"On the app, it stated that that part was optional when making a cancellation."

"Do I make you nervous or uncomfortable?"

"N-n-no."

"Then tell me."

"I have an appointment with my grief counselor that I forgot about and didn't want to cancel the session." Anndee knew she was lying. She couldn't even look her in the eye.

"I'll see you at three thirty, Lakyta." She walked out the door before Lakyta could even protest. She wasn't about to play with this woman. Fuck the rules. She would give them up for her.

5

Lakyta

"She showed up at my damn job and everything. Said something about going to her parents' grave and needed flowers. That may have been true, but still." Lakyta was still on edge about Anndee coming into the nursery earlier. She immediately called Kayla as soon as she got home.

"Well, some trainers take their jobs seriously," Kayla replied, playing devil's advocate.

"But do all trainers ask their clients if they make them nervous or uncomfortable?"

"I don't know, they might. Anyway, enjoy your session. She should be there shortly." Kayla hung up before Lakyta could get in another word. The doorbell rang and Anndee stood there looking as edible as she did earlier.

"Hey," Lakyta said as she let the woman in, closing and locking the door behind her. They headed to her sunroom and with the heat of the room, Anndee's cologne was more prominent. Lakyta didn't know how she was going to get through this session without kissing this woman. Not to mention, her pussy was still throbbing from the wax the day before. Just thinking about it caused heat to rise to her face.

"So, I wanted to try something different today," Anndee announced. She set down the duffle bag that Lakyta failed to notice she was carrying. "Strength training is a good component to add when trying to lose weight. It helps you to burn more fat. From your profile, it said you weren't a fan of weights. Given that your best friend filled it out, I have to ask if that is true."

"It is. I don't want to be bulky and look like a bodybuilder."

"I lift weights religiously. Do I look like a bodybuilder?" Lakyta examined the other woman in her muscle shirt and basketball shorts. She could tell Anndee was toned, but she wasn't bulky. She had muscles no doubt, and Lakyta would even go as far to believe the woman had a nice six pack she'd like to trail with her tongue.

"Lakyta?" Anndee called, smirking. "Are you checking me out?"

"Um…no…yes…yes, I am. You asked me if you looked like a bodybuilder and I was just checking you out to give you an honest answer."

"You are something else, you know that?" Anndee shook her head and opened the duffle bag to bring out some arm and leg resistance bands. "These shorter ones are for your thighs. After our jog, we'll work on your legs when we get back. The longer ones are for arms. And don't worry. I can tell by the look on your face you're a little apprehensive, but I will demonstrate how to use them correctly. We don't need you getting any injuries like you were going to with those things you called squats."

Lakyta rolled her eyes as Anndee chuckled. They headed out to jog around the block, but this time, they ended up doing two miles. Anndee seemed to be impressed and said as much when they got back and took a water break.

"Now that your body is all warmed up, let's take the medium resistance band. Go ahead and step in." Anndee knelt down and held the resistance band out for Lakyta to step in. She brought the band up to just above her knees. She put a hand in between Lakyta's thighs and the contact made her gasp.

"Relax," Anndee said, looking up at her. "Try to stand with your legs as far apart to where there's some resistance." Lakyta did as instructed as Anndee moved her feet to where they were parallel. She stood up and looked down at her. Lakyta wanted to look at anything else but the dark expression in the woman's eyes, but the unrelenting pull made it impossible.

"On my count, you are going to squat like I showed you on Tuesday. The resistance band is going to make it slightly difficult and your thighs and glutes will burn faster. Keep going until I say stop. Ready?" Lakyta nodded, gulping. Anndee took a couple steps back and began to count.

By the time they had done three sets of ten, Lakyta's lower body felt like it was on fire. She couldn't even get the band off without Anndee's help.

"How do you feel?" Anndee asked.

"If I answer that, I will cuss you out."

"Then my job is done. Now, we are going to have the resistance band around your calves, and you will do side and back leg lifts."

"More leg work?"

"Lakyta, you only did one leg exercise."

"Yes, and I feel the burn and the pain."

"No pain, no gain."

"Tsk." Lakyta sucked her teeth. She took the band from Anndee and pulled it up to her calves. Anndee adjusted it slightly and then showed her the intervals for both legs. She would do each

34

leg for three rounds of 15. When she was done, if she could have moved her legs, she would've kicked Anndee.

"I think I'll let you make it today with legs," Anndee said, putting the leg resistance bands away. "Now for arms." She showed Lakyta how to stand on the band and hold the ends of the bands in her arms. They went through six arm exercises just to start since this was something new for Lakyta.

An hour later, Anndee was packing up her workout equipment as Lakyta came out of the kitchen with two bottles of water.

"How long have you been a personal trainer?" she asked.

"A while. It started when I was in the military. I was a drill sergeant and then realized that I preferred working one-on-one with people to help reach fitness goals instead of combat goals."

"I bet you get a lot of women clients who want to sleep with you." Lakyta meant it as a joke, but she wasn't ready for Anndee's comeback.

"Are you one of those women?" she asked, stepping closer to Lakyta, backing her against the island and placing a hand on either side of her. She took Lakyta's water bottle and set both of theirs on the counter to the side.

"Well, I just meant that..." and before she could finish, Anndee's lips were on hers, her tongue parting them and meeting her own. She didn't know where to put her hands, so she left them awkwardly at her side. Anndee pressed into her body, an electric surge coursing through Lakyta. Anndee grabbed the woman's hands and put them around her neck as she slid her hands down the woman's arms and sides, settling on her hips, then wrapping her arms around her waist.

"I want to taste you," Anndee whispered against Lakyta's lips. The woman couldn't breathe at those words. Her brain short circuited as Anndee began to tug her yoga pants down. She took off each of her shoes and socks. Anndee let out a feral groan at the site of Lakyta's pantiless pussy.

"I...I...I haven't showered yet," Lakyta stuttered.

Anndee looked up at her with hooded eyes before she lifted the woman's right leg over her shoulder, never taking her eyes off her. She moved her face closer and could smell the musk and arousal that taunted the beast inside her.

She kissed each trembling thigh as Lakyta's sighs and low moans were a symphony to her ears. As she made her way to the apex of the woman's thighs, she looked up as her tongue swiped between the slick folds along the bulging nub between them. Lakyta's hips bucked as she gripped the edge of the island. She was already on the verge of an orgasm sooner than she wanted to be.

Anndee palmed each ass cheek to steady Lakyta as she slid her tongue up and down again.

"Please," Lakyta rasped.

"Please what? Use your big girl words."

"Please make me come in your mouth." That was all Anndee needed to hear before she buried her face in Lakyta's wet pussy. Lakyta screamed and gripped Anndee's hair as the woman went to work on the area that hadn't been touched in years.

"Agh! Oh God! Yes!" Lakyta moved her hips in sync with the tongue that was teasing her release. She felt a finger slip inside her and then another. The slow strokes and the relentlessness of Anndee's tongue had her climbing up the island.

"Don't fucking run, Lakyta," Anndee warned. Her thighs began to shake like the rumblings of an earthquake. On unsteady legs, she leaned more against the island, but it was no use. Her orgasm shattered her, bringing her to tears. Anndee gripped her to keep her up right as her orgasm continued its rampage through every nerve ending in her body. It was nothing like yesterday. This orgasm seemed to be out for vengeance for the lack of existence the past few years.

As the first one settled, the second and third came barreling in. She could feel her release running down her standing leg. Her screams turned into moans that turned into sobs. When her body finally settled, Anndee carried her bridal style up the stairs and to the bedroom where Lakyta directed.

Lakyta listened in a state of pure bliss as Anndee turned on the shower. She looked at the bedside clock and realized Cason would be home any minute now.

"You think you can get up and take off your sport's bra?" Anndee asked. She nodded and sat up slowly. Her arms and legs felt like jelly. Between the workout and Anndee's tongue, she was going to sleep good tonight and be sore tomorrow. Luckily, it was Friday and the nursery was closed the next three days for maintenance repairs and an inspection that she delegated to one of her other employees monthly.

Anndee helped her into the shower. Lakyta looked the woman up and down and bit her bottom lip. The woman chuckled and shook her head as she too got undressed and then stepped in, walking Lakyta's back to the wall. Their lips brushed against each other in the gentlest kiss before Lakyta couldn't take it any more.

She deepened the kiss as she wrapped a leg around the woman's body, their pussies meeting. Anndee moved her pussy against Lakyta's with so much need, chasing the orgasm that was a touch out of reach. Lakyta trembled as her orgasm crested, not as powerfully as downstairs, but it was still explosive. She watched as Anndee's face scrunched and her lips parted as her body shook. The woman moved against her faster and then bucked her hips and let out a moan that elicited another peak for Lakyta.

Hearts pounding, clits throbbing, breaths rasping, neither ready to let go of this moment, but Lakyta didn't want Cason to walk in and see Anndee coming out of her room. Plus her yoga pants were still downstairs.

They bathed each other and then got dressed. Anndee pulled Lakyta to her.

"I don't think I can be your personal trainer anymore. I crossed the line and mixed business with pleasure."

"I was going to fire you anyway," Lakyta smiled, wrapping her arms around the woman's neck. Anndee smiled down at her before placing a kiss on her forehead. A knock at the door made them both jump.

"Mom, if you're done getting off with my mentor, I'd like to have her back now." Lakyta's mouth fell open as Anndee's shoulders shook, not even trying to stifle her laugh. Lakyta swung open the door to Cason holding her yoga pants with the tips of his index finger and thumb. She snatched them as he fell out laughing.

Anndee walked past her and out the door, but not before giving her a peck on the cheek.

6

Anndee

"Do you really like my mom?" Cason asked as they walked through the neighborhood park. After he caught them, Lakyta agreed to let them walk the neighborhood while she warmed up leftovers.

"I do."

"Are you using me to get to her?"

"I actually met your mom before I met you."

"So you're using her to get to me?" Anndee frowned as the corners of Cason's mouth turned up. They both burst into laughter.

"Are you okay with me seeing your mom?" He shrugged.

"I didn't know she was into women, and it doesn't bother me as long as you don't hurt her." Anndee nodded.

"So, do you want to talk about your dad?" They came to a bench and took a seat. They stared into the lake that sat in the middle of the park.

"When I was younger, my dad wasn't around much. He always chose to deploy any chance he got so he could move up the ranks. His ranking was more important than us, though he always said the higher his rank the more money to support me and Mom. I thought it was all cap looking back, seeing as how my mom has always had her own money, even before meeting my dad. She came from money, and even though she had me young, my grandparents still supported her and me."

"Do you resent him for it?"

"Not really. I get the whole going after your dreams even though you have a kid thing, I just don't get putting your dreams first. I think I felt resentment when he died because he made this promise about what the next year was going to look like, and this time, he was actually going to come through on his promise, except he died during combat, the thing he loved more than me."

"I didn't know your dad, but I do think he loved you."

"I don't think he didn't, I just think he loved his job more than me."

"Growing up, I lived with Coach Jarren most of my childhood. My dad was supposed to be coming home for good after this deployment. His aircraft was shot down as he was flying back to the base. It hit my mom hard. She killed herself not too long after he died because she couldn't handle it."

"Do you resent her for leaving you and being too sad to stick around for you?"

"For a long time I did. I felt like she didn't love me, but I realized she loved my dad so much. I think she felt like in her state of mind, she was no use to me. I learned to forgive her though."

"How?"

"I think that many times people commit suicide because they feel like life is too much to handle and that leaving this world is the only way out. It's the only way to deal with or escape the pain. Sometimes the pain is too unbearable. Now, I'm not saying that people should just kill themselves because of the pain, but just like you sought me out and I know you're seeing a grief counselor, I wish that other people could as well or had people around them that would support them and help them get that help."

"Like my mom."

"Like your mom, like my aunt and uncle, and Coach Jarren. Everyone needs someone in their corner especially through the hardest and most difficult of times. My mom had that, but by the time anyone knew how much she was struggling, I walked in the house to her lifeless body with a gun in her hand and a bullet hole through her head."

"Damn, Anndee."

"Language."

"Sorry. I'm sorry you had to see that. How old were you?"

"Ten." Cason turned to look at Anndee and gawked.

"Geez, I'm sorry that happened to you." They were quiet for a while, staring out into the lake. The sun was setting further as street lights began to come on. Cason took his phone out to check a message. "Mom said the food is ready. Are you staying for dinner?"

"If you want me to."

"Trust, it isn't just me that wants you to stay for dinner." He laughed as Anndee gave his arm a slight shove.

When they got back to the house, the aroma of lasagna filled the house. Anndee's stomach growled and Cason laughed as he went upstairs to the bathroom to wash his hands. Anndee washed hers in the downstairs bathroom and then headed to the kitchen to find Lakyta swishing her hips to a slow jam on her phone. Anndee stood in the doorway and watched as she plated the food and carried the plates to the table.

She let out a yelp and clutched her chest when she saw Anndee standing there smiling. Lakyta shook her head and continued setting the table as Cason came bounding down the stairs.

"How was the walk and chat?" Lakyta asked once everyone was seated.

"That's client patient confidentiality, right Anndee?" Cason asked. Lakyta raised an eyebrow.

"I'm not a licensed professional," Anndee said between bites.

"But you are a licensed personal trainer, and you took an oath, though it seems you broke that with my mother, so this counts too." Lakyta pinched the bridge of her nose as Anndee choked on her water. Cason only laughed and shoveled food into his mouth.

"Please excuse my son and his lack of a filter. I don't know where he gets it from."

"I might have an idea." Anndee winked.

"Gross. Can we not in front of the underage child at the table?" Cason croned. Lakyta and Anndee busted out laughing. They talked and got to know each other over the next hour.

After dessert, Cason headed to his room as Anndee helped Lakyta with the dishes.

"That was an interesting dinner," Anndee said.

"It was. I didn't expect Cason to be so chill about me dating a woman."

"We're dating?" Anndee asked, stilling. Lakyta froze and her eyes shifted as she thought of something to retract her statement. When Anndee's lips turned up, she let out a breath. "Gotcha."

"You really had me thinking I was on an island by myself. I mean yeah it's only been less than a week, but I like you."

43

"Same. And since we are apparently "dating," I guess I should ask you on a date."

"You guess?"

"Okay, I will ask you. Lakyta, how about you and I go to the beach this weekend?"

"Like Galveston Beach?"

"Yeah, but we don't have to get into the water. We can go to the pier, ride rides, and eat."

"Sounds like a date, though I'm not sure how great of company I'll be since I am sure to be sore."

"Take an epsom bath and add in some marjoram and peppermint oil. It should do the trick."

"Good to know."

The dishes were done and the table cleared. Lakyta walked Anndee to the door. Once on the other side, she turned to look at Lakyta.

"I'll pick you up around seven tomorrow evening. Traffic shouldn't be as bad and we will head out to Galveston for a little weekend getaway."

"Weekend? As in staying the night?"

"Yeah. Don't act shy now. My face has been all up in your pussy, and this weekend will allow me to get to know the both of you even better without any interruptions." Anndee watched as Lakyta flushed a deep red. She pulled her in for a slow, sensual, long kiss. She could feel Lakyta's heart beating rapidly inside her chest in contrast to her resting heart beat.

She pulled back and licked Lakyta's bottom lip. She stepped back, pulling her own bottom lip into her mouth.

I'll see you tomorrow." She got in her car and headed home, reminiscing about the taste of Lakyta's pussy on her tongue, and anticipating spending a surmountable amount of time in it this weekend.

Chapter 7

Lakyta

"Mama and Anndee sitting in a tree. K-i-s-s-i-n-g." Cason cackled as he mocked her. She swatted at his arm, just missing him as he jumped back.

"Boy, hush." He went into the living room and plopped on the couch. She sat next to him, on leg on the floor, her other tucked underneath her. "So how do you really feel about me dating in general, and how do you feel about me dating Anndee?"

"Honestly, I'm happy for you. You and dad have been divorced for a long time, and you haven't dated anyone, not that I know of. So, I'm happy for you. And as for dating Anndee, I mean, she's real cool. I like her even though I just met her. Our talk earlier was really helpful and made me feel better.

"We have a parent dying overseas in common. She talked about how she was raised with Coach Jarren and his family. It was nice to have someone to talk to who wasn't a licensed professional and had things in common. I do hope things work out between y'all."

"Wow. I am amazed at the young man you have grown into. Who raised you?" Lakyta smiled and winked an eye. Cason rolled his eyes and shook his head.

"But really, the fact that she's a woman, I don't really care. Plus, she's like the coldest trainer in the city. I'm about to be ripped by the time summer is over."

"Shame. Did you finish your homework?"

"Finished and submitted. I'm going to go ahead and head to bed. I'll see you in the morning." He stood up and kissed her cheek as he jogged up the stairs. Lakyta pulled her phone out and sent an SOS to Kayla and for her to meet at their breakfast spot, Snooze A.M. Eatery on Montrose, at eight the next morning. Kayla sent back several question and exclamation marks as well as a thumbs up.

She ran a bath and did as Anndee had instructed. Being a botanist also meant she was heavily into essential oils and had a whole stash of them. She soaked for about an hour and then moisturized before slipping into bed. Her clit had a steady throb as she closed her eyes and went back to only a few hours ago to her and Anndee in the kitchen, and then them in the shower. When she woke up the next morning, her body wasn't aching as much as she had expected.

"Bitch, spill all the damn tea!" Kayla squealed. Lakyta shushed her and looked around to make sure no one else in the restaurant was paying them any mind.

"I will if you promise to pipe down."

"Ok, ok. Fine. Go." Lakyta took a sip of her coffee as a smile spread across her face. Kayla gasped. "She ate the box didn't she?" Lakyta nodded. Kayla squealed louder than she did the first time. She jumped up out of her seat and Lakyta looked up at her in horror. "My best friend finally got her pussy ate after not getting any for several years!"

Lakyta felt all the color drain from her face as the other people in the restaurant cheered. She couldn't even speak or move. Once the other patrons quieted and Kayla sat down, she seethed.

"I can't believe you just fucking did that."

"Lakyta, relax. We're in LGBTQ town. I'm sure everyone in here is legit happy for you and doesn't think of you in any type of way other than silly for waiting so long."

"I am mortified."

"You'll live. So tell me how did y'all even get to that? Did more happen?"

"I ain't telling you shit after that stunt you just pulled." She stuffed a forkful of pancakes in her mouth. Kayla scoffed.

"Whatever. I'm just glad my bestie got some."

"I need a favor. Can Cason stay with you this weekend? Anndee is taking me to Galveston."

"For the whole weekend?"

"No, for half the weekend. Yes, hoe, the whole weekend."

"Damn, y'all moving kind of fast don't you think?"

"Oh, I know you not talking after you've been hounding me for years to date or get some."

"Yeah, but I mean, it's only been four days."

"And? Kayla, I am a single mom in her mid thirties. Dating at this age is not the same as it was when we were younger. I'm in a different period of my life right now. I'm not having anymore kids, and I'm looking to get married, not date for years and then it ends up not working out."

"No more kids? Does Anndee know that?"

"That'll be something to discuss this weekend."

"Just be careful. I'm all for this just being a fling to scratch an itch, but if it's more than that, I don't want you to get hurt or be disappointed."

"Kayla, I'm a big girl. I can handle it, but thank you."

"Well, is she still going to be your personal trainer?"

"More personal than anything. I fired her, so now, she can work me out any way she wants."

"Ooooookay!" they fell out laughing.

When they had left the restaurant, Lakyta received the greenlight for the service repairs the nursery had, were completed. As she pulled into her parents' driveway, Anndee sent a text that she would be picking her up a little earlier because she wanted to take her somewhere first. Despite the different ways that Lakyta asked, Anndee refused to tell her.

She opened the door to her parents' house and immediately burst into tears. Her older brother JJ was standing there with open arms as if he had been waiting for her. She jumped in his arms as she sobbed. She hadn't seen him in two years now that he was living over in Asia.

"Hey, lil sis," he gasped as she choked him with her tight hug. Footsteps could be heard behind him and she opened her eyes to see her teary eyed parents.

"When did you get back?" she asked, letting him go.

"Last night."

"Did y'all know he was coming home?" Her parents nodded.

"Well, in that case, Cason can stay here for the weekend instead of at Kayla's. I'm sure he'll be happy to see you." She wiped her eyes with the back of her hands.

"Why does Cason need to stay with anyone?" her mother asked. "He's sixteen."

"He's also a teenage boy," Lakyta reminded.

"Aww, don't do my nephew like that." They went into the living room to sit down.

"Catch us up on what's going on with you in Asia." Lakyta said.

"Well, I found a nice house, work is amazing, and my fiancee is everything I've ever wanted."

"Fiancee?"

"What?"

"When?" They asked in unison.

"Can I get to that? Sheesh. I met her while I was on an assignment in Chiang Mai. We hit it off and come to find out, she lives not too far from me. We've been dating for the better part of a year. She wanted to come back with me, but she had an assignment in Bali, where I'll be meeting her at the end of the month. She's a photojournalist and runs her own travel blog. She is also a YouTuber."

"She sounds wonderful and I can't wait to meet her," their mother said.

"Finally, someone to make an honest man out of you. Proud of you son." JJ sighed and rolled his eyes as their father guffawed and their mother elbowed his side.

"Aww, that means I'm going to get a little niece or nephew," Lakyta squealed.

"Whoa, pump the brakes. No one said anything about kids. We just got engaged a couple weeks ago. Let us enjoy being engaged. Now, where are you going that you can't let my nephew stay home for a weekend?"

"Well, I met someone and we are going away for the weekend. That's all." She feigned coy as her mother leaned forward.

"Lakyta Linette Barnes, you better fill in those gaps," her mother scolded. "It's been years since you and Mike divorced and I've not known you to date even a piece of grass. Now you all of a sudden are seeing someone and going away for a weekend?"

"Yeah, bug," her father chimed in. "I need to meet this young man taking my baby girl away." She looked down and could see JJ eyeing her. He always knew when she was hiding something.

"Kyta?" he said.

"Well, the person I'm dating isn't exactly a man," she mumbled.

"I don't give a damn if they were a talking tree," her father responded. "I still want to meet them before they take my baby girl away."

"I agree with your father," her mother added. "How does Cason feel?"

"Cason loves her. She's a personal trainer, which is how I met her."

"What a cliche," her brother deadpanned.

"Shut up. She's not my personal trainer anymore."

"I bet she isn't," her mother eyed her. Lakyta gasped as her father chuckled.

"I am glad that you all are taking my coming out as something to joke about."

"Sweetheart, I've always known you may have been queer since you were young. It was just a feeling." She smiled at her mother's words.

"So, where is she taking you?"

"Well, she said she wanted to take me somewhere first before we head to Galveston."

"Tell her come by here first," her dad demanded.

"Daddy, I am a grown woman with a whole teenage son."

"And I am a grown man and still your father. Do it look like I give a damn?" Lakyta let out a breath and looked up at the sky.

"Fine." She sent a quick text with her parents' address to Anndee. She said she would be there in about five minutes. She happened to be just down the street at Jarren's parents' house.

When the doorbell rang, Lakyta jumped. They had moved to the kitchen so her mother could pour them some tea and put some tea cakes on a plate.

"I'll get it," her father announced from the other end of the island. He pointed to Lakyta's seat for her to sit back down. She grumbled as her mother gave her a tight hug. She could hear voices as her father and Anndee got closer. Soon as her eyes landed on Anndee, the other woman was looking at her too with a wide smile on her face. Heat warmed Lakyta's entire body.

"Well, I have never seen my daughter blush like that," her mother said.

"Mom," she retorted, snapping out of the trance that was Anndee.

"Nice to meet you Mrs. Callum," Anndee said, giving the woman a hug.

"Oh please, anyone who can make my daughter flushed like that can call me Loretta."

"I'm JJ," Lakyta's brother said, holding out his hand.

"Now, what are your intentions with my daughter?" her father rumbled.

"Daddy!" Lakyta shrieked, eyes as big as saucers.

"Oh, I'm just messing with you," he chuckled, his 6'4 frame shaking up and down. Lakyta put her face in her hands as she felt arms around her. From the smell of her cologne, she knew it was Anndee.

"I promise to take good care of your daughter this weekend, and beyond that."

Finally leaving her parents' house and heading back to hers with Anndee following her, Lakyta tried to calm her nerves about being alone with Anndee for an extended amount of time. She thought about her conversation with Kayla. Was it too soon to be going on a mini vacation with someone she had only known for four days? She shook her head as she put her car into park in the garage, letting it down.

She shot Anndee a text that she was just running in to grab her bags she had packed this morning before meeting Kayla, and would be right out. She also sent Cason a text to go to his grandparents' house instead. She didn't mention that her brother would be there.

When the house was locked up, she went towards Anndee's car and saw her standing there waiting. She walked over and grabbed her bags out of her hands and placed them in the trunk as Lakyta got in on the passenger's side.

"So, you still aren't going to tell me where we're going that you had to come and get me earlier?" she asked as Anndee got in the driver's seat and buckled her seatbelt.

"Nope," was all the response she got as they backed out of her driveway. Not even thirty minutes later, they were pulling up to Mercer Arboretum in Humble off FM1960.

"The botanical gardens?" Lakyta questioned. "Now, I know you may not know a lot about botany, but don't you think I would've been here before?"

"Just hush and get out of the car." Lakyta twisted her mouth up and got out. Anndee waited in the front of her car with her hand out. Lakyta took it and they headed in. It was a beautiful and sunny day in May, so the garden was thriving and alive.

"Hello, you must be Anndee, and welcome back Lakyta," Maureen, an older white woman, greeted. "Anndee has something special setup for you two. Follow me." Lakyta side-eyed Anndee and all she got back was a smirk.

Around the corner in a large patch of grass, a picnic was set up. Now, Lakyta knew there was no food allowed inside the garden. There was an area across the street that held picnic areas and playgrounds.

"Maureen," Lakyta feigned shock. "You let her bring food in here?"

"Believe me, she fought tooth and nail and I wasn't going to budge, but when she mentioned your name, I figured just this once, I'd make an exception. Just don't think you can make this a habit."

That last part she looked at Anndee, then patted Lakyta's arm and walked away."

"I can't believe she let you do all of this. You must have laid on the charm pretty thick."

"Or, she just loves you," Anndee responded as she guided Lakyta down to the blanket where there was a large spread of delicious looking food. There was kombucha, sandwiches, fruit, chips, and two slices of pie.

As they ate, Lakyta tried her damndest to get Anndee to tell her what the itinerary was for Galveston. With them arriving later on tonight, she knew that they wouldn't be doing anything but going to wherever they were staying. That thought alone had her shaking.

"Why do you look like a child who is about to get in trouble?" Anndee asked, observing her. Lakyta felt goosebumps as the other woman's eyes roamed over her.

"I'll admit that I am a bit nervous. I haven't dated or had sex regularly in a very long time. Hell, just a few days ago I got a wax and had an orgasm." Anndee barked with laughter as Lakyta glared. "It isn't that funny."

"Oh, but it is. I 've had plenty of waxes before I started getting laser hair removal, so I know enough to know that getting a wax is not a pleasurable thing."

"Well, tell my pussy that."

"There's a lot of things I want to tell your pussy." Anndee's gaze darkened as Lakyta suddenly felt naked under her eyes. "There's a lot of things I want to tell your body, but that will have to wait. Let's pack up and walk around a bit."

They spent the next few hours walking the garden as well as the other side across the street. When the garden closed, they hit the road, heading towards Galveston.

Lakyta didn't know when she fell asleep, but she woke up to Anndee placing soft kisses on her lips standing outside the passenger's side of the car. Lakyta looked around and noticed they were at the Moody Gardens Hotel. She got out as they gathered their bags and went to check in.

When they walked in their suite, Lakyta gasped at the size of the bed. She went to the window and saw that their room overlooked the pool. She was definitely getting in there tomorrow. She heard the door close and knew that there was no turning back now. Turning around, Anndee was leaning against the wall, licking her lips and gazing at her.

"You like the room?"

"It's nice," Lakyta croaked. "I'm going to take a shower." She hurriedly grabbed her bag and tried to get past Anndee, but Anndee stopped her.

"Lakyta, please stop trying to run from me. You tried that on the island in your kitchen and that didn't work. I won't hurt you, I promise you that." Lakyta looked at her and dropped the bag. She pushed Anndee against the wall and smashed her lips to hers. She made light work of pulling Anndee's shorts and boxers down. As she continued to kiss the other woman, she slid a finger between Anndee's folds, feeling how aroused she was.

"Lakyta, shit," Anndee moaned against her lips. Lakyta dropped to her knees and wasted no time licking up Anndee's wetness, moaning at how good she tasted. "Fuck!"

Lakyta looked up to see Anndee's head was laid back against the way as her chest heaved up and down rapidly. The woman pushed Lakyta's face deeper into her pussy. When she went to use two fingers to penetrate her, Anndee swatted her hand away and she took that as penetration was off limits. She continued to sucked on the woman's engorged clit until she was gently pulled to standing.

"I don't want to come just yet," Anndee panted, kicking off her shoes and removing her shorts and boxers that were around her ankles. She bunched up the dress Lakyta was wearing and pulled it over her head. She had chosen to wear a matching panty and bra set that day and was glad she did because the look on Anndee's face when she saw it was well worth it.

"Damn you're sexy as hell." Lakyta blushed at her words, but her pussy was too needy and she needed Anndee to hurry up.

"Anndee, I need you, now."

Chapter 8

Anndee

Anndee went over to one of her bags and set it on the bed. She pulled off her shirt and sports bra. She watched as Lakyta licked her lips and eyed her pierced nipples. She wasn't heavy chested by far, a small A cup, but Lakyta seemed highly intrigued.

"What's in the bag?"

"Remember when I said there were things I wanted to tell your pussy and your body?" Lakyta visibly gulped, then nodded. "That's what's in the bag." Anndee dumped the bag out on the bed. She reached for the strap and the bottle of liquid coconut oil. She knew Lakyta was wet, but a little more slip n slide wouldn't hurt. Watching Lakyta as Lakyta watched her, she put on the strap, making sure to secure it snuggly so the spur on the inside was on her clit. Every time she moved, it rubbed against her. She would have to make quick work of getting Lakyta off. She rubbed the oil up and down the silicone dick and then tossed the bottle back in the bag.

She looked up and Lakyta's eyes were huge looking at all the toys. Anndee made her way over and behind Lakyta and unsnapped her bra, pushing the straps off her shoulder and watched as it fell to the floor. She tugged at the band of her panties and pulled them down, making sure to bite one of Lakyta's ass cheeks on the way down. Her yelp made Anndee smile as she stood up and placed gentle kisses up her back.

Anndee placed her hands on Lakyta's hips and walked her over to the sliding door. She opened it and Lakyta hesitated.

"Don't be scared now," she whispered in her ear, feeling Lakyta shiver against her. The night air was humid and warm. They were bound to work up a sweat. Once Lakyta's hands were on the railing of the balcony, Anndee slipped her right hand down the woman's body and rubbed gentle circles around her slick bundle of nerves.

Lakyta gasped and her body began to shake as Anndee's well oiled dick pressed against her back. With her left hand, she gently pushed Lakyta forward so she was slightly bent over the railing, making sure to keep the steady movement against her clit. She positioned her strap at Lakyta's entrance and eased her way in.

"Oh, fuck!" Lakyta shouted.

"Damn girl, I'm jealous," someone from under them shouted. Lakyta tried to stand up but Anndee kept stroking her in place and fiddling her clit. She moved her left hand up to palm Lakyta's large, soft breast before squeezing her nipple between two fingers.

"Agh, Anndee, yes! Yes! Yes!"

"Yes, girl, you better take that dick!" the same woman cheered. That gave Anndee more ammunition to speed up her strokes. The spur on the inside was hardening her clit and she could feel her orgasm was about to crest, as well as Lakyta's. She pulled out and turned her around, pushing her back against the glass sliding door.

"I want to see you when I make you come all over this dick," she growled. She lifted Lakyta's right thigh and wrapped it around her waist as she plunged back into her. Lakyta's screams echoed against the night sky as the woman beneath them kept egging them on.

"I'm coming!" Lakyta screamed. The way her face scrunched up and eyes rolled back paired with her screams was all Anndee needed for her orgasm to send her into a blinding whiteness, a realm of nothingness. She came hard as was ramming into Lakyta to get the spur to rub against her clit until she finished.

The women trembled in each others' arms as they tried to catch their breaths.

"Now that's what the fuck I'm talking about!" the woman said. Both women laughed as Anndee pulled them inside, closing the door and locking it. She pulled Lakyta to her and tongued her down before walking her to the bed and lying her down. Getting to her knees and pushing the other woman's legs back to where her knees were to her ears, Anndee ate her ass like it was her last meal. Lakyta's come dripped down Anndee's face and she didn't care. Her soft moans spoke to Anndee's inner ego as she slid her tongue up and inside where her strap had been.

"Yes, baby, right there! I'm bout to come on your tongue."

"Come then," Anndee demanded, and Lakyta obliged. When her orgasm settled, Anndee moved up to her clit, making the woman squirt as her body went rigid. Lakyta was thick, but Anndee stayed in the gym for that reason. She liked thick women.

Her face full of Lakyta's cream, she moved her up the bed and settled between her thighs, digging her deep with soft strokes. They both came calling each other's names, then drifted off to sleep, neglecting the other toys on the bed.

In the morning, Anndee woke up to her clit being sucked into Lakyta's mouth. It wasn't long before her orgasm woke her up faster than a few shots of espresso.

"Well, shit. Good morning," she moaned. Bemused, Lakyta moved up her body and straddled her, kissing her so she could taste herself on her lips. The woman ground her pussy against Anndee until she met her own release, her body shuttering like a camera. Anndee held her close, feathering kisses along her jawline and then her shoulder.

"We better get up," she said. "I have a whole day planned and if we stay in this bed, I'm going to fuck you all day."

"That doesn't seem so bad," Lakyta grinned slyly.

"Shower, now." Lakyta protested with a moan, but got up anyway. They showered, having another quickie and then dressed for the day. They were going to have breakfast in one of the restaurants and then head to the spa.

Once they were dressed in their robes, they had a couples massage. As Anndee was just about to doze off, Lakyta asked her a question that ruined the moment.

"Do you want kids of your own?" she asked. Anndee felt the woman tense who was massaging her, and rightfully so. That was a loaded question.

"Honestly, I hadn't thought about it. I know we are older in age, and you already have a son..."

"Who will be graduating in a couple of years."

"I don't know. I mean, I would like to, but if not, I'm okay with that." She was lying through her teeth, but more than a child, she wanted Lakyta.

"I'm not that old, Anndee. I don't know about physically having another child, but I am open to surrogacy and adoption." Anndee sat up as both masseuses left the room. Their massage was over anyway. Lakyta sat up and looked at her, hesitation in her eyes.

"Listen, this is new, we are new. Let's just take it a day at a time."

"Anndee, I'll be real with you. I haven't dated in a long time and I am looking to settle down and get married. I'm not into just casually dating or casual sex. I know it's only been five days, but I do have feelings for you." Anndee thought for a moment. She was feeling this woman as well, and it had been four years since her last relationship, if she could even call it that.

"How about this?" she began. "Let's shelve this conversation, for now, and come back to it in say a couple of months? For us to just be starting out, I don't want it to be so heavy so quickly."

"I just wanted you to know where I stand."

"And I get that, and I appreciate it. But let's get to the rest of our weekend and get to know each other first. Deal." Lakyta nodded, but Anndee could tell this was a topic she wouldn't get away from.

Chapter 9

Lakyta

The rest of that day was amazing, spent at Pleasure Pier, riding rides, and dining at her favorite place, the Tiki Hut. She couldn't shake their baby conversation, but she agreed that for now, they just needed to get to know each other.

Entering the Galveston Railroad Museum and taking a tour was easily her favorite part, other than the gardens. She was a double major, getting a bachelor's in history. Learning about the railroad and its history not only in Texas, but the U.S., was eye-opening.

The next stop was Bishop's Palace, a Victorian-style home in the East End Historic District. Being born and raised in Houston, Lakyta had never done an actual tour of Galveston and never knew all its history. She was glad that Anndee had made this happen and pegged her as a history buff before really getting to know her.

Throughout their sightseeing, they talked about everything under the sun, stopping to eat or get ice cream in between sites. By the time they made it back to the hotel, Lakyta was wiped. They showered the day off and headed to one of the restaurants for dinner.

They were both quiet after they placed their orders, looking at everything and everyone but each other. Lakyta felt awkward and wondered if bringing up babies so early was such a good idea.

"Okay, listen," Anndee started, slicing the silence. "This is clearly important to you and you aren't going to let it go. I'm okay with not having kids. I really am. I've made it this far without them, I can continue."

"I'm not saying I don't want to have kids, I just physically don't want to birth another child."

"You don't wanna have my baby?" Anndee asked, and then smirked as Lakyta frowned. The waitress came with their food, saving Lakyta from having to answer, even if only for that moment. They ate in silence, but Lakyta felt Anndee's eyes on her quite a few times.

Dessert came and went and Lakyta still hadn't answered. When Anndee took care of the bill, she pulled Lakyta with her. They ended up at the hotel pool. Lakyta had put on a swimsuit at Anndee's request under her dress. Fortunately, the pool was empty. They shed their clothes and got in, the water warm to the touch. Anndee pulled Laktya to her, and Lakyta wrapped her legs around the woman's waist.

"You still haven't answered my question," Anndee said against her lips as she slid her bikini bottom to the side and painted her already bulging clit with her thumb. Lakyta gasped into the woman's mouth as two fingers were slid in her.

"Oh shit, Anndee."

"I'm not letting you come until you answer me."

Lakyta's orgasm was just about to erupt when Anndee stopped her advances. Then she started again and stopped right when Lakyta knew she was going to fall apart.

"Oh, cat got your tongue?" Anndee let go of Lakyta and went underwater, lifting her up onto her shoulders. Lakyta yelped as she tried to regain her balance. She placed both hands on Anndee's

64

head as her bikini bottom was slid to the side again and this time, a tongue strummed her clit.

"Someone might see us," Lakyta whined, pushing her clit closer to Anndee's mouth. She was going to lose it if Anndee kept this up.

"Ah, ah, shiiiiiiiiiiiiiit!" Anndee stopped again. "What the fuck, Anndee? Let me fucking finish." She glared down at a smiling face and watched as Anndee licked her tongue out against her pearl that was on the verge of making everyone in this hotel know she was getting fucked.

"Dammit I'll have your baby, just eat my pussy till I come." Anndee buried her face in her essence and not even a minute later, Lakyta was screaming as she fucked Anndee's face.

"Yeah girl, let it on out!" a familiar voice shouted. Anndee eased an embarrassed and satiated Lakyta down.

"Honestly, I would've let you finish even if you said no," she admitted.

"What?" Lakyta shrieked, splashing Anndee.

That night, after they'd showered and tried out some of the other toys until Lakyta literally ran into the bathroom and locked the door, they lay tangled in each other, Anndee rubbing her back.

"This has been a really great weekend. I don't want to go home tomorrow."

"I'm glad you enjoyed it," Anndee responded. "But the weekend isn't over yet. I have something planned for you tomorrow as well."

"You keep spoiling me like this, and I'll drag you to the courthouse next week."

"Promise?" Lakyta giggled as Anndee tickled her before rolling on top and kissing her ever so gently. They ground their hips into each other, chasing one more orgasm before they both fell asleep.

On Sunday, they had breakfast by the pool and then headed to do some shopping. Lakyta tried to buy several outfits and some shoes for Cason, but Anndee insisted since she invited her on this trip.

By noon, they were both famished, and Anndee led them to the Rainforest Pyramid. Lakyta was in awe of all the animals. They walked down some steps and over to a little water reservoir that was lined with flowers that looked like they didn't belong there. There were so many different ones. Lakyta turned to look at Anndee who stood with her hands in her pockets.

"What is all this?" she asked.

"I just wanted to give you your flowers and show you how special you are. I know we've barely known each other for a week, but there is something about you that I just can't shake, and I am all in for seeing where this goes."

Lakyta ran and flung her arms around Anndee's neck, their lips crashing into each other, craving that connection.

"I'm all in, too," she panted.

"Good, because this is where we're eating lunch."

"With all these birds?"

"There's food for them, too." Lakyta just shook her hand and placed hers into Anndee's outstretched one, and let her lead the way.

The End.

Playing Games:
Kayla & Jayshaun

In Between Chapters

With my Hot Stepmom Summer series, I purposely didn't add any epilogues because I wanted to write in between chapters for prominent side characters. Everyone loved Kayla from "I Wanna Give You Your Flowers," so I knew she had to have her own story. That being said, these in between chapters are meant to be short, funny, sexy, and fulfilling.

Xoxo

M. L. Sexton

Kayla

"I still can't believe you're getting married," I said to my best friend, Lakyta. "And since I'm the one that hooked y'all up, I better get a shout out in y'all vows." Lakyta shook her head. She may have thought I was joking, but I was serious. Her pussy will still look like it needed a weed whacker to find it if it wasn't for me setting ehr up with Anndee.

"I appreciate all that you've done, but I will not be shouting you out in my vows. Besides, I'm too nervous to even think about that. The wedding is the day after tomorrow, and I feel like there are a million things to get done."

"Bitch, please. I confirmed with the caterers and the bakery. The flowers are sitting in the fridge at the venue. It is fully decorated, boring, and bland just like you like it, and Anndee's tux was picked up this afternoon according to the text she sent me. Cason is with your parents and your brother is coming in tonight." I did my best to reassure her and stick to my maid of honor duties, but her face was still stuck in a frown. "What's the real reason that you sitting over there looking like Anndee ain't eat your pussy in a month?"

Her head whipped up and the horror on her face had my sides hurting from laughter. The corners of her mouth turned up as she began to smile. It wasn't long before she was laughing with me. By the time we settled down, my cheeks were burning.

"It's just, we've only been together for less than a year, and we are already getting married."

"That's because you hoes are some U-Haul lesbians."

"Some what?"

"U-Haul lesbians. You know how they say that lesbians move faster than the speed of light? I mean y'all moved in together after like two months. And then by month three, y'all was talking about having a baby through IVF and how she was going to carry it. And then…"

"I get the point, Kayla," she groaned.

"I'm just saying, when you know it's love, you know it's love."

"Well, now that I've found my person, it's time for us to focus on you."

"You who?"

"You, bitch. I know that you don't want to be single forever, and I know you have your little sneaky links or whatever, but I want you to be happy."

"I get my back blown often. I have my own house and my own news segment on the local news, which by the way is nationally syndicated. I just bought my second car and third rental property, so the money is flowing. I am happy. I don't need nobody dusty, crusty, skidmarked draws son coming in and fucking up what I have going on."

"You say that now, but don't you get tired of sleeping alone at night?"

"Hell naw! I don't have to hear anybody snoring, and ain't nobody to kick out in the morning. Now, I have to get ready for work. I will see you tomorrow morning."

I gave her a hug and kiss on the cheek as she walked me out of her house. I really hated having lied to her like that. Everything she said was true, but little did she know, I had been fucking her brother, JJ.

Ever since he and his fiancee split, we had been talking. It was innocent at first, but one of his visits home, we got drunk and I let him sniff my pussy, and then he ate it, and then he slung that anaconda all up and through my ovaries, uterus, and fallopian tubes, rearranging shit without permission.

Jayshaun, Jr. aka "JJ"

"Fuck, Kayla, damn," I sputtered as she played "peek-a-boo" with my dick in her mouth. The way she swallowed and sucked at the same time had my eyes rolling in the back of my head. When my plane touched down, she picked me up after her news segment and brought me to her house. We wasted no time getting straight to business. I hadn't been home in two weeks.

My toes cramped as my ass tightened, my load shooting down her throat. My hips jerked to no particular rhythm as my balls spasmed. I swear my soul left my body for a second and I was looking down at me sitting on her couch and her on her knees.

When soul and body met, she popped my dick out her mouth and licked her lips. She was nasty as fuck, but that was why I had feelings for her. What initially started as just us fucking when I was in town for business as I prepared to move back here from overseas, turned into me developing feelings and not knowing if I should or shouldn't tell her.

As she walked towards the kitchen, I stood up with my dick swinging on hard and followed behind her fat ass that jiggled and rippled like waves in the ocean. She pulled two bottles of water out of the fridge and handed me one. I unscrewed the top and downed half as she leaned over the island and sipped on hers. Setting my bottle down, I stood behind her and slammed into her, water flying out her mouth as she dropped the bottle on the island, water spilling everywhere.

74

"Fuck, JJ!" she screamed as I gripped her left hip and pinned her down by the back of her neck with my right hand, her titties slapping against the water on the counter, splashing it like a little kid jumping in puddles after it rained. Her shit was tight and my balls were already tensing up. I ain't want to come yet, so I did what I had to in order for her to get hers: I pinched her clit hard and her body jolted like someone slammed on the brakes in the car too hard.

"Agh! Shiiiiiiiiit!" Her walls contracted around me, and I was done for. She milked me like I wasn't worth shit, had me screaming like a bitch as my strokes became like a kid coloring all outside the damn lines. I pulled out and spilled my seeds on her back, still holding her up as her orgasm settled.

Nothing could be heard but bated breaths and long sighs, the water dripping off the counter onto the tile floor.

"And you better clean that shit up," she said as she attempted to walk towards the stairs. All I could do was smirk and shake my head as I got some paper towels and did as she said.

We both showered, fucked, and showered again. She had quickly become my addiction over the past ten months. I would fly her out to whatever country I was living in, never staying anywhere for more than a month. I wasn't on no scary or in love type shit, but I was definitely feeling her, and I know she had her reservations. My sister was her best friend and she was getting married the day after tomorrow, well, tomorrow now since it was early the next day. This was Lakyta and Anndee's weekend.

Not to mention, I hadn't exactly told my parents or my sister that my fiancee and I had decided to go our separate ways. More so

75

that she was already married with six kids, and had a husband and a few sister wives. She used me to get away and for some attention. Imagine my surprise showing up to a restaurant that I frequented in Japan to see her and the whole family there. The look on her face told me everything I needed to know.

Kayla snuggled up to me and laid her head on my chest. Our heartbeats competed to be in sync until I felt her breathing slow as she drifted off to sleep, and I wasn't too far behind her.

A few hours later, we got up and got dressed. I called an Uber to take me to my new place where my car was waiting. Once I put my bags and things inside, I hopped in the car and headed to my parents' house before I met up with Anndee for the "bachelorette" party, which I told both her and Lakyta that it's weird to have a "bachelor" or "bachelorette" party in the day time. I know they weren't trying to get lit before the rehearsal dinner.

Stepping into my parents' house made me miss being home even more. Ma was clearly throwing down for breakfast. The aromatic aroma of biscuits, sausage, eggs, grits, and pancakes could be smelled at the door.

I tiptoed in the kitchen up behind my mother and wrapped my arms around her waist placing a kiss on her cheek.

"Oh, what the hell?!" She turned around and had her spatula ready to hit me with it.

"Ma, it's just me," I said, taking a few steps back and laughing.

"Boy, I was about to Molly wop your ass." My eyes narrowed at her and my head cocked to the side.

"Molly wop?" I questioned.

"Yeah, ain't that what the kids say now?" I shook my head and cautiously went in for another hug as I swiped a biscuit out of the pan behind her. The spatula met the back of my head as I took a bite.

"Ow!"

"That's what your ass gets for not telling me you were home, sneaking up on me in my own house, and stealing a biscuit without washing your hands. Ain't no telling where your hands been."

"Anyway, where's Pops?"

"He went to meet up with Anndee and her uncle. Something about...hell, I don't know. Anyway, wash ya hands and then come sit down and catch me up."

After washing my hands, she had plates set at the dining room table. I heard the front door open and in came Cason and Lakyta.

"Oh, Grannie you cooked breakfast?" Cason asked, and then ran to the restroom followed by Lakyta.

We ate in a comfortable silence before Ma asked me the question I had been trying to avoid.

"So, when do we meet this fiancee of yours?" Cason and Lakyta looked up, anticipating my response.

"Uh, well, you won't. We broke up."

"Oh no," Lakyta said, her face frowning up.

"That sucks ass," Cason said. "Ow!" Lakyta slapped him upside his head. She was definitely our mother's child.

"Watch your mouth, boy," she scolded.

"Well, it was kind of a saving grace. She had six kids, a husband, and she was a sister wife." Their mouths dropped as expected. "Yeah, I was shocked, too."

"That hussy," my mom seethed. Cason snickered followed by me and Lakyta. It was rare my mom cussed or used derogatory words, but she was in rare form today.

"I guess we had better get going to these "bachelorette" parties," I announced as I stood up and took my dishes into the kitchen, placing them in the sink.

"I still can't go?" Cason asked. He was only 17 and thought he was grown enough to hang with the big boys.

"No," Lakyta said. "You'll stay here with your grandmother and help out around the house."

When we got outside, Lakyta stopped at my car. She had that look on her face that let me know she was up to something.

"I know you said you broke up with your fiancee and all, but I know a "just got some pussy" face when I see one."

"You wild'n, you know that?"

"You can play coy all you want, but I will find out who she is." And that was what I was afraid of.

Kayla

I don't know why Lakyta thought it was a good idea to have a damn bachelorette party in the middle of the day before the rehearsal dinner, knowing that day drinking is my shit. About to have me lit all the way up and accidently throw my coochie at her very married daddy. That man was fine as fuck to have two kids, a grandson, and a wife.

I went along with this idea to tour the Montrose area and go to different restaurants. This shit would've been so much more fun had we done this at night when all the clubs were open.

There were five of us since she decided to invite some of her college friends. She swears that I knew these girls, but college was a blur. Dicks and alcohol was all I remembered. I don't know how I passed all my classes, let alone walked across the stage at graduation.

"Oh, this is sooo cute!" said the white girl. Yeah, she had a white friend, and her name was Becky. How ironic.

"Oh, this is sooo cute," I mocked, thinking no one heard me until Lakyta elbowed me.

"Play nice," she whispered.

"I am playing nice, but you know my issue with white women."

Back in college, I competed against this white girl for a spot on our campus's radio show. The host was fine as hell, and I had fucked him a time or two. It wasn't like I was trying to date him or anything. I needed this for my internship hours. Anyway, they gave it to the white girl and she ended up taking over the whole show, the dude losing his spot.

I've been at the news station for ten years and last year, they hired a new producer, a white woman. She came in thinking she was about to run things during my segment, trying to insert her tasteless opinions where they were not needed. We got into it, I may have reached out and touched her one good time, only to later find out she was sleeping with one of the other news anchors and pregnant for him when she had a whole wife who was the producer of another show. She tried to sew me and I told her I'd split her wig. She told me she ain't wearing a wig, but the look I gave her was enough.

The next morning, she came in playing nice and brought me coffee. I should've known it was a trick. She had laced it with a damn laxative. I was shitting bricks, literally. My booty hole was so raw. After the show, I caught her in the parking lot and whooped her pregnant ass. She quit after that.

Later that evening, after the bachelorette party, I headed to Lakyta's house to get dressed. She and Anndee had moved into a mini mansion because Anndee claimed they were going to fill it with kids. Lakyta told her she better marry a few other bitches because she wasn't popping out any kids and she would only suffer through Anndee's needy ass being pregnant with one. The plan was for Lakyta to carry, but she found out she was in early onset menopause, and no longer had a period. The news was devastating for her, and me. I even offered to carry the child, which is some shit I'd never thought I'd do since I don't want kids, but for her and Anndee, I would.

Luckily, Anndee shut that down real quick. She said that if Lakyta couldn't carry, she would. I got on my knees for something other than sucking dick that night and thanked God she said "no."

"I really thank you for putting up with me and my wedding shenanigans," Lakyta said to us as we threw back a shot in her kitchen.

"You owe me," I responded.

"I owe you what?"

"I was ready to pop my pussy on a handstand in a half-naked nigga's face." Becky's face reddened as her eyes widened. "Yes, Becky. I was going to pop. My. Pussy. On. A. Handstand." I clapped in between each word as she visibly looked like she was going to pass out. The other two women, Taneea and Raquel, fell out laughing. Lakyta shook her head.

"Ignore her. She has no couth. She was raised by wild animals."

"Bitch, a pack of alpacas showed me how to pop this juicy pussy. Besldes, this my pussy I can do what I want. I'm a big girl." I had to laugh at my damn self along with Taneea and Raquel.

An hour later, we pulled up in the limo at the hotel where the rehearsal dinner was and where we would be staying the night since the wedding was there. With my bestie being a botanist, it was flowers everywhere. Flowers that I had never seen before. But what really caught my attention was JJ and his fine ass in that tailor made suit. He was standing with Anndee and a couple of other guys at the entrance.

"Damn, my wife look good," Anndee hollered as she pulled Lakyta in for a sloppy kiss.

"Watch your hands on my baby girl, Anndee," Lakyta's father warned. Her hands had slid down to Anndee's ass.

"Yes, sir," Anndee responded, holding her hands up, surrendering. She and Lakyta snickered as they headed inside. JJ stood by the door and gently pulled my arm.

"Here's my room key. Room 317." He handed me the card and then walked in. I smiled to myself and slid it in my clutch.

Dinner was literally a five course meal, and I was stuffed. I didn't realize that so many of their guests would be here for the rehearsal dinner, but there were some fine men in here, including Anndee's cousin who coaches at the high school.

After dinner, the DJ really went in on all the latest hits, even throwing it back to 99s and 00s. I hit that dance floor hard with Lakyta and the bridesmaids with my Megan knees. Well, all the bridesmaids except for Becky. She sat at the table and snapped her fingers off beat.

I could feel JJ's eyes burning into me as I ground my ass all on one of the bridesmen's dick. It was hard and big, too, but JJ was just going to have to deal. We weren't together, and I didn't want Lakyta to know that we had been fucking around for months quite yet. I had never kept anything from her. A few minutes later, my phone buzzed and it was a text from JJ.

JJ: Meet me in hall, right the fuck now.

I looked up and he was glaring at me, and then got up to leave the ballroom. I thanked the guy I was dancing with, then excused myself. Once I stepped into the hall, a firm hand grabbed my arm and dragged me into a nearby family bathroom.

"What the fuck, JJ?" He pulled me in and then slammed it shut, locking it.

"What the fuck were you doing out there?"

"It's called dancing."

"You were backing yo ass up on anotha nigga in my face."

"And? We ain't together." There was a pregnant pause as he looked at me, his gaze softening.

"Okay, so what are we then? What is this?"

"We fuck, that's it. We've talked about this several times, and we agreed that it was just sex."

"Well, that doesn't work for me anymore."

"The hell does that mean, it "doesn't work for you anymore?""

"It means, no touching other men, or women, because I know you into that, too."

"I don't know where you got off thinking that you're my daddy, but I can do what I want with my ass, hands, pussy, mouth."

"Don't fucking play with me, Kayla." His eyes darkened, and funny enough, my ass was turned on. "I don't want to play these games. It ain't just sex no more. I want you, and we are going to be together. I don't like other men having access to you."

"Nigga, I don't give one fuck, I don't give two fucks. I don't give a red fuck or a blue fuck. I don't give a Horton Hears a Who fuck about what you don't like about what I do or what you don't want me to do." He gave me a blank stare. Before I could blink, his hand was around my neck, and he had my back against the cool tile wall, his tongue down my throat. He reached under my dress and snarled against my lips at the fact that I didn't have any panties on.

"You was rubbing your pantiless ass against another nigga's dick?" he questioned, brows furrowed and breath coming in fast. I couldn't answer as two fingers plunged into me making me scream out. He loosened his grip on my neck as his fingers gently massaged my walls, and his thumb teased my clit.

I began to see stars as my orgasm coated his fingers and gushed like thick honey down my legs. My thighs were shaking as he continued to play in my release, pulling two more orgasms out of me. I went blind momentarily with the last orgasm, having to lean my head against his chest until my vision cleared.

"Now, go back out there and act like nothing happened," he demanded.

"But I need to clean myself up first," I said, my head jerking up.

"Nu uh. I want you to feel what I did to you as you play in them other niggas faces." He smacked my ass and waited for me to head out first. I had to walk with my thighs close together to keep my juices from running further down my legs. I could hear him laughing behind me. Pay back was going to be a bitch, and his ass had another thing coming. Since he was the best man, we were seated right next to each other. Game on, my nigga.

♌♌

"Alright everyone, it is time for the best man and I to make a toast," Kayla said, grabbing everyone's attention. "And I will go first. I've known Lakyta forever. She's like the sister I've never had. When I sent Anndee to her house, I legit thought it would just be for her to get her kitty scratched, but it turned into something more. And I am tooting my own horn since she said they weren't going to thank me in their vows." Everyone laughed.

That was one of the many things I loved about her. She wasn't afraid to speak her mind, and she was funny as hell.

"A love like theirs is rare and needs to be celebrated. To Lakyta and Anndee!" Everyone raised their glasses and took a sip. As soon as she sat down, her hand was on my dick. It caught me off guard and I jumped, hitting my knee underneath the table.

"You okay, son?" my father asked.

"Uh huh," I squeaked out.

"Your turn,' Kayla smiled as I bricked up and she found her way inside my pants.

"I'll be saying, ah hm, my speech, sitting down. The uh, wine has me a bit buzzed." Light laughter could be heard as her hand went up and down my shaft. I felt the tip bead with my precum as she stroked it so painfully slow.

"I uh, ha, um, love Anndee for my sister. And um, she seems like a nice, mmm, person." Kayla was not playing fair at all, and I guess this was her payback for earlier. "I hope to one day, gah, have a love like theirs."

"JJ are you sure you're okay?" my mother asked.

"Yeah, JJ, you look a little, peakish." Kayla smirked as I tried to glare, but the way she had a grip on my dick and how soft and coincidently lubricated her hand was, my face contorted on its own.

"I'm fine." I cleared my throat as I felt my release building up. "IjustwanttosayhowthankfulIamforAnndeewalkingintomysisterslifean dImhappyyoumakeherhappy, eeeee, agh fuck!" I spewed my words out the same time my seeds did, all over my lap. I looked down and was glad she had thought to put a napkin down. She gave a few more jerks and my balls tightened as my fist slammed on the table.

"JJ!" my mother scolded.

"Sorry, Ma. I just got a little too…excited and overwhelmed. I'm so happy for y'all." Anndee and Lakyta both frowned at me as everyone clapped slowly.

After the rehearsal dinner was over, I headed straight to my room to get out of my clothes. Kayla had another thing coming as soon as she got in this fucking room. I heard the lock on the door click and looked up as she came in with a huge grin on her face. She shut and locked the door as she bent over laughing. I stood there butt ass naked with my hands on my hips glaring at her.

She stepped out of her shoes and threw her purse on the couch. Walking over to me, tears ran down her face as she wrapped her arms around my neck.

"That was the worst best man speech if I ever heard one," she chuckled.

"I'm glad you were amused. I can't believe you gave me a handjob in front of my parents."

"I can't believe you made me walk around and sit in my own orgasm. So, we're even."

"Not even close." I ripped her dress off as she squealed and threw her on the bed. I could still smell her orgasm from earlier as I spread her legs and had her knees to her ears, swirling my tongue in her pussy and getting it wet again.

"Jayshaun, gotdammit!" Her leg muscles trembled as her pussy squeezed my tongue. I swiped up to her clit and it throbbed as she thrashed through a strong orgasm. Her thighs clamped so hard around the sides of my head, I could barely hear her screams as she gushed against my mouth.

I rolled over so that I was sitting on the floor with my head back so she could ride my face. I was the throne to this goddess who tasted like my future.

She came twice more before I got up and crawled between her legs, rocking into her gently. I looked in her eyes as she looked into mine before she sucked my bottom lip into her mouth. The feeling threw my hips offbeat, but I quickly regained it as our tongues wrestled for dominance.

"I want you, Kayla," I whispered.

"I want you, too."

We entangled ourselves with the sheets and each other for the rest of the night. Nothing else needed to be said.

Kayla

Wedding Day

I woke up the next morning, and JJ was still snoring loudly. I put it on his ass several times last night and had him sleeping like a baby. I really can't talk because my ass was knocked out, too.

I crept around and found a shirt of his to slip on as I gathered my things. I tiptoed backwards out of the room, and closed the door gently. I relaxed and let out a breath, resting my forehead against the door.

"You dirty ho." I screamed as I jumped and turned around, coming face-to-face with a smirking Lakyta.

"You're not mad?" I asked.

"No, though next time you decide to give my brother a handjob, make sure that it's only your forearm on down that is moving."

"You think everybody knows?"

"Probably, but I don't care. Let's go so you can wash the ho off and get into hair and makeup." She turned and sauntered off down the hall to the bridal suite.

I took a long ass hot shower since I had an hour before we were to get our hair and makeup done. Room service delivered breakfast, and I scarfed down my food to replenish from last night and this morning.

"I see someone was putting in some work last night," Raquel quipped.

"Or someone put some work in on her," Taneea added.

"What does that mean?" Becky asked. We all looked at her.

"It means…" Lakyta began.

"It means I sucked some dick, threw some ass, and sat on a niggas face. I let him eat my ass, too."

"Ewww, Kayla. That's my brother."

"And? You act like he don't fuck."

"I don't need to know the details of him fucking, damn."

"So, are y'all a thing?" Raquel asked.

"I think so. We talked about it, but I mean we were also on the brink of an orgasm, so it may not have been something we should've discussed while his python was swimming inside me."

"For fuck's sake, Kayla!" I laughed as Raquel and Taneea joined in. Becky just looked lost.

Two hours later, hair fried, dyed, and laid to the side, we were lined up and ready to walk in and get my bestie married. Since I was the maid of honor and JJ was the best man, we walked in together.

The room was set up nicely with sheer material draped from the ceiling, the tables were lined with cream runners and an assortment of rainbow colored flowers, and the chairs had rainbow colored covers. Everyone was told to wear solid color attire in various colors of the rainbow.

Cason, despite being nearly grown, was the ringbearer. When it was time for Anndee to walk in, she had her uncle on her arm. She wore a lavender tuxedo and some black and lavender Chucks. Her hair was freshly braided back with gold hair jewelry. I stood there nervous, excited for them to see each other as if it were my wedding.

I looked over and saw JJ staring at me. He smirked as I smiled back, heat rising to my face. When the music changed, we both looked towards the door to see Lakyta with her father on her arm. My vision blurred as tears swelled in my eyes.

As her father gave her away and she took her place by Anndee, I could literally say that I have never seen my bestie so happy.

"When you showed up at my door that day, and I slammed it in your face," Lakyta began, "I knew instantly that I was not going to be able to let you go. You worked me out, and then you *worked me out*." Little laughs could be heard.

"Your daddy is still in the room, Kyta," her father grumbled. Her mother swatted his arm as Lakyta rolled her eyes and turned back to Anndee.

"What I love most and what made me really fall for you," she paused, getting choked up, "is how you have been there for Cason. He adores you and looks up to you. The bond you two have makes my heart feel like it's going to burst out of my chest. You are my person, and I'd move mountains and part seas just to keep you in my life."

"You ain't Jesus," I blurted out. She gave me a scolding look as the audience roared. "My bad."

"Lakyta, having a door slammed in my face was something I never experienced before. I was like, is this woman crazy? But when you opened it back up, it led to you opening up your heart to let me in. You've loved me so hard, harder than I've ever been loved before. I see you with Cason and the kind of young man he is, and I know that our future kids are in good hands."

"Kid," Lakyta corrected. Anndee chuckled.

"Anyway, I don't know how I was living or navigating life before you, and I don't want to go back to that. You are my present, you are my future, you are my forever."

There wasn't a dry eye in the house as they exchanged rings and jumped the broom. I was glad when pictures were done so we could turn up at the reception. After the first dance, father-daughter dance, and bride-mother/auntie dance, I got to get out on the floor and shake my ass. Everybody joined in, even Becky, though she probably should've sat this out too like she did last night.

The last song of the night, *Teenage Fever* by Drake, came on and I felt arms turning me around and wrapping around my waist, pulling me into a hard chest.

"Hey," he said.

"Hey," I responded.

"I have the room for another night, if you want to move your things into it and stay with me."

"Is that so?" I questioned.

"It is."

"I'll have to think about that. One of the other bridesmen asked me to come to his room and Netflix and chill." He raised an eyebrow and narrowed his eyes.

"I'm going to take a page out of your book and say, I don't give one fuck, I don't give two fucks, I don't give no ifs, ands, or butt fucks."

"Nigga, did you just quote Weezy?"

"I don't give a Horton Hears a Who fuck about nan nigga that wants to do anything with you. I'll lay his ass out and then fuck yo pussy up so bad, it'll start queefing my name."

I howled and shook my head. This man just didn't know what he was getting into fucking with me.

The end.

Long Walks on the Beach

M. L. Sexton

Chapter 1 (Gelisa)

"Dammit!" I screamed, slamming the keys on my laptop. This was the third photographer that had backed out of going to Mexico with me because they didn't have a passport. One of the others was an ex-con who couldn't leave the country, and the other offered to bring her husband in hopes of a threesome. I deaded that situation immediately. There were all kinds of creeps in this world.

I was thinking of giving up on the idea because it didn't seem like I would find any photographer who could pay their own way to get to Mexico for the shoot. Now, my best friend, Bleau, had told me that maybe I should offer to pay their way, but I said that it would be best not to since someone might try to scam me or use me to get the most outrageous things to eat or bring back to the country.

Next month's theme for my blog was all about Mexico and its beautiful scenery and culture, but especially the beaches. I had already toured different parts of the country, but I took those shots myself. For this particular trip that was sponsored, I wanted a professional photographer, and someone I could use long term, which meant I needed a real photographer.

My phone rang and I picked it up to see Yahir's, my son, face. I smiled as I answered his video call.

"Hey, lovebug."

"Hey, Mommy. Mimi said to call you."

"Why does your Mimi have to tell you to call me instead of you calling me on your own?"

"Well, I want to keep playing my video game with my cousins and Paw Paw even though he's losing. He's really bad, Mommy." Gelisa laughed and shook her head.

Yahir was staying with my parents for the summer in Dallas along with his three cousins, my sister's kids. My parents had me and my twin at a young age, so they weren't too old to take care of four boys under eight. They were in better shape than I was.

"Well, don't stay on that game too long."

"I'm not. Mimi said we are going to Six Flags Over Texas in a little while with Uncle Byron." Byron is my younger brother who still lives with my parents. He was about to graduate high school next May.

"Okay, well you have fun and behave for your grandparents."

"I will. I love you, Mommy."

"I love you, too, baby."

When we hung up, I texted Bleau to meet me for drinks later on that evening. I needed to get out of the house and destress from finding a photographer.

"Why don't you make a post on Instagram or TikTok?" Bleau asked as we sipped margaritas at Los Cucos. That was our favorite happy hour spot, and we tried to go there once a week. "I don't even know why you didn't do a search on social media before making that ad."

"I don't know either. I guess I didn't want to seem like a creep sliding in people's DMs."

"It isn't creepy if you are seeking a job opportunity. Just try it and see what happens." While we chatted, I simultaneously made

98

a quick ad on Canva and posted it to Instagram and TikTok, then locked my phone. I was hoping Bleau would be able to go with me to Mexico, but she had plans for that week. "Tell me why you can't come with me again?"

"Well, I met someone. I don't want to get into too many details, but just know that this person is really sexy, and they have a lot of money."

"You golddigging hoe," I snickered. She swatted at me, but I dodged her. "Who is she and where did you meet?"

"She's a billionaire, and I met her at work." I shook my head. Bleau was an interior designer, so I can only imagine she met this woman while designing her house.

"I hope she's better than Tierney."

"Ugh," she scoffed. "Don't remind me about that trick. I still can't believe she swindled me into booking her two tickets to Madrid for her to end up taking her damn wife."

"I wish I could've been at the airport that day," I laughed.

"Have you talked to Makayla lately?" she raised an eyebrow as I quickly looked down at my drink. Makayla and I were currently separated. We had gotten together while I was pregnant with Yahir. She took a job in another state and wanted us to go with her, but I didn't want to leave Texas. She treated Yahir as her own, and he loved her like a second mom.

I got pregnant with Yahir through IVF because I wanted a kid. He is the best thing to ever happen to me, and then Makayla walked into our lives and rounded out our family. I still love her and want to be with her, but I told her that long distance was not what I signed up for.

"I did, last week. She said she would fly down to Dallas to spend some time with Yahir. Legally, she did sign his birth certificate, so she technically can see him whenever. My parents so desperately want us to get back together, but I don't want to do long-distance."

"I get that, Gelisa, I really do, but I really think you should reconsider. Even Melisa agreed."

"You've been talking to my sister about my love life?" I narrowed my eyes at her.

"Yes, and she's concerned. She said you won't talk to her about it and she wants to know how you are really doing." I examined her face and she let it slip in her eyes, and I immediately knew. "You're fucking my sister!" She jumped at my accusation, but didn't deny it. "How long?"

"A few weeks."

"And when were you going to tell me?"

"If it got serious."

"I always knew eventually you two would get together."

"How so?"

"You've had a crush on her since forever, and if we weren't fraternal twins, I'd think you had a crush on me, too."

"Don't flatter yourself."

"So, tell me more about how you're fucking my sister."

Chapter 2 (Makayla)

As soon as I saw the ad pop up on my "for you page" I immediately sent a DM. Since Gelisa and I had separated and I moved to California, I had taken up photography and was actually really good. In the past year, she and I hadn't talked much. When I would call, she would just hand the phone off to our son, Yahir. I missed him like crazy, but with my new venture as a photographer, I spent a lot of time traveling.

I looked around at my empty apartment, and then closed and locked the door behind me. A couple of weeks ago, I decided to move back to Houston to get my family back. I missed the fuck out of my wife and being able to hug and kiss our son, read him bedtime stories and play with dinosaurs. I hadn't told her that I was moving back, but I did mention it to her parents who were more than happy to hear it.

The airport wasn't too crowded as I went through the pre-check line. The flight wasn't bad either. Soon as I landed, my car was waiting for me. I had it shipped ahead of my arrival, so I would have it when I got here. I already had an Air BnB set up for Yahir to spend the week with me before heading to my hotel in Houston. I decided not to get an apartment because I knew within the depths of my soul that my wife would take me back.

In the past year, there has been no one else. I took a vow of abstinence and shot down every woman who tried to snatch me up. My mind, body, and soul were only for Gelisa Marquette. I only had eyes for her.

The driveway to my in-law's house was about a quarter of a mile long. They lived in this bourgeoisie ass Black neighborhood, and I loved that for them. Before I could even shut the door, the front door burst open and Yahir came flying out, screaming, "Mama!" I squatted down and held my arms open for him to jump in. My heart threatened to beat out my chest as tears swelled in my eyes.

I whirled him around as he squealed and giggled. This boy was my world, and I don't want to know life without him in it. I carried him to the door where his grandfather waited with his hands in his pockets, smiling.

"What's up, Pops?" I greeted as he brought us into a hug.

"My third daughter is here to make my other daughter realize her mistake," he beamed.

"We can only hope."

"Is that my Makayla?" my mother-in-law asked, coming from the back of the house with a huge smile. She kissed my cheek and hugged me tight. I heard little footsteps coming from around the corner.

"Auntie Kayla!" they screamed. I don't know how Gelisa's parents put up with all four grandkids, but I commend them for that. I knelt down and wrapped all four boys in my arms.

"Alright, that's enough," their grandmother, fussed. "Y'all gon on and play now while I fix Makayla a plate." The boys ran off towards the oversized playroom they had. In the kitchen, Byron, my brother-in-law, got up from his seat and dapped me up.

"What's good, sis?"

"Man, just trying to see how I can get your big-headed sister to see what's up."

"Don't talk about my baby like that," Mama Dukes said, placing a plate for me on the island. I swear this woman could cook her ass off. I missed the holidays I spent here in Dallas eating on good ass food. Gelisa could throw down, almost as good as her mama, though I would never tell her that.

"So, what's the plan?" Pops asked.

"Well, she posted about needing a photographer for a shoot in Mexico. Y'all know I've been doing photography and traveling. I responded to her post and said that not only could I go, but I could pay my own way and was able to be full time."

"Won't she know it's you, though?" Byron asked.

"Naw. My business page doesn't have photos of me, nor can anything be traced back to me. I think my anonymity is what keeps people intrigued. I want them to know my work, not me."

"But your work is you, sweetheart," Mama Dukes said softly.

"I know, but I just want the focus to be on my work."

"How do you think this is going to play out when you get there?" Pops inquired.

"I'm not sure, but at that point, she won't have a choice but to work with me. She hasn't responded to my inquiry yet, but I think she'll say yes."

"Man, I wish I could be there when this shit blows up in your face," Byron guffawed then winced when his mother slapped him upside his head.

"Watch your mouth," she warned. When I finished eating, I went to get Yahir and we headed to the Air BnB. I had bought

103

some stuff for him while I was still in Cali so that his grandparents wouldn't have to worry about packing anything.

By the time we made it, he was fast asleep in his carseat. I grabbed him and the bags and headed inside. He woke up long enough for me to bathe him and then get him into bed. After my shower, I put on a pair of boxers and a sports bra. When I finally checked my phone, I saw that Gelisa had responded. She hadn't even asked for a photo, but she praised my work and my online portfolio. I booked my ticket and called the hotel that she said she was staying at.

I made sure that they booked us in the same room. I was told that it was a sponsored stay, but I explained and sent proof that I was her wife. I knew she would be pissed, but I didn't give a fuck. She was, is, and will always be mine.

Chapter 3 (Gelisa)

I was thrilled when I got the notification from the photographer on my post. They messaged me their flight details and hotel reservation. In just a few days, I would be going to stay in this five star hotel in a penthouse suite, just to promote it on my blog. I was finally going to get professional photos done, and given their social media and catalog, I could definitely see this person being with me long-term.

Through a few hours of research, I could not find the face behind "Long Walks on the Beach Photography". They specialized in beach photography, and I was even able to find some of their work in countless magazines and blogs.

When I spoke to Yahir a few days ago, and everyday since, he was telling me all the things he was doing with Makayla. She went with them to Six Flags Over Texas and a carnival at the AT&T Stadium where the Dallas Cowboys play. They were having some summer camp as well for kids.

The times that I did speak to Makayla on the phone, my pussy stayed soaking wet. She looked fine as hell. She was the definition of tall, dark, and handsome, with mocha skin, dimples, juicy lips, a fade around the sides and back of her head with her hair in a messy bun at the top, and her fucking muscles.

She still looked at me the same as when she was here and we were happy. But I had to push my feelings to the side and remember that we are co parents. That's it.

The doorbell rang, and I was pleasantly surprised to see my twin. "Best friend fucker," I said as I pulled her into a hug as she laughed. She was dressed in this floor length sundress that put all her lady lumps and bumps on display. We were the same height, 5'11, and same build, we just didn't quite have the same face.

"Where are you taking my best friend?" I asked as we headed to the living room so she could help me pack the rest of my things. I was only going to be gone a week, but I had to have options. There were clothes all over the couch, the floor, and the coffee table, and three empty suitcases.

"I am taking her to Miami," she responded as she started putting clothes that were on the coffee table in the suitcase that was on the floor beside it.

"How long have you liked her?"

"Since we were kids."

"And you never said anything because?"

"She was your best friend. You kept claiming how she was the third twin, or the triplet as you put it. It felt weird. Then I met Salim, and we had the boys, and now, I'm here."

"I still can't believe it."

"Well, bitch, believe it." I could tell there was something she wasn't telling me, but I wasn't going to push the issue. I was just glad that she was here and that she seemed happy.

Once everything was packed, we ate some pizza and drank margaritas and had a slumber party. My flight was first thing in the morning, and the photographer had messaged me to say that they were already in Mexico. They went a day early to take some photos for themselves before I had them on call the entire week.

The flight to Cancun wasn't bad, but the two hour drive was miserable. My driver nearly got us killed three times. When we finally arrived at the hotel, which I now realize is in fact a beautiful resort (the website did it no justice), I could not get out of that car fast enough. A bellhop came out and grabbed my bags as I took in the ivory stone exterior, the brown framing of the windows, the luscious palm trees and large boulders that lined the sides.

"Hola, senora," the concierge greeted. "Do you have a reservation?"

"Yes, I am a sponsored guest, Gelisa Marquette." He typed on the computer and then looked up at me and smiled.

"I have your reservation here. I am Juan Pedraza, the assistant manager. I am so glad to have you stay with us, and my hope is that your trip is marvelous and the accommodations are to your liking. Here is your room key, and please, follow your bellhop."

"Gracias," I said and followed the man with my bags to the bank of elevators. We went up to the second floor and to the right down a long hallway.

"Here is your room," the man said. "Please leave your cart outside the room and someone will be by to get it later on."

I gave him a tip and then swiped my keycard and headed inside, bringing one of my bags with me. The suite was brightly lit with the french doors to the veranda wide open, the breeze from the ocean blowing the cream linen curtains. When you walk in, to the left is a small table and a mirror. I placed my purse and key card there. Down to steps you are in the living room which is completely furnished with a u-shaped couch that faces a big flat

107

screen television mounted on a brick wall. There's a faux fireplace for aesthetics. Off to the left is a kitchen with a small island that could seat four. To the right is the door to the bedroom.

I walked in and saw a suitcase by the bed. It wasn't just any suitcase. I know that suitcase.

"No," I gasped.

"Hey, Gelisa," came that familiar panty melting voice behind me. I slowly turned around and came face-to-face with Makayla, and then everything went black.

I felt something cool being pressed to my forehead as someone stroked my hair. My eyes fluttered open and I knew I hadn't been dreaming.

"What are you doing here?" I croaked. She pressed a straw to my lips and I sipped the cool cucumber lemon water. She set it on the table and then her deep brown irises pierced into me.

"I am the photographer."

"What?!" I tried to sit up and instantly felt dizzy.

"Gelisa, relax."

"You're the person behind "Long Walks on the Beach"?"

"Yes."

"When did you get into photography?"

"Well, if you weren't always so quick to get off the phone, you would have known that I've been doing travel photography for a while and I'm really good at it."

"I saw your portfolio, and you are, but why would you respond to my post, and why are you in my suite?"

"Our suite, and you said you needed someone full time, and I can be that."

"Back up. What do you mean our suite?" I tried to sit up again and she helped me lean against the headboard.

"Don't get mad, but I called the resort and asked them to put me in the same room as you."

"Makayla, are you fucking kidding me? This is a sponsored trip. I'm getting paid for this!"

"Well, I am too. I explained and had to prove that I am your wife, and then I talked to the manager about my photography and sent over my portfolio, so this is a sponsored trip for me as well."

"I need to call the front desk. You need a separate room." I reached for the phone and she grabbed my hand.

"I want to make a deal," she said. I tried to pull my hand away, but she pulled it to her mouth and kissed my palm like she used to always do, sending chills through my body and making my pussy throb. I clenched my thighs and she smiled against my hand, her eyes settled between my legs.

"Glad to see I still have that effect on you."

"What is this deal?"

"I want us to reconnect. I moved back to Houston, and I am currently staying in a hotel. I want my family back, and I am not giving up without a fight."

"I thought you did that when you left us."

"I wanted you both to come with me."

"You took a job and said yes before even talking to me."

"I did, and I am sorry for that. That was the first big mistake I made. The second was leaving you and Yahir." I nodded in agreement. "I want us to spend this week together, rekindling our marriage, while working together. This is a big opportunity for both of us that can open more doors. I will not get in the way of that."

"What do you want me to do?" I asked.

"I want you to try."

"I can't make any promises."

"I'm not asking you to, I just want you to try."

"Fine. But where will you sleep?"

"The fuck you mean where will I sleep? You're still my wife, and we will sleep in the same bed. We will cuddle. I won't fuck you unless you say I can, but you will sleep in my arms. Best believe that." The smirk on her lips let me know she smelled how aroused I was. I clenched my thighs tighter. "Now, go shower so we can head to dinner." She got up and left the room, closing the door behind her. I pulled my phone out of my pocket and went to my suitcases that she had brought in while I was passed out.

Groupchat with best friend and twin:

Gelisa: Code red, bitches! Code red!

Bleau: Makayla must be there.

Melisa: Yep.

Gelisa: You heffas knew she was going to be here?

Melisa: Yeah, she told Mom and Dad and then she called us. We met with her a couple days ago.

Gelisa: And y'all didn't think to tell me that?

Bleau: Now, why would we do that and ruin the fun?

Gelisa: I hate you both. This woman just told me that I WILL sleep in the same bed as her in her fucking arms.

Melisa: ???

Bleau: And?

Melisa: Y'all are still married. Hell, let her eat that pussy too.

Bleau: And fuck you seven ways till Sunday.

Gelisa: I hope that the first time y'all get ready to fuck, that your periods start.

Bleau: Did you forget I am in early onset menopause?

Melisa: And I had a hysterectomy due to cancer?

Gelisa: :| I'm done talking to you hoes. I'm going to shower as she demanded so we can go to dinner.

Melisa: Have fun!

Bleau: And let her dick you down! LMAO!

I sent the middle finger emoji and then threw my phone on the bed. I took a cold shower and that did nothing to my pussy. Just being in the mere presence of this woman had her betraying me. I walked out of the room and she was sitting on the couch with her back to me.

When she turned to look at me, her gaze set me on fire the way she drank me. She slowly stood up and licked her lips, not taking her eyes off me as she rounded the couch until she was standing right in front of me.

"You look good enough to eat," she groaned. I couldn't take my eyes off her. They always had this way of holding me in place. She grabbed my hand and intertwined our fingers. She never let it go even when we got to the restaurant around the corner. It was an outdoor restaurant and we had a table that allowed us to see the beach and the water. It was very intimate and I was unnerved.

When it came to Makayla, no one else compared. She was an amazing wife and is an amazing mother, but she hurt me when she left. Her expectation of me to follow was assuming. I usually couldn't say no to her, but that time, I did. I didn't want to move to Cali. Both our families were here. Her parents are heading up to Dallas in July to spend time with Yahir and my sister's kids who they also claim as their grandkids.

This being here with her is beyond unexpected and a little unsettling. How am I supposed to concentrate and work with her when I know for a fact that through that camera lens, her eyes are fucking me into oblivion?

"You ready to order?" she asked. I nodded and ordered some fish tacos with a margarita with two shots of Patron, while she ordered steak fajitas and a beer. When the waitress left, I was left exposed under Makayla's gaze.

"So, when you answered the ad, you knew it was me," I began. "Why didn't you tell me it was you?"

"Would you have agreed to it?" I didn't answer because I knew I would've declined, and she did too.

"I don't like being deceived, Makayla."

"And I'm sorry, but I was desperate. Whenever I would try to talk to you about us, you would change the subject or hang up. Being here, you don't have a choice but to talk to me."

"I do have a choice."

"Not when you're lying in the bed next to me, wrapped in my arms with nowhere else to go." I glared at her as the waitress set our drinks down and then left.

"Listen, Makayla. Do I still love you? Absolutely, so much it's still all consuming. But by no means does any of this mean we will all of a sudden get back together. I said I would try, but you don't have access to my body like that. Not anymore." Her eyes seared into me as she swirled her beer around.

"Yeah okay. I'll let you think that, but please, and I mean as respectfully as possible, I stamped all seven letters of my name all over that pussy, in that pussy, and everywhere else on your body, and nobody, no motherfucking body, can even come close to erasing that." I sat there stunned and in shock as she took a swig of her beer. I was royally fucked.

Chapter 4 (Makayla)

Looking at the shock on her face was worth it. Priceless. I'll be damned if she thinks that I am going to make this next week easy for her. I bet myself I'd give her until the end of the night before I am face deep in her pussy, tattooing my name over and over again until she cries.

She looked away from me, staring out into the ocean. Even the profile of her face was a work of art. The slight sliver of light from the moon across her face made her glow brighter than the stars in the sky. Was I simping for this woman? Hell yeah, and I would until my last breath. Even in death I'd simp for her, and I know she knows that. No matter how much she has tried over the past year to keep me at arm's length, she knows I'd go to war for and over her and Yahir.

"Here's your order," the waitress said, placing our dishes on the table. "Enjoy." She walked away and my eyes found hers looking back at me.

She quickly looked down and began eating her food. She's lucky we weren't in a booth or I'd fuck her pussy while she ate and watch her try her best not to scream. I remember we used to do all kinds of voyeuristic shit before the separation. Gelisa was a wild woman, and a fucking freak. But she was and is my wild freak.

We ate in silence for what seemed like forever. Once we were done and the table was cleared, I paid the bill.

"I'm going to take a walk on the beach," she said quickly as I turned to head back to the resort.

"No matter how long you try to prolong this, you will be in the bed with me tonight, in my arms, naked." Her head whipped towards me.

"You never said anything about me being naked."

"As long as we've been married, you have never slept with clothes on, so don't even try that shit with me." I turned and walked towards the resort before she could say anything.

It was two hours before she came walking through the door. I had spent that time editing some of the photos on my laptop that I had taken the day before. Tulum was such a beautiful place, and we had been here when Yahir was around one. We took a family trip. We took many family trips, and I miss the fuck out of those.

I had been stalking her social media the past year and saw all the trips she took with her family, feeling left out and exiled. Despite her folks always inviting me, it was Gelisa who needed to invite me, and I told them as much. I remember my parents even telling me that Yahir was my son too, and that I should be included, but to be honest, as much as I wanted to be, I knew it wouldn't be the same as before.

Gelisa tried her best to avoid me as she went into the bathroom and did her nightly routine. She spent over an hour in the bathroom. Now either her routine had changed, which I highly doubted, or she was trying her hardest to extend being in the bed with me.

When she came out, I was butt ass naked in the bed, her side of the bed turned down waiting for her. She had on a silk robe and stood in the doorway to the bathroom. I watched as she strode over

115

to the bed and got in, covering herself as she took the robe off. I shook my head and chuckled.

"Goodnight," she said, turning the lamp off on her side. I turned mine off and slid under the covers, wrapping my arms around her waist and pulling her back to my front. Her body stiffened as I held her close, our warmth cocooning us. I could smell her pussy and how much she was turned on, but I wouldn't make a move until she said something. I kissed her shoulder and nestled my face into the nape of her neck.

Her body began to relax as she moved my top arm to between her legs. She used my fingers to part her wet ass pussy. I smiled as she moved me up and down her clit.

"Move your hand," I whispered. "I know what the fuck to do to my pussy." She shuttered and moved her hand, widening her legs, giving me more access to her.

I stroked her clit and felt it harden. Her body gave little shakes as she moaned, bucking her hips and rubbing her ass against me. Her breaths told me she was close. I pinched her clit and held her close to me as she unraveled, screaming my name. I could've came just from that alone. I went to move my hand as she settled and she stopped me.

"I'm going to need you to use your words," I whispered against her shoulder as my fingers continued their triste. Her breaths were ragged as her hand covered mine. She tried to slide my fingers in her pussy and I stopped her. "Gelisa, baby I will do whatever you want me to do to your body, but I'm going to need to hear you say it. Please say it. Use me how you want, but tell me. I want to hear the words come off your lips."

She was silent. I was wet as hell and silently begging her to tell me to fuck her. The desperation to eat her pussy was unsettling. To move my body against hers made the ache in my core unbearable. But it was what she said that killed all of that.

"We have to be up early tomorrow. Let's go to sleep." She moved her hand from mine and I slid it from between her legs, but not before rubbing a few circles on her sensitive clit. She gasped as I rubbed a little longer, and then moved my hand to cup her breast, her nipple between my fingers. My other arm was under her head and gently around her neck, her hands holding on to me. Her soft snores began as I then drifted off to sleep.

The next morning, the sun was shining bright and hot against my face. We were still wrapped up in each other, but my face was in line with her breasts. I smiled as I took one in my mouth and sucked hard. Her body jerked as her hand went straight to my head to pull me closer. I wrapped my tongue around her taut, chocolate nipple and tugged.

"Oh, God! Shit!" I knew what I was doing and I was going to keep teasing her until she used her words. I continued my assault on her other nipple, and I knew she was about to crest. I rolled her on top of me, keeping her nippled in my mouth. I moved my hips beneath, rubbing my pussy against hers until she took over, grounding against me.

"Makayla," she moaned.

"Use your words, Gelisa." I sucked and bit down hard on her nipple and she shattered, her screams echoing against the walls in conjunction with the crash of the waves. I don't care if I never hear

117

anything else in life as long as I hear her screams when she comes.

"Shit! I'm bout to come again." Her body was quaking as she moved her hips faster. I held both breasts together and sucked both nipples into my mouth.

"Makayla, shit, Makayla! I'm comin! I'm fucking comin!"

"Come then. Gimme that shit." I locked eyes with her as she squirted while she came. I saw the tears and my vision blurred. I wrapped my arms around her until she finished as she placed her face beside mine. She tried to move, but I kept her in place as she sobbed. Feathering her with kisses along her shoulder, I rubbed circles in her back until she quieted.

Gelisa raised her head and looked down at me. I wrapped my hand around her neck and brought her lips gently to mine. I sucked on her bottom lip until it was swollen and then slid my tongue into her mouth. She was hesitant and then gave in, completely relaxing her body against me.

I loosened my grip on her as she lifted up. We stared at each other for a moment. I could still see the hurt in her eyes, but I also saw something else: hope, longing, and the love for me that never left.

"You aren't going to make this easy, are you?" she asked.

"Anything that's easy getting, isn't worth having," I responded. She shook her head and placed a peck on my lips as she got up to go to the bathroom. I let her have her time by herself before it was my turn. I didn't want to push her too far too fast. I was going to follow her lead, and if that meant using my body for her pleasure, then so be it. She can use it.

After washing up and getting dressed, I put my hair into two long french braids which was easy since I only had hair at the top of my head. My braids ended at the middle of my back, but decided to wear them over each shoulder. I dressed in a white, linen short set with some loafers and some sunglasses.

At the front door, Gelisa had her suitcase that had her clothes and portable changing room. She was cooking breakfast when I came into the kitchen and took a seat at the island. I watched her as she moved around the kitchen, reminiscing about watching her do this all the time, before. Except, this time was different. I wasn't sucking on her neck and rubbing her pussy while she cooked, being interrupted by a miniature version of her.

She plated our food and sat down next to me. I took at sip of the coffee and closed my eyes, reveling in its rich flavor.

"That good, huh?" she asked, watching me with a smirk on her slightly swollen lips.

"Not as good as you." She looked down at her food.

"What happened last night and this morning was…"

"I swear if you say it was a mistake, Gelisa…"

"No, I wasn't going to say that. It wasn't a mistake, not in the slightest. It was amazing, and I wanted it and I still want it and more, but we still need to talk, and I don't want you to think that us having sex is all it's going to take to repair things."

"Gelisa, don't try to tell me what I think. I know sex won't make everything right. But what I am saying is, whenever you want to come, let me know. I will make you orgasm until you are satisfied. I know I have work to do, a whole helluva lot of it, but shit, I can work on me and fuck you at the same time."

"You're relentless," she sighed, taking a forkful of her eggs.

"And your pussy misses me." She rolled her eyes and continued eating as I cleaned my plate.

Once we finished, we headed out to Playa Paraiso. There was a yacht there waiting for us.

"Hola," the woman who would drive the yacht greeted us. "Are you Gelisa and Makayla Marquette?"

"Yes. I'm Gelisa, and this is my…my…"

"Wife and photographer." I smirked as Gelisa folded her arms across her chest.

"You are a beautiful couple. Let's get going." We followed her onto the yacht as she showed us around. What Gelisa didn't know was that since she had sent me the itinerary, I made minor adjustments to the trip. For starters the room situation, and now the yacht. I reserved the yacht for the whole day, so there was a crew cooking below deck and we would have lunch, snack, and dinner on the yacht, as well as spend the night in the ocean.

The captain showed us to the bedroom where we could change and then left out. I closed the door and turned to find Gelisa staring at me, eyes shifting.

"What are you doing?"

"I have to confess something."

"What did you do now?"

"Well, I reserved the yacht for the rest of the day and the morning. There is a crew to cook lunch and dinner, as well as breakfast."

"You what? Makayla, you were only supposed to be here to take the photos."

120

"And I will do my job, because again, this is for my business too. But I am also here to get my family back, which means I will do whatever it takes, and I mean whatever it takes. If it means you telling me how much I hurt you and how much you hate me, I'll listen. If it's to tell me that you fucked other people while we were separated, baby I will listen." I closed the space between us. "If it means eating your pussy on the deck of this yacht in the moonlight, I will do it. I will do whatever."

Her lips parted as her chest rose and fell quickly. I backed her into the wall of the room, slipped my arm around her waist and parted her lips wider with my tongue. She moaned into my mouth and wrapped her arms around my neck. The yacht began to move as I deepened the kiss. My clit was aching like a motherfucker, but I will deny myself as long as she is satisfied.

I pulled away from her and watched as she tried to catch her breath. I smiled and pecked her lips a few more times.

"Get dressed in your first look and meet me up on the deck." I grabbed my camera bag and headed out the room.

Chapter 5 (Gelisa)

I scrambled around the room on gelatin legs as I looked for my phone. When I found it I sat on the edge of the bed and brought up the group chat.

Gelisa: 911!!!!
Melisa: This bitch. What did she do now?
Bleau: Y'all got back together? I got my sissy back?

I told them about what happened last night and what happened this morning. I also told them about the whole yacht situation.

Melisa: So why are you texting us? Get your wife back.
Bleau: And let her eat yo pussy. Hell, open your damn mouth and eat hers. Sounds like she's begging to be on bending knees.
Melisa: (crying laughing emoji) She probably trying to be on bending knees with Gelisa bent over. Be like Rose, but bend over the railing and get your back blown out. Just don't fall in.
Bleau: But if y'all fall in, make sure she survives too. Don't be selfish like Rose.
Melisa: Yeah, because I'm sure Yahir loves her more.

I watched as they continued their shit talking using *Titanic* references before I just locked my phone and threw it in my bag. I rummaged around and pulled out my newest swimsuit from

Fashion Nova. It was a bright yellow thong bikini. The top barely covered my whole breasts, but my nipples and areolas were covered. I was going to play her at her own game. I pulled my hair out of my scrunchie.

Spraying some moisturizer in it, I puffed it out. I then spread on some gold glitter body glow and then made my way up to the top deck. When Makayla saw me, she nearly dropped her camera. She caught it in time and watched as I made it to the bow of the yacht and looked out over the water. I could hear the camera being snapped in my direction. I know most photographers liked taking candid shots at first. I turned to look at her as she stepped closer to me.

"You ready?" she asked as she pulled her bottom lip between her teeth, leaning over to the side to get a better look at my ass. Using one finger, I put it under her chin and lifted it until her eyes were on me.

"I'm always ready." I dropped my hand and then positioned myself against the railing. She watched me and then took a few steps back. She knelt down and turned the camera and snapped in a few different directions.

"I can get a photo of you both if you would like," said one of the male crew members bringing up some drinks. He set them inside the eating area and then came over.

"Oh, that won't be necessary," I said.

"Thank you so much," Makayla said as she handed him her camera. She pulled my arm gently until we were pressed against each other. She palmed each of my ass cheeks as I looked up at her. She smiled as the camera snapped, and then dipped her head and stole my breath in a kiss that had me ready to get out of this dental floss and fuck her in front of the crew. She lifted me up and I wrapped my legs around her.

I pulled back slightly and could see the man moving around us snapping photos. She laid me on the floor of the deck and settled between my legs, grabbing underneath one thigh as she rested on her forearm. I gazed up at her and the look in her eyes had me ready to melt through the floor.

"You two are naturals," the man said, still snapping away at us. I pushed Makayla up and she didn't resist.

"Time for a wardrobe change," I said, but really, I would use any excuse to be out of her presence for a moment to breathe and gather myself.

I hustled back down to our cabin and changed into a one piece that was connected at the sides with the back and my stomach exposed. It was hot pink with bright orange and green flowers. I pulled my hair up in a matching hair tie and changed the jewelry.

This shoot was to be taken while enjoying a nice, cold, mixed drink. Makayla was damn good with her camera. When she showed me the pictures after a few more outfit changes, I was speechless. She captured me the way I had dreamt in my head. Maybe there was a perk to your photographer being your wife who was madly in love with you.

Around noon, we were eating some bomb ass quesadillas with refried beans, tortilla chips, and guacamole. The margaritas were to die for. The captain said we would be at the perfect snorkeling place in a couple of hours.

"I'm going to take a nap," I announced as I stood.

"Okay," Makayla said, not making a move to follow me. I went down to the cabin and undressed, sliding into the bed. I was almost asleep when I felt familiar hands around me, pulling me close. My eyes fluttered open as I watched her raise one of my breasts and put my nipple in her mouth and sucked.

"Shit," I hissed.

"Go to sleep, Gelisa. I am just sucking on your titty, that's it." I frowned and she chuckled. "I told you. You have to use your words." I wanted her to eat my pussy so fucking bad, but I didn't want to go that far again until we talked, so I had to settle for her sucking on my nipples, and she always sucked so damn hard. I felt myself squirt when she bit down. I almost caved until she pecked me on my lips and then closed her eyes, drifting off to sleep. I was fuming, but what could I do other than go to sleep?

An alarm woke me up to an empty bed. I looked around and Makayla was nowhere in sight. I assumed she was up on the deck. I turned the alarm on my phone off and got dressed to go snorkeling. The boat wasn't moving, so I assumed we had made it to the cave. When I got to the top, I saw the most beautiful rock structure. It was a large arch, and I could see the entrance to the inside of it.

Makayla was putting on her snorkeling gear and encasing her camera in some sort of plastic contraption. She looked over at me and smiled, licking her lips. I went to where my gear was waiting for me and put it on. We had been snorkeling many times before, so it was nothing new.

"We will stay here for four hours and then continue out before being on cruise control back which will get us back at around seven tomorrow morning," the captain said. Before I got up here, it was almost four. I nodded my acknowledgement and got ready to jump off the side. Makayla walked up to me and held my hand.

"I got you, baby," she said. She counted to three and we jumped in. Under the water was crystal clear. We saw so many different fish as well as colorful coral and rocks. I turned to see Makayla with her camera pointed at me. I tried striking different poses. She gave me a thumbs up when she was done and turned to snap pictures of the sea life. I swam towards the cave, and when I came up, I was inside. It was blue from the reflection of the water, and so quiet. I climbed up onto the side and took off my gear.

I took a seat and just looked around. I still couldn't believe this was my life, and I couldn't wait until Yahir was a little older to enjoy this with us...me...enjoy this with me.

Makayla came in a little while later and took off her gear, snapping a few pictures of me. She set her camera down and then sat down beside me.

"Penny for your thoughts?"

"Why did you really leave, Makayla?"

"I wanted more opportunities. I thought moving to California would be the best option for all of us. I mean, I figured you could just blog from anywhere, but I didn't take into consideration that you didn't want to leave."

"And when I told you that I wasn't leaving and neither was Yahir, you still left."

126

"I was being selfish and I assumed you would give in and follow. I was naive to think that you would just give up your life for me. I was also wrong."

"I begged and pleaded with you not to leave, and I felt like you weren't listening."

"I was listening, I just ignored it. I just thought that you would get over it. When I got to Cali and realized that you were serious, I should've moved back, but I was so mad at you. Mad at you for not wanting this as much as I did."

"Not wanting what?"

"My dream. I had expressed wanting to take up photography for a while, but you kept saying I had a good job and why give up a good job for something that was a hobby. I tried showing you my work, but you weren't having it."

"So, you're trying to blame me now?" I asked.

"No. What I'm saying is, I left anyway and stayed because I wanted to prove to you that I could do this, for real. That photography wasn't just some hobby. I never once mentioned how blogging was just a hobby."

"Makayla, I was doing this long before we had even met. You cannot compare the two."

"You didn't believe in me, Gelisa, and that shit fucking hurt." Seeing her now, saying all of this, I realized that I was part of the problem as well. I didn't support her, and all this time, I had forgotten about that and thought she had just left just to leave, not because she was hurt.

"I'm sorry, Makayla. I guess I was too wrapped up in my own career that I didn't realize I was dismissing you."

127

"I get it, and I forgave you a while ago, but I still shouldn't have left. I could've made photography work in Houston. I was never in Cali much anyway. I was always traveling. My pride is why I didn't move back sooner."

"You are so fucking selfish," I whispered, tears blurring my vision. I was pissed that she tore our family apart and let her pride get in the way. I was pissed at myself for ignoring what she wanted, and also for my being selfish. I was pissed that we made Yahir suffer for a year when this could've been resolved. I got up and put on my gear.

"Where are you going?" she asked.

"I need to go for a swim. Please don't follow me." I dove back into the water and out of the cave.

Chapter 6 (Makayla)

It had been two hours since I had been back on the yacht, and Gelisa was not back yet. *You're so fucking selfish.* Her words replayed over and over in my head. She was right, but she was also selfish. I think that's why we fit so well together because we are both the same.

I sat at the little desk and edited some photos. I had showered and dressed in my linen shirt and pants set so she could have the bathroom free when she came back. I had my headphones on, but I heard when the door opened. I didn't even look up as she got her stuff and went into the bathroom.

When she came out, she had on this lime green dress that was cinched at the waist, flowy to her mid thigh, and the straps came over the shoulders, crossed her chest and covered each breast and then tied in the back. I stood up and pulled her to me, pecking her lips. I know she was still mad and we had a long way to go, but my heart didn't care.

"I love you, Gelisa."

"I know you do. Let's go eat." She pulled back from me and headed up.

The crew already had the dining area set for us. They had their own area where they ate. It was dark and all we could hear was the water splashing against the side of the yacht.

"I want to come home, Gelisa. Tell me what I need to do." She took another forkful of food. I sipped my drink and waited. I wasn't really hungry. I watched as she finished her food. When she was done, she took a huge gulp of her drink.

"You didn't eat your food," she noticed.

"It's not what I have a taste for."

"Makayla," she whined. I smiled at her. I was wearing her down. I miscalculated about being face deep in her pussy last night, but I was getting it tonight.

"Just tell me. Therapy? No sex? Separate place? What? Tell me."

"It's not that simple."

"It really is. Either you want me or you don't."

"That isn't fair. You know damn well I want you."

"You never said it."

"I want you, Makayla. I really do."

"But what?"

"I don't want us to rush this. It's been a year. There's no telling who you've been with and you don't know who I've been with."

"Actually, I know you haven't been so much as on a date in the past year."

"How do you know that?" I raised an eyebrow and she sighed. "I'm going to kill Melisa and Bleau. Why were you keeping tabs on me?"

"Because you're my wife. Why wouldn't I?"

"You're a stalker."

"I don't give a fuck. I'm making sure no one touches what's mine." I stood up and held my hand out to her. She took it and I led her out to the deck. There was a blanket laid out, and I sat down, pulling her gently into my lap. The only light was from the moon and the stars. She sat between my legs with her back to me.

I nestled my face into her neck and breathed in her scent of cocoa butter and lemongrass. She leaned more into me. I watched as she pulled down the straps exposing her breasts. My breath caught in my throat. As many times as I've seen her naked, it never got old. A breeze came and lifted her dress, showing she had no panties on.

"Gelisa, I need you to use words, and I need you to use words right fucking now," I demanded, pinching her nipples between my fingers.

"I need you to fuck me, Makayla." No sooner had she said that, I had her lying on her back with her legs spread, dipping my tongue inside her. Her fingers were in my hair the minute I sucked her clit into my mouth hard. Her screams were the only thing that could be heard out in the open waters.

"Kayla, fuck!" She creamed against my mouth, then started gushing. My clit ached and I reached in my boxers and strummed it as I lifted her ass up and ate it. She played with her clit as I ate her ass until she came again, her pussy spazing as my hips jerked and bucked agaisnt my hand, cresting along with her. I removed my hand from my boxers and dipped two fingers in her pussy as I lapped up her orgasm, pulling another one from her. Her moans were barely audible as she came, wrapping her thighs around my neck.

I moved over her and was pleased with how sated she looked. I kissed her, allowing her to taste how fucking amazing she was on my lips. Our love for each other transcended time. She was my one and only.

"Let me take you to bed and fuck you properly," I whispered against her lips. She nodded with a smile on her face. I lifted her up and carried her bridal style to our cabin. She undressed while I did. She moved to her knees on the floor and looked up at me.

"I love you, Makayla," she said. "Now spread your legs." I swallowed hard as I did what she said. My hands fisted and opened as she swirled her tongue between my lower lips. There was tingling in my toes that went up my legs and to my clit as she worked her mouth on me.

"Fuuuuuck!" I swore as she ate my shit. I fisted her hair and fucked her face until all I saw were stars. She took that moment to dip her fingers inside me, bringing me even harder over the edge. My eyes rolled back as my body went rigid.

"Ah, shit! Good girl," I choked out. I had never come so hard. Before the separation, we fucked everyday. And going from fucking everyday to no fucking at all, I expected to come hard, but not this hard that I temporarily went blind.

I let go of her hair and staggered back until my back hit the wall. She liked me off her lips and smiled at her handiwork. She went to the bathroom and I heard the water running. I went in after her and we got cleaned up before getting in the bed.

"I love you too, Gelisa," I whispered before popping a titty in my mouth and sucking hard, causing her to gasp before we both settled and fell asleep.

Chapter 7 (Gelisa)

I woke up sore the next morning with my titty still in Makayla's mouth. Last night was much needed. I know we talked in the cave, but we didn't talk about what to do moving forward. I tried to move, but Makayla sucked my nipple hard causing my pussy to throb and my thighs to clench. She knows how my body reacts when she does that.

"Good morning," I moaned as she moved her hand between my thighs and rubbed my clit. In no time I was falling apart. She knew I was horniest in the mornings, so she really wasn't playing fair. She let go of my titty and pecked my lips.

"Something smells good," she said, stretching out on the bed. I, too, began to smell some sausage and pancakes. "Let's get up. We have a long day, and I am worn the fuck out." I giggled as she pulled me into a hug and kissed me again.

After getting dressed and eating breakfast, we got off the yacht and headed back to the resort. We packed another bag and headed out to our taxi that was taking us to Tulum Beach where we were having a private Cacao Ceremony. It was something that I always wanted to try, and I knew it would be great to document the ceremony for the blog.

At noon, there was a beach party to celebrate the beginning of summer. Besides snapping photos, we did allow ourselves to join in the festivities and live in the moment.

That evening, on the beach, we had a romantic dinner under the stars, compliments of Makayla. She was really going out of her way to wine and dine me this entire trip. I was truly blessed to not only have her in my life, but to have her in my life as my wife.

Dinner was my absolute favorite Mexican dish: Costillas al agave. It was pork ribs marinated in agave. They were so juicy and sweet. We took several Tequila shots. It was still light out, so she took me by the hand to get some shots along the beach as the sun was setting.

When she was satisfied, we walked hand in hand in the water. It was so nice to just be here with her, though I missed Yahir something terrible. We spoke to him earlier after the beach party and he was just having a grand ole time.

"Your thoughts are loud," Makayla said. "I miss him, too." She pulled me into her side as we kept walking.

"He is just growing up so fast. I almost want to have another one." She stopped short and looked at me.

"Would you?" she asked, looking me in my eyes. We had talked about having children, before. I didn't think that was still on the table.

"Yes," I said, before I could even think about it.

"With me?" Her eyes watered as mine did, too. I nodded. "Words, Gelisa."

"Yes, I would. Baby, we discussed this before. When Yahir turned six, we would have another baby. He'll be six in August."

"What if I said there was sperm already waiting for us?"

"What do you mean?"

"I contacted the sperm bank where you went and asked them to preserve a vial for us. I want Yahir to have a full blooded sibling."

I melt into complete sobs against her chest. She held me for what seemed like forever.

"Why are you like this?" I asked when I was able to speak again.

"Because I love you, and I want to grow our family together. This whole separation was never going to end in divorce, and you know it."

"It could have," I teased. She twisted her mouth to the side, and we both fell out laughing. We walked for about another hour and then got a ride back to the resort. We made love to each other until the sun was peeking from behind the clouds the next morning.

The next few days were a blur. We went to a few more beaches, and I was sure I had enough photos and content for my blog and social media to create a mini series. With Makayla's photos alone being posted to social media, the increase in resort bookings and bookings in general afforded her a nice, fat check. Part of our sponsorship was that we would receive a 20% commission for bookings, which meant that we had steady checks for the months to come.

Our last day was a bit odd, or should I say that Makayla was acting a bit odd. We had sex that morning, and it felt rushed. I asked her what was going on, but she said nothing. I knew she was lying. She said she had some places to go, so I spent the day shopping. That afternoon, I got back to the resort and a dress was hanging on the closet. There was a note pinned to it.

Wear this for me, with no panties. Meet me on the beach at 5:30.

135

Xoxo

Your Wifey

I looked at my watch and it was already 4:45. I hurried and showered. When I was done getting dressed and made up, it was 5:27. I tried my best to get to the beach through the sand. In the distance, I saw Makayla standing near the water. I smiled and rubbed her back. She turned to look at me and smiled.

"You look amazing," she said.

"I would say thank you, but I think your opinion may be biased since you bought the dress." I noticed she was dressed in a fitted white tee, red linen pants, and barefoot. "So, what's the occasion?"

"We've been married for five years, and this last year has been the fucking hardest without you and Yahir. I fucked up, and I own that, and if it has taught me anything, I can't live without y'all. I don't want to live without y'all. Y'all are the air I breathe, and I've been suffocating.

"When we got married, I vowed for better or for worse, and I stand behind that. You are my wife, Gelisa, til death do us part." She got down on one knee and I couldn't breathe. "This was supposed to be about work and winning you back, but I realized you never left. I did. So, it became about me getting back to my family. Baby, will you take me back so we can put our family together again?"

She pulled out a box from her pocket and opened to show a new band that matched the one I already had on my finger. Despite the separation, I always wore my wedding rings. I held my hand out and she looked at me.

"What I tell you about that shit? Words, Gelisa." I giggled at her being upset.

"Yes, Makayla, come home to us." She put the band on my finger and I heard screams behind me. I turned around to see my parents, her parents, our siblings, our friends, and Yahir running towards us. I scooped him up in my arms as I let it all out. I felt hands around me as our family and friends embraced us. What was supposed to be me going on an all expenses paid trip, turned into me getting my little family back, while looking forward to growing it.

Makayla

I was nervous as hell when I proposed. I knew she would say yes, but I was scared that I would fuck it up. It was risky deceiving her to go on this trip, but when the opportunity arose, I had to jump on it. Not only did I get my family back, we were going to be adding to it and becoming a family of four.

After I proposed, we had a ceremony on the beach. It was small and intimate. We spent another week in Tulum while our family and friends flew back.

Once the honeymoon was over, we went back to Houston and had my stuff moved back in. We fucked for two weeks straight to catch up on lost time. That involved drinking a lot of water, eating a lot of fruit, and some waterproof sheets because baby is a squirter.

With the success of my photos and the first part of her series, we decided to join our business, naming it "Long Walks on the

Beach Travel Co.". We also started family counseling which has helped a lot in our communication.

The saying goes, if you love someone, let them go. If they come back, it was meant to be. I rock with that shit.

The end.

Bonus Epilogue

Gelisa

"Push, baby!" Makayla coached me. I was going to beat her ass if she told me to push one more got damn time. I was sweating, exhausted, and these damn contractions were no joke. I don't ever remember them being this painful with Yahir.

"P…"

"If you tell me to push, Makayla, so help me God, I will cut out your tongue and shove it so far down your throat, you won't be able to taste anything until it is already digested and turned to shit," I seethed. Her eyes widened and I heard Bleau on the other side of me snicker. I whipped my head around towards her, and she clamped her hand over her mouth.

"Alright Gelisa," my midwife said, bringing my attention back to her. "The head is out, and I need you to give me one big push." I nodded in understanding.

"So, she can tell you to push, but I can't?" Makayla asked. I gritted my teeth and bared down to push and roared at her. She jumped back in fear but never let my hand go. Our baby shot out of my vagina and into the hands of my midwife.

I was so glad I opted for a home waterbirth. My midwife held our baby girl under water for a little while until she began to move. She slowly brought her to the surface, and cleared her lungs when she let out a shrill cry. She handed her to me, and I laid her on my chest. Makayla climbed in the pool behind me.

"She's so beautiful," Bleau sobbed, rubbing my shoulder. Yahir came bursting into the room with my mom and sister.

"Yay! I have a sister!" he cheered, coming to kneel beside the pool by Bleau.

"Gelisa, I need a small push for the placenta," the midwife spoke. I pushed gently and felt something slide out. Makayla then cut the umbilical cord.

Melisa held her arms out with a blanket to take baby girl so that I could get out of the pool and cleaned up. Helping me to the bathroom, Makayla sat me on the bench in the shower and bathed me ever so gently.

Once clothed and in bed, Melisa handed baby girl back to me and I nursed her. She latched on a lot quicker than Yahir had.

"What's her name, Mommy?" he asked, climbing into the bed next to me.

"Yaritza," Makayla responded, kissing the top of his head.

"Can I hold her?" I looked down at Yaritza who clearly seemed to be done nursing. I burped her as Makayla nestled Yahir into my side. I placed her in his arms as he looked down at her. My vision blurred as tears swelled into my eyes.

Makayla kissed my forehead, and it was more than just a kiss of affection. It was a long road to get here.

Makayla

Watching my wife, son, and daughter, pulled at my heartstrings. We went through hell to get Yaritza. It had been almost two years since Gelisa and I had gotten back together after that trip to Mexico. Things were better than they were before. There's extensive and open communication about everything so that there are no misunderstandings. We go to therapy twice a month, but in the beginning it was more like two to three times a week.

We had a lot of issues to work through that weren't just surface level. Once we were in a better place, we decided to have a baby. We went through several rounds of IVF, becoming discouraged and considering getting a surrogate.

After the last round, we were shocked and overjoyed that it stuck. She was on bedrest her entire pregnancy, and I was grateful that we both worked for ourselves and from home. We had enough content for our shared business that it lasted the entire term of her pregnancy.

"Babe, what are you thinking about?" Gelisa asked. We were lying in bed after everyone had left. I fed, bathed, and put Yahir to bed after Gelisa read him a story. Yaritza was sleeping in her attachable bassinet.

"How far we've come as a family," I responded, wrapping my arms around her. I was about to go in and pop her breast in my mouth like I did nightly and she popped my hand.

"Don't," she said, giggling. "Milk comes out of them now."

"So."

"These breasts are for Yaritza for however long she nurses, so you'll have to wait."

"Are you serious?"

"Yes." The way she smiled, I couldn't even be mad at her. Watching her give birth to our second child made me fall in love with her even more.

"Okay, so since I gotta wait to suck on your nipples, how long I have to wait to stick my tongue in your pussy?"

"Kayla!" she laughed.

"What? I'm dead ass serious."

"I know you're serious, which is why it's funny. The midwife said about three weeks or until I feel comfortable, and that's only for my clit. As for penetration, six weeks, missy."

"How are you feeling right now?" I grinned.

"Like I just birthed a whole damn human!" I laughed and she joined in. I kissed her deeply before sliding my tongue into her mouth. She moaned and that shit had my head gone.

"You can't be moaning like that when I can't suck on your clit."

"I can suck on yours," she said seductively.

"Naw. I'll get mine when I can give you yours."

Three weeks later...

Gelisa

Since giving birth to Yaritza, life has not slowed down like I thought it would. Makayla could not be a better wife. She's done the cooking, cleaning, making sure Yahir is fed, cleaned, and entertained, and has been keeping up with his school things.

It was Friday, and Yahir and Yaritza were with my parents who were staying at my sister's house to give us some alone time and privacy. I had just showered and cooked dinner while Makayla worked on things for our business.

"Damn it smells good in here," she said, coming into the kitchen and wrapping her arms around my waist, sucking on my neck. "Shit, you smell good, too. And you got on some lace lingerie." She stepped back and pulled my hand to spin me around, taking in the view. "You trying to tell me something?"

"Today marks three weeks, and my pussy is wet." She went still and her eyes darkened. I laughed as she pulled me into her.

"Cut all this shit off and let's go upstairs," she demanded.

"Babe, no. I worked hard on this dinner to show my appreciation."

"Well, can you sit on the table so I can have dessert first? Baby, I am dying over here." She looked at me with pleading eyes.

"I'm not sitting on the table, but you can get on your…" and before I had the word "knees" out, she was on hers with her tongue sliding in between my folds through the seamless lace panties. "Shiiiit!" I dug my hands into her scalp and pressed my pussy further into her face, back arching away from the counter.

"Damn, I missed this," she mumbled, lips not leaving my clit. "You taste even better after having a second baby."

My head fell back as she continued her assault on my clit, sucking it into her mouth, hard.

"Makayla!" I screamed as I grabbed the back of her head and held on to the edge of the counter. I was coming hard, harder than I ever had.

She lifted one of my thighs over her shoulder and gripped my eyes, not letting up at all, intensifying the pleasure so much so that I just knew I was going to black out. I didn't even feel like my feet were on the ground. I was floating in and out of consciousness on cloud 9.

"Baby, are you crying?" she asked, wiping her face. I looked down and burst out laughing. I held on to the counter with both hands as she lowered my leg, both legs still feeling like jelly. "What is that?"

"Breast milk," I panted, laughing even harder. She placed both hands on my breasts and felt the dampness of the bra.

"You mean to tell me I ate you so good I made your titties nut?" At this point, I was unable to breathe. The cross between confusion and satisfaction that spread across her face was hilarious. There were droplets of milk in her hair as well.

When I finally settled down and caught my breath, I told her to keep an eye on the food while I went to go pump. It was time for a pumping session anyway which was why I was leaking.

Back in the kitchen, she had plated our foods and had them on the table. She pulled my chair out and I sat down. She took her seat and said grace. She put a forkful of roast in her mouth and moaned, closing her eyes.

"This roast, mixed with the lingering taste of your pussy, is magnificent. I wonder what else your juices taste good mixed with."

The End

M. L. Sexton

Falling in love with
your best friend
ain't easy.

Dance for me

Playlist

Teenage Fever - Drake
Surprise - Chloe Bailey
So Sexy - Luv Jones
My Type - Sweetie
In My Bed - Rotimi
Texts Go Green - Drake
Break My Soul - Beyonce

1
Jessamyn

"And again. 5…6…7..8." We ran through the dance number for what felt like the hundredth time and Milani Fae, still wasn't here. She has a show in less than a month and has been late to rehearsals everyday this week. Luckily enough for me, she paid me in advance so I could also pay my dancers. Essentially, time wasn't money, but I still hated my time being wasted. When the music stopped, I hustled over to her manager who was looking down at her phone.

"Where is she?" I demanded.

"I-I-I don't know. I've called, texted, and left several voicemails. It rings once and goes straight to voicemail."

"Look, my dancers are tired. I know she paid us in advance, but she signed a contract that included a strict schedule. She has been late everyday, and we still haven't rehearsed at the venue because she doesn't even know all the moves. And when she does decided to show up, she's hungover or high as a fucking kite. You need to do your job as her manager and get her ass here, so I can do my job as her choreographer so she doesn't have a repeat from a few months ago at Essence Fest."

At Essence Fest, Milani performed and damn near became a part of "cancel culture," and honestly, her performance should've been canceled. Not only did she not know the choreography, she was sloppy and stumbling across the stage, slurring her words. Social media dragged her for filth, and rightfully so. Many people demanded their money back for her piss poor performance and she

149

went on a hiatus for quite a while, canceling the rest of the shows on that mini tour.

We were gearing up for her show in Emancipation Park in Third Ward for the annual Summer Block Party that celebrated the beginning of summer. This year had big names coming, and I refused to have her up there, embarrassing me and ruining my reputation.

"Listen, Jessamyn," Alani stated, "I have to pick my daughter up in less than an hour. I nodded my head and then turned back to Milani's manager whose fingers were flying across her phone screen.

"If she isn't here in the next ten minutes, we are done for the day," I warned.

Fifteen minutes later, I was closing up the studio as a limo pulled up. Milani came stumbling out talking loud and walking like her feet didn't know how to move forward.

"Hey, Jessie girl!" she slurred.

"It's Jessamyn, and where the hell have you been?"

"What? I'm here aren't I?"

"Yeah, four hours late. Everyone has gone home." I headed to my car as she stumbled after me.

"But y'all work for me," she said, somewhat sobering up.

"If you keep pulling this shit, I have no problem refunding your money. I'll be damned if you get on that stage and tarnish my fucking name. Stop all this partying all night, day drinking, and popping pills, and get your shit together, or you won't have a career." I got in my car, slamming the door. I sped off to my house in a hurry to get to Kayden before he jetset across the globe with my parents.

"Jessamyn, we almost missed you," my mother said as I hurried out of the car.

"I know, I'm sorry. Milani was late to rehearsals and we stayed an extra hour waiting for her to only show up as I was locking up."

"Well, he's still in the house grabbing his electronics," my dad said, kissing me on the forehead. I ran inside to see Kayden coming down the stairs.

"Hey, Mom," he smiled, running to hug me.

"Hey, Baby. I'm going to miss you so much," I told him, squeezing him tight and placing kisses all over his face. He laughed and tried to push me off.

"Okay, okay, okay, Mom, I think that's enough," he laughed. I held him at arm's length and just stared at him. He looked so much like his dad. He usually went with his dad for the summer, but since his grandparents were world travelers now, he opted to go with them and his cousin Corbin, my sister's son.

"Make sure you behave and call me everyday."

"I will," he promised, giving me one last hug before running out the door. Tuesday, my sister, was pulling up and Corbin got out of the car before she even put it in park. He and Kayden began chatting up a storm as they got in my parents' car. Tuesday hopped out and took his bags out, giving them to my dad.

"Hey sis," she said, throwing an arm around me.

"You missed rehearsal today," I side-eyed her.

"I heard Milani did, too, so I'm good." I rolled my eyes and shook my head as our parents backed out of the driveway. They and the boys waved and we waved back.

"Two and a half months with no kid, sounds like a hot mom summer to me," she cheered, dancing into the house heading straight to the alcohol. I closed the door and followed in behind her.

"Who all is coming tonight?" she asked, pouring us each a shot.

"Chey, Sydney, and Kahlani," I responded as we clinked glasses and took it to the head.

"Is Sydney's girlfriend coming?"

"I don't know, probably. Why?"

"You know I can't stand that bitch."

"Come on, they've been dating for years."

"No, they've been dating on and off for years. I don't know why Syd can't let her go. She's like a damn leech." I fell out laughing as she poured another shot. The doorbell rang and she grabbed some more glasses as I answered it.

"Shots! Shots! Shots!" Chey, my cousin, sang as she gave me a hug with two bottles of tequila in her hands. I laughed and hugged her back.

"Your ex-husband must've come and got the kids," I said as we headed to the kitchen.

"Hell yeah, he came and got them bad ass kids. I love my babies, but bitch, I'm mufuckin tiiiiiiiiiiiiiiied!" Tuesday howled from the kitchen. As we walked in, Chey sat the bottles down and they hugged. We all took another shot as the door opened and we ran to the hallway to see who was coming up in my house.

"It's Kahlani up in this bitch!" Kahlani screamed as she stood in the doorway. I shook my head as Chey and Tuesday screamed, running to hug her. They headed towards me as Kahlani pulled me in.

"Hey, supposed to be sister-in-law," she teased.

"Not that shit again," I groaned, rolling my eyes.

"You know damn well I will always ship you and my sister." We headed into the kitchen and sat down.

"Speaking of sister," Tuesday began, "is Syd bringing Khoralyn?"

"I hope not," Kahlani stated. "I swear, every time Syd calls me, I dread answering the phone because I know she about to be on that dumb shit and complain about Khoralyn."

"Y'all are being too hard on the girl," I said.

"Bitch, do you know this bitch drinks shots with a fucking straw?" Chey asked.

"Like who the fuck does that? It ain't a shot if you have a straw." I chuckled at Tuesday.

"I'm trying to keep my teeth bright and white," Kahlani mimicked Khoralyn. We fell out laughing.

"Did she say when she would be here?" I asked Kahlani. "I'm ready to get the games started and the pizza will be here any minute now."

"Shit, fucking with that girlfriend of hers, maybe never. You know she don't like you like that."

"Umhm," Tuesday and Chey said in unison.

"I don't know why." I took another shot.

"Bitch, don't feign stupid," Chey said. "You know she does not like Syd's friendship with you."

"Okay, but she's friends with the both of you," I said, pointing to Chey and Tuesday.

"Yeah, but they don't like pussy like you do," Kahlani responded, tipping her head towards me.

"Y'all really think she doesn't like me because I'm a lesbian? That sounds stupid as fuck."

"You may see it that way," Chey said.

"But just wait until she gets here," Tuesday added.

2

Sydney

"I don't know why I have to spend my Friday night at Jessamyn's house," Khoralyn argued as I drove.

"You don't have to. I didn't even invite your ass. You decided to tag along."

"Yeah, because you're going to *her* house." I shook my head. I had a long day at work, having to put out a fire at this big ass building downtown that took a few hours to finally put out. No one was hurt, thankfully, since it was a construction site.

"What does that even mean?" I frowned, keeping my eyes on the road.

"You know what it means." We had had this argument since Khoralyn and I first met. It was only supposed to be sex, but some way somehow, she bamboozled me into a toxic ass relationship. I mean, I could've broken up with her for good, but she does this thing with her tongue that has me seeing stars and my toes throwing up gang signs. Shit was ridiculous.

"All I know is when we get here, don't be on that bullshit," I warned.

"Excuse me?"

"I didn't stutter, Khoralyn, and I'm not fucking playing. We are here to have a good time with my friends and my sister. Don't fuck this up."

"You got me fucked up," she started and I tuned her ass out. She didn't stop talking for the next ten minutes until we pulled up outside.

155

I got out of the car and she slammed my door, still running off at the mouth. I put my key into the door of Jess's house and that's when the talking stopped. I turned around to see a scowl on her face.

"You said you gave the key back," she said, barely above a whisper.

"What?"

"A month ago, you said you would give her her house key back."

"I don't remember saying that," I retorted, genuinely confused.

"We were having sex, and I was doing that tongue thing you like and I asked you to give her key back and you said you would."

"If we were in the middle of having sex, you can't take anything I say seriously."

"So when you say you love me, you don't mean it?" she screeched. I rolled my eyes.

"Here we fucking go." I turned the key and opened the door walking towards the kitchen as she slammed the door and was going off. There were three shots already waiting for me as Chey, Jessamyn, Tuesday, and Kahlani sat there eyes wide. Ignoring them, I took all three shots and sat next to Kahlani.

"Give the key back, right the fuck now!" Khoralyn yelled.

"The fuck is she talking about?" Chey asked.

"Sydney has something to give to you Jessamyn." Khoralyn put her weight into one hip and crossed her arms, looking at me. I looked up at Jessamyn who looked completely confused.

"I ain't giving shit back, Khoralyn, so either you deal with it, or you deal with it."

156

"Bitch…" and before she could finish her sentence, I had her by the throat.

"Listen here. Like I told your ass in the car, act like you got some fucking sense." A smile crept across her face as she smirked at Jessamyn over my shoulder.

"Yes, daddy," she moaned, kissing my lips. I kissed her back and then let her go, going back to my seat.

"Who's ready to sing karaoke?" Jessamyn asked.

It was two in the morning, and we were winding down. Khoralyn had left early in an Uber because her attitude was fucking with the vibes. I made her leave and we argued about that. I don't know how much more of this I can take. I had love for the girl, but I wasn't in love with her. I don't think I ever was.

"Damn, they asses are knocked out," Jessamyn said, referring to Chey, Tuesday, and Kahlani sprawled out on her ridiculously large couch. I helped her clean up the mess we all made, and then we headed to the backyard. We sat next to each other on her wicker couch that faced the massive land that stretched far and wide on the other side of her pool.

"Thanks for coming tonight," she said.

"You know I wouldn't miss this."

"You could've left Khoralyn though," she giggled.

"Funny thing is, I didn't even invite her. She just tagged along."

"Why is she always like that?"

"Man, I don't know. You know that's how she's been since we first met."

"Yeah, but she's not hostile towards Chey or Tuesday." I just shrugged my shoulders. "You remember when we used to all play truth or dare, and you dared me to jump in my neighbors' pool, butt naked." We fell out laughing at the memory.

"Man, you got in so much trouble, but your neighbors' daughter didn't mind." She laughed even harder. "You remember when Chey dared Tuesday to drink your dad's bottle of Hennessy, like the whole bottle?"

"I still can't believe Tuesday did that shit. Kahlani cried so hard thinking that Tuesday was going to die, and I sat there in shock. We were grounded for what felt like years."

"And we stayed at the hospital for hours, vowing to never drink alcohol."

"And now look at us? Drunk as fuck!" We giggled as we stared up at the stars. I looked over at her and her profile was breathtaking. I don't know when I fell in love with my best friend, but this girl had my whole fucking heart. I don't know if it was the alcohol or my emotions, but I leaned over and kissed her. She jumped back slightly, shocked, but then cupped her hands around my face and pulled my lips back to hers.

Our tongues fought for dominance as she ran her fingers through my blowout. I climbed between her legs and rested my hands under her ass cheeks. She smelled like cinnamon and good decisions.

Abruptly, she pushed me up and jumped up. She stared at me with wide eyes, her chest rising and falling quickly.

"Jessamyn, breathe," I said, standing to my feet. She backed up and then ran in the house without a word. I followed after her

158

until she slammed and locked her bedroom door. I was about to knock and felt it was no use. Seeing her look at me like that, I almost felt regret. I knew that nothing would be the same after this.

I walked in the fire station, and my coworkers whistled at me. I was still in the outfit from last night: black pleather shorts, a crop top, opened toed sandals and my crossbody purse. I shook my head and rolled my eyes at them as I went to my locker, grabbed my uniform and headed to the showers. Wrapping my hair and putting on a shower cap, I took a long ass hot shower. I got maybe four hours of sleep in Jessamyn's guest bedroom.

She avoided me this morning, and thankfully, Chey, Kahlani, and Tuesday were still there to break up the awkwardness. I knew Jess and I would have to talk about this, eventually, and I had a feeling it wasn't going to blow over very well.

As soon as I was dressed, we were called to a fire in Midtown. We hustled to the fire trucks and sped to our destination. With as many fires we were putting out, you'd swear we lived in California, but this Texas heat was nothing to play with.

The smoke could be seen from a couple miles away, and as we got closer, what we saw had us all gawking. The newest highrise apartment building was 27 floors high and the entire thing was up in flames. There was a large crowd outside as we rushed out to get the building blocked off.

"Alright, keep those people back," I yelled. "Chase, get on the ladder. Langston, call the chopper. We will need overhead. Morrison, call Stations 68, 16, and 28. We need all hands on deck." I was made lieutenant of my station, Station 54, two years ago. In those two years, we have had no casualties of any fire fighter, and I take damn good care of my team.

"Are you in charge?" a man asked who looked to be in his early 50s, dark skinned, salt and pepper beard, and about three inches taller than my 5'11.

"I am. How can I help you?"

"I'm Morris Carlson, the owner of this building."

"Nice to meet..."

"Listen," he interrupted, but before he could finish, there was an explosion as the building started to come down. I yanked his arm and ran as the crowd began to quickly disperse.

"Everyone, abort, abort!" I radioed to my team. I looked behind to see that the debris from the building exploding was quickly catching up to us. Something that felt like a shockwave had me and Mr. Carlson flying in the air. I landed on my back in the grass, somewhat cushioned by my fire gear and helmet.

I could hear Mr. Carlson groaning a few feet away, which meant he was alive.

"Everyone, check in! Over!" I listened as each one of my team members let me know they were okay. I saw my sister running towards me, screaming my name. She worked for Station 28.

"Sydney!" She crashed to her knees beside me, lifting my head up. Pulling my helmet off, I could see the tears streaming down her face.

"How's my blowout?" I asked. She smiled even as more tears came streaming down, hugging me to her chest.

Eight hours later, I was soaking in my bathtub at home. There were so many injuries and deceased people. A two mile radius was

160

blocked off around the building. So much damage was done to surrounding businesses, and the city was going to take care of cleaning up.

"Oh my gosh, Syd!" Khoralyn cried, coming into the bathroom. Her face was puffy as tears streamed down her face. I was happy for her sympathy, but she wasn't who I wanted to see.

"Hey, Khoralyn," I moaned, my joints aching and screaming as she hugged me. I had been checked out at the hospital and given some painkillers, which seemed to be doing nothing for my body.

"Baby, I'm so glad you're okay. I saw what happened on the news, and I tried to get away from work, but my boss threatened to fire me."

"It's okay, really."

"What can I do for you?"

"Nothing, really. Kahlani made me dinner and got everything set up for me before she left."

"Okay, well, I'm here now, and I'm going to take good care of you. I can play nurse, and you'll be my patient."

"Khoralyn, I really just want to eat and go to sleep. My body hurts and I'm exhausted."

"Well, I can just stay the night and hold you." I didn't even have it in me to argue. Once I was out of the tub and full, I took a pain pill, and drifted off to sleep, ignoring Khoralyn as she tried to kiss me and get me to fuck.

3

Jessamyn

"Oh, look who's on time today," I said. It was Saturday afternoon, and we had rehearsal from 2pm-7pm. Milani, for once, was on time and seemed to be sober, but only time would tell.

"Hey, I don't need all of that sass," she retorted. "Remember that I am paying you."

"No, you remember that I can refund you, but there is no other choreographer in the city who can have you right in the next two weeks." She looked me up and down and smirked.

"You know, you're really sexy when you're irritated," she admonished.

"Positions everyone." I turned away from her and stood a few feet to her right. I looked at Tuesday and Chey in the mirror and both were giggling. The music started and we went through each dance routine of Milani's performance. She wasn't bad for someone who had missed a lot of rehearsals, but she wasn't near execution either.

After rehearsal, I worked with her one-on-one until she seemed to be able to do it without me dancing alongside her.

"I think that's enough for today," I said as I downed a bottle of water.

"Hey, Jessamyn, I decided to go ahead and record a music video while I'm here. I want to use a few of these dance routines for the video. Do you think you can round up some of your best dancers to go with my back up dancers?" I cocked my head to the side, eyeing her. She laughed. "I'll pay you double what I paid for the show."

"Okay, bet," I said. We both laughed.

"Listen, I respect the fuck out of you and your professionalism. No one has ever spoken to me the way you have over the past few weeks about getting my shit together. Just know that I heard you."

"Good. So that means my time won't be wasted moving forward?"

"I promise, it won't be wasted." She pulled her bottom lip between her teeth. I'm not gon lie. Milani was sexy as fuck. She was tall and always wore her natural hair. Her skin was like a rich milk chocolate, sunkissed golden. Her eyes were deep brown and almond-shaped. The pants she wore were tight and showed off her curves, and her sports bra pushed her breasts together. In another life, I'd definitely fuck her.

"Since there's no rehearsal tomorrow, I'm having a party at the mansion I'm staying at. You should come, and invite whoever."

"I'll let you know." She winked and walked out of my studio.

"BITCH! Hell yeah, we going!" Tuesday was too excited about the pool party.

"I'm about to snatch me up a rapper," Chey added.

"Ain't your baby daddy a rapper?" Kahlani asked.

"Yeah, and?"

"He ain't shit," I reminded.

"Fuck you hoes. Y'all some haters." We fell out laughing as I pulled in my driveway. "How's Sydney?" Kahlani had texted us earlier about the fire and the explosion.

"She's fine. Khoralyn is over there now."

"Ugh," Chey grumbled.

"I bet you Syd is feeling even more miserable than she was before," Tuesday added. We talked for a few more minutes as I got in the house and turned the oven on to heat up some leftover pizza.

I took a shower and poured a glass of wine as I watched a few episodes of *Stranger Things.* Sydney and I usually watched each season together, but since she was hurt today was with Khoralyn, and after that kiss last night, I watched it alone.

I had thought about that kiss all fucking day. I don't know what Syd was thinking. Maybe it was the alcohol, or the weed we had smoked. But I couldn't get out of my head what my girls had been saying for years about me and Sydney being a thing. I've known Syd and Kahlani since I was 12. We had always been friends. I wouldn't say I saw her as a sister or anything, but we had just been friends.

We never flirted or came close to any of that. When I came out as bisexual in high school, she was thrilled, almost too happy now that I think about it. She had been lesbian all her life and it never dawned on me that there was even a possibility that she had feelings for me. She was supportive through all my relationships, even my longest relationship which was with Kayden's dad. I was delusionally in love with that man, and vice versa, but I think we both realized that despite being in love with each other, a friendship was as far as we should have taken it.

I cleaned up and got in bed, taking two edibles. Rehearsals had been kicking my ass, and since we didn't have rehearsals

164

tomorrow, I was about to get some good ass sleep so I could be well rested for this party. I grabbed my phone and opened a separate message to send to Sydney. Usually, we text in the group chat, but I didn't need the group to know this.

I'm glad you're okay. We need to talk about last night.

I knew she was asleep and wouldn't respond. I'd just check in the morning. It wasn't long before I passed out, them edibles sneaking up on me.

"Aye, pass me the pepper!" someone yelled. I jolted up in bed and looked at my clock. It was ten in the morning. I slept damn near 12 hours. Pots and pans could be heard clinking and clanking downstairs and I knew it wasn't anybody but Chey and Tuesday. All my girls had keys to my house, and I was starting to regret it.

I could smell breakfast being made and my stomach told me to get my ass up. I took care of my morning routine and headed downstairs to surprisingly see Kahlani in the mix.

"Hey, ya'll," I said, hugging each one. Tuesday was at the stove and Chey was cutting up fruit.

"The Keurig is ready, creamer already in the cup," Chey said. I pushed the button to brew me some coffee.

"I thought you would've been at Sydney's," I said, talking to Kahlani.

"I would but Khoralyn was still there and they were arguing. I didn't feel like hearing that, and I knew Tuesday would be over her throwing down in your kitchen."

"And you know this," Tuesday cheered, not looking up from the pan.

"At this point, she might as well live here," Chey said, popping a grape in her mouth.

"Don't give her any ideas," I grumbled, taking a sip of coffee. Chey had got the creamer to coffee ratio just right, per usual. "Are y'all going to have time to get y'all stuff for the pool party?"

"Girl, bye," Kahlani said. "Look by the front door." I saw three medium sized tote bags neatly lined up. I just smiled and shook my head.

We spent the next hour and a half eating, talking, and making summer plans since the kids were gone. Kahlani didn't have any kids, but she was glad there was no potential babysitting of her nieces and nephews.

Around 11:45, we piled in my jeep and headed to Kingwood Estates. I typed in the code as the iron gate opened up to the subdivision.

"Dayuuuum," we said in unison as we drove through the gate. These houses were more like palaces than mansions. I don't know what strings Milani pulled to rent one of these out, and I can't imagine how much she was paying. We pulled up to the house that she had texted to me, and there were cars that lined the driveway. The music could be heard before we even got out of the car.

"Don't she know it's a lot of white people that live over here?" Kahlani asked.

"It's Milani," I said. "She don't give a fuck." We got out and took our totes with us, heading to the front door. Chey pushed it open and we were instantly hit with the smell of weed, Tequila, and body sweat.

"She sure knows how to throw a party," Tuesday said, looking around.

"Let's head out back," Kahlani suggested.

We made our way through the crowded living room and kitchen to the backyard. There was a huge pull and right on the other side was a gate that separated it from the lake the house sat on.

"Over there!" Chey yelled, pointing to a free cabana. Yeah, that's how large the backyard was. We staked our claim and set our bags down.

"I'll go get us some drinks," Tuesday offered. As she walked off, I saw Milani in the distance.

"Hey, I'm going to go talk to Milani and thank her for inviting us," I said.

"Okay," Chey and Kahlani nodded. I headed over and her eyes landed on me as I got closer. A wide smile spread across her face.

"If it isn't a ray of sunshine to add to an already bright day," she said. We hugged and she looked in my eyes with this look that made me want to melt even more than I already was in this heat. She had on this hot pink thong bikini that complemented her dark skin.

"I just wanted to say thanks for inviting us," I smiled.

"No problem. Let me know if there is *anything* I can do to make you enjoy your time even more." She winked at me before she headed inside.

"Keep it professional," I muttered to my throbbing clit. As I made my way back over to our cabana, I realized I hadn't had sex in a while, and I was horny like a dog in heat.

I arrived at the cabana the same time as Tuesday did with our drinks. We clinked cups and took a swig of the punch. It definitely had a kick and would probably sneak up on us.

"I'm going to take a swim before we get too lit and drawn," I announced, coming out of my cover up. I chose a black bikini with gold trim to wear. I had braided my hair into two french braids so it wouldn't get in the way. Besides, it was too hot to be wearing thick tresses loose and wild all over my head.

Right before I dove in, my eyes landed on Sydney in a yellow bikini, with her hair pulled into a ponytail. Being a firefighter meant her body was toned as fuck, and her muscles were on full display, skin glistening. Her appearance caught me off guard and since she had caught me in mid jump, I fell into the pool, mouth and nose full of water.

I came up gasping and choking as a splash was made near me. I looked over and Milani had jumped in, holding me up by my waist.

"Are you okay?" she asked. I put an arm around her neck to calm myself. I just had to jump in the deep end.

"Yeah, I'm good," I nodded. I looked up and Sydney was staring at us, her face expressionless. Khoralyn came up behind her and kissed her cheek, throwing me a sour glance. They went over to our cabana and sat down with the girls.

"You sure?" Milani asked. I turned to look at her.

"Definitely." She guided me to the side of the pool and we both got out.

"You hungry?" she asked. I nodded and followed her to the grill. We sat and ate for who knows how long as I got to know her

168

as Milani the person, and not Milani Fae, the artist. She was real down to earth and animated when she spoke. We talked about everything from childhood, to relationships, to careers, and even kids, though she didn't have any.

"I wanna take you out," she admitted, her hand on my thigh, eyes piercing into mine.

"Milani, I don't make it a habit of going on dates with my clients. I don't mix business and pleasure."

"Okay, well, how about since this is my first time in Houston, you show me around the city."

"Do you know how big Houston is? That could take days."

"I'm here for the next few weeks, Jessamyn. I have time." Against my better judgment, I agreed. I told her I had to get back to my girls since I had abandoned them. She understood and went over to her crew.

"Oh, now she remembers us," Chey feigned being upset.

"Hush," I said, flopping down between her and Kahlani.

"You and Milani looked mighty cozy over there," Khoralyn spoke, seeming a little too excited about it.

"We were just talking," I responded. "This is her party and she is my client."

"Umhm, seemed like more than that," Tuesday said, eyeing me over the rim of her cup.

"Doesn't she date a lot of women?" Sydney asked, changing the energy in the air.

"And?" I asked. "That has nothing to do with me."

"I'm just saying, you don't want to be known in the media as one of her latest conquests."

169

"Why do you care?" Khoralyn demanded, sitting up and swinging her hair as she turned to the side to look at Sydney.

"Ah shit," Chey mumbled, taking a bite of her hot dog.

"I don't. I'm just saying."

"You just saying what? Jessamyn is a grown ass woman. You shouldn't even be worried about another woman when your woman is sitting right here. I'm getting sick of this shit."

"If you so sick of it, then leave. I knew I shouldn't have invited your ass."

"Are you serious right now, Sydney?" Khoralyn was on her feet now and people were starting to stare.

"Khoralyn, people are watching," I whispered, trying to get her to calm down, which was apparently not a good idea because the look she gave me when she turned to set her eyes on me, I knew she was about to say some slick shit."

"I don't give a fuck about anybody watching me! I'm trying to have a conversation with my girlfriend, and don't you ever address me." I was out of my seat and so were Chey and Kahlani as they held me back from jumping on her. "Oh bitch, I know you weren't about to touch me."

I pulled and yanked to no avail as Chey and Kahlani's gripped tightened around my arms.

"You just gon sit there and let this bitch try to run up on me?" Khoralyn asked Sydney. Syd was on her feet in an instant, yanking Khoralyn by the arm.

"I'm warning you. You ain't got too many more times to refer to her as a bitch."

"Let me go! Help! Help! She's hurting me!" I noticed that the music was off and everyone was looking at us.

"I think that is our cue to leave," Tuesday said, standing and grabbing our bags. Chey and Kahlani finally let me go and followed her out. On my way to the sliding door, I ran into Milani.

"I am so sorry about all of that," I apologized. She only smiled.

"No worries. Made the party a little more interesting. I'll see you tomorrow?"

"On time?" I asked. She knew I was referring to this party possibly keeping her from being punctual.

"On time, I promise." We hugged, and I headed out the door.

4
Sydney

"I'm so sick of you always defending her!" We had made it back to my house after the embarrassing scene Khoralyn caused at that party. I was pissed. After the shit at work yesterday, I just wanted to relax and have a good time at the party. I was still sore and bruised, but that wasn't going to stop me.

"And I'm sick of you and whatever this shit is you have against Jessamyn. We are just friends, like I've been saying since I first introduced you to her. She and I are just friends."

"So, you don't ever think about fucking her?" She was following me around as I got undressed and into the shower. I had wrapped my hair beforehand and was kind of glad I didn't get it wet since I was not in the mood to go through a wash routine having to deal with her bullshit.

I didn't respond to her ass. Literally, everytime I hung out with my sister, Chey, Tuesday, and Jessamyn, it was the same old thing, but she was stuck on Jessamyn, who I still needed to talk to about the kiss.

"You don't hear me talking to you?" she asked.

"How can I not when your loud ass?" She glared at me through the shower door as I bathed and exfoliated. I turned the water off and grabbed my towel, hanging the shower cap on the hook on the shower wall. I dried off and threw the towel in the plastic hamper and went into my room to moisturize.

"You know what? I hate to have to do this, but I have no choice. It's either me or Jessamyn. Pick one." She stood in front of me as I stared at her trying to figure out if she had lost every ounce of her mind to give me an ultimatum like that. I continued putting on my shea butter and then slipped on my boy shorts and tank top.

"I'm not even going to entertain that stupidity, Khoralyn. The way you be buggin out over Jessamyn, it's almost like you are obsessed with her. Who is at my house right now? You. Who have I been dating for several years? You. Who do I spoil and take on vacations? You. I don't know why you continue to have this fixation on her when you're the one right here with me."

She stared at me for a moment, letting that sink in. Her face softened as she wrapped her arms around my neck and pecked my lips with kisses.

"I'm sorry. It's just that I love you so much, and I get jealous sometimes." She kissed my neck and squeezed my pierced nipples as she made her way to her knees, pulling my shorts down. I spread my legs and gasped as she slid her tongue between my pussy lips, wrapping it around my clit.

"Fuck, Lyn!" My legs were already shaking as she sucked me in her mouth, rolling her tongue back and forth across the bundle of nerves. I was ovulating, so it wasn't long before I was screaming and fucking her mouth, coming hard as my muscles tensed. My orgasm was chased by another, my ass cheeks cramping up. When I could see straight again and gently moved her, I went to the bathroom and cleaned up.

"You still didn't give me an answer," she said, coming out of her clothes and turning the shower on.

"And I'm not going to. If you want to be with me, and continue this relationship, you're going to have to get over whatever this is

173

and accept my friendship with Jessamyn. Period. I don't want to hear shit else." I walked out of the bathroom before she said anything and got in the bed. When my head hit the pillow, it was all over for me.

The next morning, I smelled bacon burning. I jumped up out of bed to Khoralyn in the kitchen attempting to cook, knowing good and got damn well she can't.

"Are you trying to burn my fucking house down?" I fume as I throw the pan in the sink and turn the water on after turning the stove off.

"I'm sorry. I was just trying to do something nice for you after the way I acted yesterday."

"You can't cook, Khoralyn. What the fuck?" The smoke alarm was blaring, and I grabbed a cup towel to fan it. She was crying now, but I was pissed. What the hell was she thinking? When the smoke alarm went off, I threw the towel on the counter. I opened a few windows and the back door to let the smell find its way out.

"Look, I have to go to work. I appreciate what you tried to do, but please don't do that again. I will see you later." I walked to the front door and held it open for her. Her eyes met mine after she had grabbed her stuff and was standing in front of me at the door. Khoralyn kissed my cheek as she walked out, and I slammed the door to get ready for work.

By the time I arrived at the station, the trucks had been cleaned and equipment put away. We had been named the number one fire station in Houston for the second year in a row. Ain't nobody fucking with my team.

174

"Sup, lieutenant," Morrison greeted. "Any publicity stunts this weekend?" He cackled with Langston. I narrowed my eyes at them.

"What are you talking about?" Langston walked over to me and gave me her phone. I scrolled and saw countless videos from Milani's party, all of them showing how Khoralyn was acting. My blood was boiling. I should've known that as big as Milani was, that there were people recording at her party.

I threw the phone back to Langston and stormed off to my office, slamming the door. I threw my purse and bag in my chair and placed my hands behind my head. This girl was going to fucking ruin me. I had to break up with her today.

The morning was filled with me filing paperwork, and around noon, I was about to head out the door to get some lunch when Khoralyn came walking into my office. I closed my eyes and let out a long breath.

"What are you doing here?" I asked.

"I came to bring you lunch. I thought you might be hungry. Don't worry, I didn't cook it." She gave me a small smile and handed the bag to me. I placed it on my desk and then turned to look at her.

"We need to talk."

"Okay, but before you say anything, I want you to know that I am really sorry for my behavior. Like I said last night, I get jealous sometimes, and I..."

"That's just it, Khoralyn. You don't just get jealous sometimes. You get jealous all the time, and after yesterday, I refuse to keep doing this with you. We're done. I can't live like this. The arguing is stressing me out. The accusations are getting on my last fucking

175

nerves, and you seem to not want to hear anything I ever have to say because you keep doing the same shit over and over."

"Are you choosing her over me?" she snapped.

"That!" I yelled. "That right there is what I was just talking about. I didn't mention shit about Jessamyn and you ask me that dumb shit. This doesn't have anything to do with her." I pulled out my phone and went to social media. I showed her the video from yesterday. She watched as her eyes watered. "Do you know how this shit makes me look? I am the youngest and first Black female lieutenant of this station. Your bullshit is fucking with my job, how I eat. This shit is what I can't keep doing."

"Well, if you had just been honest about that bi- I mean Jessamyn, none of that would've happened."

"So you want to blame her for your actions? You want to blame her for not being able to control yourself and talk like a fucking adult instead of yelling, screaming, and throwing a tantrum like a fucking child? You never take accountability for any of the shit you do. You always want to blame other people for how you feel instead of checking your damn self. Grow the fuck up, Khoralyn."

Her lips trembled as she glared at me, and I didn't feel a thing. Not an ounce of emotion, except relief that this was over. This had gone on for too many years, and I wasn't putting up with it anymore.

"You can't break up with me," she whispered.

"I just did. You need to leave." She shook her head, and the look she gave me ran a chill through my body. Possessed didn't even compare to what I was seeing.

"You will regret this," she seethed through gritted teeth. After storming out and slamming the door behind her, I let out a breath. I stood there a moment before I went to get something to eat. This bitch was crazy.

As I walked back from the deli, my phone started ringing. I pulled it out of my purse and saw Langston's name come across the screen.

"Hey, Langston. What's going on?"

"Hurry and get back! Jessamyn's studio is on fire!" All oxygen had been sucked out of the air. It became hard to breathe. I knew she had to be at the studio around this time.

"Lieutenant!" Langston yelled. "Lieutenant!" I couldn't speak. I held on to the side of the building, becoming lightheaded. I couldn't lose her, especially not before telling her I loved her.

Against protocol, I got myself together enough to run to my car and speed to her studio. I don't even remember if I hung up on Langston, but all I could think about was Jess.

5

Jessamyn

True to her word, Milani was here on time, bushy tailed and bright eyed. I gave her a quick hug and saw Chey and Tuesday smiling behind her. I rolled my eyes as I let her go.

"Told you I would be on time," she smiled.

"I appreciate it. Listen up everyone." Everyone gathered around so I could make an announcement. "So, I got an email this morning and the block party has been canceled." There were groans and shouts of dismay.

"I know you all were looking forward to it, but with there being record high heats in the next few weeks, the organizer didn't want to risk any lawsuits from people dying of heat strokes. It is just too hot. But our efforts haven't gone in vain. Milani still has her music video that she wants to shoot, so we can still keep rehearsing for that."

There were loud cheers as that was something to be excited about. My dancers needed to be excited since quite a few of them were new and needed the exposure.

"With that being said, let's go ahead and get started on the first track, *Black Heart.*" Everyone got into position as I stood next to Milani. Her gaze met mine in the mirror, sending chills down my spine, and goosebumps everywhere. The music started and our bodies moved.

In the video, there was a love interest. Auditions would be held this coming weekend for the spot, but until then, I was to be the stand in. When our bodies touched, it was electric. Since Milani hit

178

the music scene, I never saw her in a way other than an alcoholic who was selfish and thought her good looks were enough to get her by. The past few days though, I have seen a completely different person.

The way our bodies moved with fluidity to the music was something to be seen. She sang over her song, but only I could hear her voice since I was closest to her, and she sang loud enough for only me to hear, as if she was singing to me. Everyone else seemed to fade into the background as we moved across the room, hips grinding, fingers grabbing, breaths bated, skin tingling, pussy throbbing.

And the way she smelled, like a rainy day and a hint of a rainbow. I had never had these sorts of thoughts or feelings, ones that I could even remotely describe or put into words. It was kind of shaking me up.

The part was coming up where we were supposed to kiss, and my knees felt weak, but the music and Milani's eyes seemed to carry me like a feather. The instruments stopped and it was only Milani's voice on the record, acapela, as she gently placed her lips on mine, and I moaned softly into her mouth.

The applause snapped me back to reality, and I took a step back out of her embrace. We just stared at each other as everyone else began to chatter, their indecipherable.

"I want you to be the love interest in my music video," Milani admitted.

"What?"

"I don't think we need to hold any auditions for the part. It's yours. I'll let my manager…" An explosion cut her off, as ringing

179

pierced my eardrums. I instantly felt pain everywhere and my vision was cloudy. No, not cloudy, smokey. There was smoke everywhere and it became so hot.

The air was suffocating me and I couldn't breathe. Through the ringing there were screams, but I didn't know where they were coming from. *Kayden.* My baby was the first thing that came to mind. I can't die.

I put my face into my elbow crease and coughed several times. I tried not to inhale too deeply. A stinging pain shot through my leg as I looked down and saw shards of glass sticking out of it. I pulled out the larger pieces that I could see, and blood came pouring out.

My voice was caught in my throat as I tried to scream, call out, anything. The smoke was too thick and engulfed my lungs. I felt around in front of me and I was close to a wall. I reached up to find something to hold onto and was lucky enough that I was by the wall that had the ballet bar. Still coughing, I pulled myself up, not quite standing. I leaned against the wall and looked around at the smoke and bright orange, yellow, and red flames.

When I turned, something was moving fast towards me in the smoke. I went to run as hands tightly wrapped around my throat from behind. I clawed at the person's hands as I tried to suck in air, which was no use since the smoke was all that came in, cutting off my airways even more.

My head was slammed against the wall, a splitting headache rendering me dizzy. I felt the wall connect with my head two more times before the darkness consumed me.

Khoralyn

When she slumped against the wall, I could hear the sirens. I'm glad I thought to tie a scarf around my nose and mouth and cover my eyes with safety goggles. I heard voices getting closer and took off running towards the back of the building.

I made it out of the exit into a back alley and yanked the scarf off, finally being able to breathe. I looked both ways before running to the next block over to hop in my car and speed off. I don't know what Sydney thought she was doing breaking up with me. There was no way I was going to let them be together. Sydney could say all she wanted that she and Jess were just friends, but I knew better.

Hitting 59 N, I jumped on the HOV and made my way to Conroe. Thank goodness the speed limit was 65 so I could push 75 and get as far away from the studio as possible. I also needed to switch cars in case Sydney needed my support. I knew her best friend dying would mean she needed a shoulder to cry on.

Making sure the doors were locked and the alarm was on, I peeled out of my clothes and hopped in the shower, letting the last week or so play back in my head. I was retracing my steps to make sure there was nothing to trace back to me. I'll be damned if I go down for this.

Laying in bed after drying off, I placed my phone on my stomach and stared at the ceiling, waiting for it to ring. It would be any minute now.

6

Sydney

There was an explosion as soon as I pulled up to the studio, I slammed my car into park as I hopped out and pushed my way through the crowd. I ripped through the caution tape as my name was being screamed by my team to not go in the building. Ignoring them, I flew through the front door and was instantly hit with the thick smoke and heat from the fire. I put my shirt over my nose and tried to feel my way to the larger dance room that I knew they rehearsed in.

The walls were hot to the touch, and I had to use my fingertips to graze it until I felt an opening. I stepped over debris and glass. Luckily, I had my work boots on.

"Jessamyn! Chey! Tuesday!" I waited a few and didn't hear anything. I called out again and heard a crash coming from down the hall.

"Agh!" I screamed as something grabbed my ankle. It was a hand. I knelt down on the floor and saw that it was Milani. She was coated in blood. I grabbed her underneath her arms and dragged her outside as paramedics came rushing forward.

"Lieutenant," the fire chief boomed. I turned to look at Chief Wilkes. "You are not to go back in there without proper gear. You are on duty and this goes against the rules."

"My best friends are in there!" I screamed, tears burning my eyes as they streamed down my face.

"Don't make me have you detained. You get your ass to the station and you stay there until I get there, or that is your career." I danced with the idea for a moment, and headed to my car. All I felt was rage, anger, and hopelessness. I couldn't save her if I died.

Four hours later, the chief walked into my office and closed the door gently. I jumped up from my desk, eyes still puffy and watering.

"Everyone made it out alive and was accounted for," he said, his gaze softer than it was earlier.

"Everyone?" I croaked. He nodded.

"Your friend is smart. Anyone who comes into the building has to swipe a key card. We were able to pull the information from her cloud or whatever and were able to match them all except for one."

"What do you mean?"

"According to Jessamyn…"

"She's awake?" He nodded.

"One of the key cards was reported stolen a few days ago and was used to get into the building today, however, the person who the key card belonged to went out of town yesterday."

"What are you saying?" He eyed me as the wheels began turning in my head. My eyes widened as I realized what he was insinuating.

"This was intentional," I gasped.

"Footage from the cameras is still trying to be restored. We noticed that the back of the building was still intact and believed that whoever did this was intentional so that they had a way out. The back door was left wide open. Go ahead and get to Hermann Memorial." I was out the door before he could even turn around.

In the car, my phone rang and I answered instantly.

183

"Where are you?" Kahlani asked.

"I'm on my way to Hermann Memorial. Where are you?"

"Still stuck at my station. The explosion was something serious. We are waiting to hear word from forensics and the bomb squas. Whoever did this, was smart as fuck."

"I just need to see Jess," I sobbed.

"Aww, sis. I wish you would just tell her how you feel."

"We kissed."

"What?! When?"

"The night she invited us all over."

"Before or after Khoralyn left?"

"After, obviously."

"Listen, this conversation isn't over, but I have to go. Let me know how they are."

"Will do." I hung up as it rang again. It was Khoralyn. I did not want to talk to her.

I swung into an empty parking space and through the sliding doors of the hospital.

"I'm looking for Jessamyn Coules."

"Are you a family member?"

"I'm her sister."

"Says here her sister is also a patient."

"A person can have more than one sister. Tell me where she is."

"Room 310, third floor," she mumbled, rolling her eyes. I ran to the bank of elevators and pushed the button several times. "Come on, come on, come on."

When I turned to see the sign for the stairs, I swung the door open and took them three at a time. Jogging down the hall, the numbers got smaller.

"320, 318, 316...310." I barged into the room to see Jessamyn just lying there, bandages everywhere. I took one step at a time, and as I got closer, the tears poured down my cheeks.

"Jess," I choked out. Her eyes fluttered open and she looked at me, a smile spreading across her face. She held her hand out, and I grabbed it. She pulled me closer to her to where I was sitting on the side of the bed.

"Hey bestie," she croaked. I grabbed the water on the side of the bed and put the straw to her lips. She took a few sips and moved her head. I set it back on the table.

"What happened?" I asked.

"I don't know. One minute I was dancing with Milani, the next there was smoke, blood, fire, and someone was choking me. She pulled the hospital gown away from her neck, and I saw the dark marks surrounding it. My mouth fell open. I moved my hand to her neck as she winced.

"I'm so sorry this happened."

"It's not your fault."

"I wish I had been there."

"Why? So you could be laid up in the hospital like me?"

"Jess, I need to tell you something. About that the other night. I..." The door burst open and Milani limped in. She went around to the other side of the bed and choked out a sob.

"They finally let me get out of bed. I had to come see for myself that you were alright." She leaned down and placed her forehead against Jess's. Their lips lightly touched as they engaged in a kiss. I was too late.

I stood up and walked towards the door. I turned around one last time to see them sobbing and staring in each other's eyes. I closed the door behind me as my phone rang again. It was Khoralyn.

"Yeah?"

"Oh my gosh, is Jess okay?"

"What?"

"I saw the fire at her studio. It was all over the news. I've been calling and texting you."

"Oh, yeah, sorry. Yeah, she's fine. I'm at the hospital now, but I'm about to leave. You free?"

"Yes, what do you need?"

"Meet me at my place." I hung up, and walked out of the hospital. I needed a pity fuck.

Three weeks later...

There was a banging on my front door that woke me up out of my sleep. I looked at the clock and it read 5:30. I looked out the window and it was dark outside.

"Who the fuck is at my door this damn early?" I slowly sat up as the banging continued. I grabbed my gun that was snapped underneath the side of my bed and crept down the stairs. The banging got louder and more frequent.

"Open this damn door, Sydney!"

"Jess?" I put my gun on the table as I swung the door open. She pushed past me and went straight to my living room. Closing

186

and locking the door, I walked after her. "Jess, what are you doing here this early in the morning?"

"Why have I barely heard from you?" she cried, tears streaming down her face.

"We just hung out a few days ago."

"Yeah, because Kahlani invited you. You removed yourself from the group chat, you haven't come to either of the game nights."

"Jess, I needed space."

"Space from what? Me?" I didn't say anything. That gave her her answer. We stared at each other, her face full of confusion, hurt in her eyes. "Why did you need space from me?" I shrugged.

"The day I came to see you at the hospital, it seemed like you were in good hands. Besides, you had Chey, Tuesday, and Kahlani. They kept me updated on your recovery. Congrats on the upcoming kickback by the way."

"Fuck all that, Sydney! Why did you need space from me? What did I do to you?"

"You made me fall in love with you." Her breath caught as she took in my words. It wasn't until now that I noticed that she came over here in her bonnet, boy shorts, a cut off tank with no bra, and house slippers.

"Syd...I..."

"Don't insult me with whatever bullshit you're about to say, Jess. It doesn't matter anyway. You're with Milani, right?"

"I..."

"Look, it's early, and I'm tired. I have to be at work in a few hours, and I want to go back to sleep. I'll talk to you later." The look

187

she gave me felt like a knife in my chest. One thing I prided myself on is that I would never hurt her, and I failed at that, miserably. I knew I was going to regret this, but my heart broke in that hospital room. I wasn't about to let it shatter.

When she walked out the door, I doubled over in screams. Not only did I lose my best friend, I just lost the love of my life.

7

Jessamyn

Two weeks later...

Tomorrow was a big day. The summer fest was back on, despite the heat index. Too many people complained, and even protested, so the organizer added some safety measures, including having several large coolers placed around the park for people to get water. Oversized outdoor solar fans were donated, and the pool would be open.

The dancers, Milani, and I were at a dance studio I was renting out for the time being until my new studio was finished being built. We still don't know what happened to my old one other than there were several explosives, and they used the key card of one of my dancers to gain access. I was still pissed about it because I worked my ass off for that studio and the location.

My parents had called me everyday since to make sure I was okay, and so that I could talk to Kayden. He was having a good time going to different countries, eating lots of food, and enjoying different cultures. Even his father called to check on me every other day.

But Sydney keeping her distance drilled a hole in my heart. Her telling me that she was in love with me was unexpected. We were friends, best friends. She can't be in love with me. We kissed once and that was it.

Someone bumping into me knocked me out of my thoughts. I looked up and saw Milani frowning at me.

"You okay? You seem deep in thought."

189

"Yeah, I'm fine," I lied. She had been so good to me. We had gone on a few dates and had sex twice. It was good, but it just didn't feel like I thought it would. Aside from rehearsals, I had been avoiding her the past few days, making up excuses for why we couldn't hang out afterwards.

"Hey, I was wondering…"

"Let's take it from the top one more time," I interrupted. I didn't want to hear what else she had to say. Her eyebrows cinched together as we got in position. Thank goodness this was the last rehearsal before the summer fest.

Later that night, I was sitting on the couch watching a movie on Netflix when I heard my door open and loud voices. Chey and Tuesday.

"Jessamyn," Tuesday sang, "we have food!" They came into the living room with Chinese takeout bags and two bottles of wine.

"Y'all know we have a performance tomorrow right?" I laughed, opening up the bags to take out the food.

"Party pooper," Chey sulked. I laughed as they began taking out their food.

"We need to take a girls' trip," Tuesday said, slurping up a noodle from her lo mein.

"Yes!" Chey exclaimed. "It's been so long since we went on one. With the kids gone and we're about to be done with the fest, we have a break until we have to get ready for KC Mane's tour."

"Let me call Kahlani and Sydney," Tuesday said, tapping away at her phone.

"Y'all, wait…" but it was too late because I heard Kahlani's voice.

"Hey, boo," she said.

"What do you think about a girls' trip?" Chey asked, scooting next to Tuesday.

"Yasssss! When and where we going?"

"When can you and Sydney get off?" Tuesday asked.

"I don't know about Sydney, but I can get off any time. Let me text her right quick." As they continued to chat, I ate my food and sipped my wine. I was not in the mood for a girls' trip. I just wanted my best friend back.

I woke up feeling jittery the next morning. It was a mix of excitement and anxiety. After the fest, Milani would be heading back to Cali. I got dressed and grabbed my duffel bag. I opened the door to find Sydney standing there.

"Hey," I said.

"Hey," she responded. "You have a minute?"

"Um…sure." I stepped out on the porch and locked the door. Setting my bag down, I sat in one of my egg chairs as she sat in the other.

"I just wanted to say that I am sorry for the way I've been acting and not telling you how I felt. I should've come clean sooner."

"Sydney, where are these feelings coming from?"

"You and I have been friends for a long time. We know everything about each other. We are closer to each other than we are to our own sisters." I watched as she tucked her hair behind her ear. "I realize now that we will only ever be friends. Khoralyn and I have been making things work. She's in anger management and going to a therapist, and I make sure she sticks to her appointment. She's much better now."

"Is she going on the trip with us?"

"No, she has to work that weekend and can't get time off." The tension in my shoulders went away. I was glad. I wanted all my girls to myself this coming weekend. "How're things with Milani?"

"Great, they're really great," I lied. I've never lied to Sydney, so why am I now?

"Good. I wish I could make the summer fest, but since Langston will be there, I have to fill in for her."

"It's fine. It'll be live streamed, so you can check social media, if there's not a fire of course."

"Cool. Alright, I'll see you Saturday."

"Okay." She got up and walked to her car. As she drove away, I couldn't help but feel like I was just dumped, and my heart was bleeding.

The venue was already packed. You would've sworn we were at Black family reunion. The stage that was built wasn't that big, but it was big enough for Emancipation Park. The stage faced the recreation center. There were numerous booths of Black owned businesses. It was a legit celebration.

I headed backstage to find Milani and the rest of the dancers. Most everyone was already there. I set my bag down as I saw Chey and Tuesday walking up.

"Finally, you got here," Tuesday said, giving me a hug.

192

"What's wrong?" Chey asked.

"What do you mean?" I responded.

"You look like you just lost your best friend."

"Naw, just nervous about the show."

"Bullshit, bitch. You're never nervous. What's really going on?"
I was about to answer Tuesday when Milani walked up.

"Hey," I said, nodding at her so the girls would shut up.

"Hey," Milani smiled.

"Yeah, heffa this conversation ain't over," Tuesday warned as
she and Chey walked off.

"I just wanted to say thank you so much for everything you've
done from the music video to this performance. I don't know if we
would've made it here without you whipping me into shape. Even
after the fire and everything."

"It's my job, Milani. It's no biggie."

"No, but it is. You have made me see things in a different light.
These past few weeks have been nothing short of amazing." I
didn't say anything back, just giving her a small smile. "But you
don't feel the same."

"I'm sorry, Milani. It's just I really do like you, but with the fire,
and things between Sydney and I..." She cracked a smile as I
frowned. "Why are you smiling?"

"Because I kind of figured that it was something with Sydney. I
tried to ignore it and pretend that you were all in with me, but I
knew I didn't come close to her."

"Wow. I didn't know I was being that obvious."

"You going to try to make it work with her?"

"I wanted to, but she got back with her ex and they are working on things. I missed my chance."

"If it was meant to be, your chance will come around again." I nodded and smiled. "But right now, let's go kill this performance."

By the time Milani's part of the show was over, I was tapped out. I could not feel my feet. I forced myself to stay with Chey and Tuesday for an hour before I headed home. I was too beat. Plus, I still needed to pack for our trip in a couple days.

Once I was done, showered, moisturized both my body and box braids, and set my alarm. I grabbed my Kindle to read the latest fantasy romance by Angela J Ford. She knows she can write her ass off.

8

Sydney

"I think I know what to pack, Lani," I groaned. My sister had arrived early as fuck this morning to check what was in my suitcase.

"I just want to make sure that you have some cute panties and outfits to seduce Jess." I whipped my head towards her. "Bitch, don't give me that look. I know something happened between you two."

"Kahlani, even if it did, I'm with Khoralyn now."

"Is she going on the trip?"

"No, but…"

"Then that hoe don't matter."

"Are you…condoning cheating?" I feigned shock.

"It ain't cheating if it's with a crazy bitch that you shouldn't be with in the first place."

"Come on, you know she's been in anger management and therapy." My phone buzzed and it was an email from Chief Wilkes. I opened it and there was a video attachment. Before I hit play, the doorbell rang. I clicked out of it and went to see who it was.

"Hey, baby!" Khoralyn shouted as she threw her arms around my neck. "I got this weekend off. I can go on the trip." I looked down and saw she had a suitcase.

"Are you fucking kidding me?" Kahlani grumbled behind me before she stomped back up the stairs. I did not know how this weekend was going to go.

When we got to Great Wolf Lodge, Kahlani, Khoralyn and I were the first ones there. I checked into our room which slept 5 people. Jessamyn and Tuesday would share a room, me and Kahlani would and Chey got her own room. Now it was looking like Chey and Kahlani would share while Khoralyn slept with me.

The fact that the rest of the women didn't know Khoralyn was here, especially Jess, had my palms sweating and brows perspiring.

Each bedroom featured a king sized bed, a walk-in closet, an en suite bathroom, a desk, two night stands, and a floor to ceiling window. Our suite sat off in a corner of the lodge, so the views and lighting were impeccable.

"Which room is ours?" Khoralyn said, snuggling up to my side.

"Well, we have to do some shifting around," I responded. "We didn't know you were coming, and Kahlani really loved the room that she and I were supposed to share."

"Yeah, I did," Kahlani mumbled as she walked past us with her suitcases into the room that she and Chey would share. We were able to view the bedrooms online, so we had chosen them before getting here.

"Problem solved," Khoralyn cheered. I could here Kahlani cursing under her breath.

"That's our room over there," I pointed to the right. Khoralyn walked off as I walked into Kahlani's room.

"Close the door," she demanded. I closed it and turned to find a scary ass scowl on her face. "What the fuck, Sydney?"

"What?"

"Why didn't you tell her the room was full? That there was no space for her?"

"Because I want some pussy on this trip, and I for damn sure know I wouldn't be getting it from Jess."

"You're that fucking horny that you couldn't wait a couple of days?"

"Listen, I am ovulating and my hormones are raging. I was not about to be walking around here, pussy dripping, because Jess is in some skimpy clothes."

"You were about to when Khoralyn said she had to work."

"Now, I'm not." Kahlani exhaled a long groan. I know she was furious, but it was too late now.

"Hey, y'all!" Khoralyn shouted. The rest of the ladies must be here. Kahlani and I rushed out to see Tuesday, Chey, and Jess standing in the doorway, looking confused.

"What is she doing here?" Tuesday asked.

"Don't ask about me like I'm not standing here," Khoralyn retorted. "If you have something to say, say it to my face." Her hands were on her hips and her neck was rolling. Tuesday, Chey, Jess, and Kahlani all looked at me.

"She didn't have to work so she joined us," I finally said.

"Did she pay?" Chey asked.

"Did I pay?" Khoralyn recoiled. "I don't have to pay shit if I'm rooming with *my* girlfriend."

"I don't have time for this," Jess said as she walked past us all to her room. I wanted to run and talk to her, but I didn't feel like hearing Khoralyn's mouth.

197

"Everybody has to pay, that's how this works," Tuesday responded.

"Baby, tell them that…" Khoralyn began, whining, before she was cut off by Chey.

"No, everybody pays or you will have to get a separate room."

"Chey, really?" I asked.

"Really. I don't give a damn that she is your girlfriend. Either she pays, or the both of you can find another room."

"Let's go, Khoralyn," I seethed, pissed the fuck off. I know they didn't like her, but what the fuck? Kicking me out, too?"

We grabbed our bags and headed down to the front desk. Luckily, they had a room open. When we got to our room, it wasn't nearly as nice as the suite the other women were in. I was even more enraged.

"I can't believe they kicked you out. Some friends they are." I glared at her, pissed because this was really her fault, but then again, I took her ass back. All those hormones that were raging earlier, were no longer existent now.

"How about we take a shower and christen the room," she smiled, wrapping her arms around my neck. I removed them and shook my head no.

"I'm tired and I really want to take a nap before we meet for the first excursion in a few hours."

"Seriously?" she whined.

"Yes, Khoralyn. I just drove four hours and I am tired."

"What if I just eat your pussy then?"

"Fine," I grumbled.

My alarm went off, and I groaned. Khoralyn gave me back to back orgasms that had me knocked out. I got up and used the bathroom. As I went to my suitcase to pick out a dress, I hadn't even realized that Khoralyn wasn't in the bed when I woke up. I looked around and her stuff was here, but she wasn't.

I continued to get dressed, opting for a cotton, body con dress that was strapless, some matching slides, and matching jewelry. Since the dress was so fitted at the top, I didn't need a bra. In the bathroom, I combed my hair up into a ponytail. My blowout was lasting longer than I expected.

As I came out of the bathroom, Khoralyn was walking in the door, smiling. She had changed too, wearing a yellow sundress, yellow flip flops with a flower in between her two toys, and her afro pulled back by a yellow and black headband. Khroalyn was a gorgeous woman, but that beauty was only on the outside. It was seeping inside, but not as fast as I wished it would.

"Where were you?" I asked.

"Oh, just walking around and taking in the sights."

"I thought we were all going to do that today?"

"I know, but I felt bad for barging in on y'alls vacation last minute, and for getting you kicked out of the suite. Go ahead with the girls, and I'll just chill here."

"You sure?" I asked, confused as to where this new attitude came from.

"Oh, I'm sure. Have fun." She placed a kiss on my lips and then went into the bathroom, closing the door. I grabbed my purse and headed to the suite. I knocked once before Chey opened it, glowering at me.

"I know, Chey, don't even start." She opened the door wider to let me in. Kahlani and Tuesday were chilling on the couch. "Where's Jess?"

"In the room," Tuesday said, nodding to my left. I knocked on the door and entered when she yelled to come in. I didn't see her in the room, so I went over to the bathroom. I stopped short when I saw she had on this red bra and thong laced set. Her ass cheeks looked palmable and the way her titties sat in the bra had my pussy purring. She eyed me in the mirror and smirked.

"I don't think your girlfriend will appreciate you looking at me like that." I licked my lips and smiled as I leaned against the doorframe.

"Maybe so, but she ain't here right now, so I'm going to continue to look." She shook her head and grabbed her dress from the hanger on the shower door.

"Why didn't you tell us she was coming?"

"I didn't know she was until she showed up at my door this morning. I was just as surprised. But I don't want to talk about her. I just want to make sure that we're good."

"We never weren't good other than when you said you needed space from me and ignored me for days."

"And I apologized." She pulled the dress over her body. It was white with red roses and green stems all over it.

"Can you zip this for me?" she asked. I walked over and began to zip the dress, but found my lips placing kisses on her shoulder, the nape of her neck, and her bare back.

"Syd," she gasped. I wrapped my hands around her waist and sucked on her neck, making sure to leave a mark. "Sydney."

My name on her lips had me ready to take this dress off and lift her up, sit her on the counter and eat her pussy. She leaned her head back on my shoulder and closed her eyes. Pulling up her dress, I dipped my hand into the front of her thong. She grabbed my hand and stopped me. I looked at her in the mirror.

"Sydney, if we do this, there's no turning back. This will change everything."

"Move your hand." She moved her hand as I dipped my fingers between her pussy lips. She was soaking wet. Her moans were soft as her body shivered against me.

I continued sucking on her neck as she placed her hand on top of mine, to guide my fingers where she wanted them.

"Move your hand, Jess," I growled into her neck. With my other hand, I pushed the strap of her dress off her arm, and then turned her around as I pulled her breast out. Sucking her nipple into my mouth and pushing her against the vanity, had her moaning a little louder.

"Shhh," I hushed. "You don't want them to hear you. We will never hear the end of it." Her lust filled eyes on me had my heart stuttering. She was fucking gorgeous.

I put her nipple back in my mouth and bit down, making her body jolt. My fingers below dipped inside her as my thumb massaged her clit.

"Syd, I'm gonna come, fuck I'm gonna come."

"Come then, and don't hold back." She let out a low shriek as her body hummed out her pleasure. My fingers were coated with her orgasm. As she settled, I pulled my hand out and licked them clean. I watched as she watched me, eyes hooded, lips parted, breaths raspy. I pulled the other strap down off her shoulder until the dress hit the floor. I grabbed behind her thighs to lift her up before she stopped me.

"Sydney, wait. I'm too heavy." I shook my head and smirked as I lifted her up. She let out a squeal as I walked us over to the wall and lifted her higher to where the backs of her thighs were on my shoulders. She grabbed on to my head as I dove head first between her legs, sliding her thong to the side with my tongue.

Jess moved her hips to press her pussy further in my face. She was so dripping wet from that first orgasm, and I was about to make it pour with her second and third. I pulled her clit into my mouth with my lips, and flicked it lightly with the tip of my tongue.

To have my best friend open and wet like this had me pulling my dress up and reaching into my panties to strum my clit. My other hand was placed against the wall as I worked my mouth on her. She smelled and tasted as good as I imagined. I don't know how we would move forward after this, and I didn't care.

It was this moment right here that had my complete focus and attention. Her clit began to harden and bulge as I gave her slow strokes with my tongue. Her legs were shaking and her thighs were tight around my head. When her hips bucked and her juices flooded into my mouth, my own hips jerked against my fingers as I crested with her.

My moans were muffled against her pussy which vibrated against her clit and made her come harder. She pulled my head closer to her as she fucked my face to satisfy her increasing pleasure. I removed my hand from my panties and stuck two fingers in her, mixing my essence with hers. She writhed some more until she began pushing my head away. I lifted her off my shoulders and pulled her down to where we were face to face, her legs wrapped around my waist.

I didn't even give her a chance to speak as my lips were immediately on hers, tongue pushing into her mouth. She hesitated at first and then began to kiss me back, wrapping her arms around my neck. I walked us into the bedroom and placed her on the bed. Pulling her thing off, and mine, I climbed between her legs and rested my sensitive bud against hers.

9

Jessamyn

"Fuck, you're so wet, Jess," Sydney moaned into my neck. I don't know if it was shock or something else, but I was still stunned that I was fucking my best friend. How the fuck did this happen?

Her hips began to move as our slick centers rubbed up against each other. I moved my hips to create more friction and apply more pressure. My clot was sensitive as fuck, but I need this. I wanted this. And I didn't want it to stop.

"Stop overthinking, Jess," she whispered against my lips, her eyes on mine. "Give it to me." And like that, I came undone again. I dug my nails into her back as I rocked harder and faster against her, riding out my orgasm. I tried to be quiet, but the shit was intense. She swallowed my moans and screams, and in turn I swallowed her as she came.

We were both a trembling mess as our orgasms settled. She rolled off me and pulled me into her arms.

"Sydney…" I began.

"Don't. Let's just let it be for right now." I nodded and rested my head against her as a knock came at the door.

"Hey, Khoralyn is looking for you, Sydney," Tuesday whispered. Sydney jumped up and went to the bathroom to clean up, grabbing her panties on the way. I slumped back into the bed. What the fuck had we done?

After getting cleaned up and getting myself together, we left the lodge and went shopping. I was so happy when Khoralyn and

204

Sydney decided to go off on their own. Khoralyn had been giving me dirty looks as if she knew what Sydney and I had done. When I came out of the dressing room to show Chey, Tuesday, and Kahlani the dress, they were sitting on the couch, fists tucked under their chins, waiting for me.

"What?" I asked.

"You fucked my sister," Kahlani cheesed. I went to deny it, but heat rose to my cheeks and a smile spread across my face.

"I knew it!" Chey squealed.

"Shhhhh!" I said. "Can y'all keep it down? Yes, we did have sex, but it just kind of happened. I asked her to zip my dress up and then next thing I know, she was between my legs."

"So, what does this mean?" Tuesday asked.

"I don't know," I shrugged. "She's still with Khoralyn."

"For now," Kahlani grinned.

We went to a few more stores and went back to our rooms to get some socks to go bowling. I hadn't been bowling in forever. After that, I didn't know what else was on the agenda.

Later that night, we all had dinner at one of the local restaurants. It was a good time until Khoralyn got upset about something and made Sydney leave. I hated that she was still with her after what we did this morning. I am usually not the jealous type, but when it comes to Sydney, the green monster is on full display.

Back in the room, I changed into some workout gear: leggings and a sports bra. I put on my slides and carried my heels in my hand.

"I'm going down to the gym," I called out. I got mumbles of acknowledgement as I headed out the door. Inside the gym, there was a dance room with mirrors on each wall, and a ballet bar that stretched around the room. By the speakers was a USB cord for my specific phone. I plugged it in and let the music rush over me as I moved my body.

I used to spend countless nights in my dance studio just vibing out to the music. Dance was something I was born with. I remember when I was younger, my dad would take me on Daddy/Daughter dates and they always included dancing. I feel like he was the one who kept pushing me towards dance because he knew I loved it.

When he injured his back playing golf, he wasn't able to dance as much anymore. It sucked, but I kept at it. Now, I was a nationally renowned choreographer, and I had celebrities from all over seeking my services.

The song ended and faded into the next. I don't know how long I had been down here, but when I disconnected my phone and went to the door, it was locked. I pushed several times and it didn't budge. I went to call one of the ladies and saw that I didn't have any service. I started banging on the door and screaming, but there was no one down here that late. How was I supposed to get out of here?

Khoralyn

I went to look for Sydney this morning, and when I found her, she was coming out of Jessamyn's room, her dress frumpled. I didn't say anything then, but when I went in to kiss her, I could still smell pussy in her lips with a hint of soap. She tried to wash away the evidence, but didn't do a very good job. I was going to have to up my tactics when it came to Jessamyn.

When the ladies all wanted to hang out, I told Sydney that I wanted it to be just us. She obliged, but I knew she wasn't happy about it. It was supposed to be a trip with her girls, but I wanted to make her see that she really didn't need anyone else but me.

Now, I'm standing outside the dance room door watching Jessamyn move her body so fluidly. I wasn't blind. I could see why Sydney would want her. She's gorgeous. In another life where Sydney didn't exist, I'd definitely push up on Jessayn, but right now, in this current life, she is a threat that needs to be eliminated. I took out a hair pin from my hair and tampered with the locks. I pulled both doors to open them and they didn't budge.

Smiling to myself, I sauntered off, heading back to my room. On the way, I made a phone call.

"Hello?"

"Hey, I need a favor," I responded.

10

Sydney

The next morning, we were all going to spend it at the indoor waterpark. Khoralyn wasn't in the room when I woke up, and I just assumed she had gone down for breakfast. I took care of my bathroom routine and put on a bikini, and a cover up. I grabbed my small tote bag and headed to the suite with my girls. I knocked and the door flew open.

"Where's my sister?" Tuesday demanded.

"Huh? What?" I asked.

"Where is Jess?" Chey chimed in.

"What are y'all talking about?"

"She never came back to the room last night," Kahlani added. "We thought maybe she would've been with you."

"How could she when Khoralyn was with me? Where did she say she was going?"

The three of them thought for a minute, looking around the room for an answer.

"She screamed she was going somewhere as she walked out the door," Tuesday remembered. "But I don't remember what it was."

"The gym!" Chey shouted, bolting out of the suite. We were on her heels taking the stairs a few at a time. We went through the door to the stairs and down the hall to the gym, and there was no one in there.

"She's not here," I said.

"Let's check that room over there," Tuesday pointed out. We ran to the double doors and looked through the window. Jess was lying there in what looked like a puddle of her own piss.

"Jess!" I screamed, banging on the door. She sat up and looked at us, eyes wide as she ran to the door.

"Get me out of here!" she cried.

I took off out of the gym and to the concierge's desk. There was a woman standing there at the computer, typing away.

"How can I help you?" she asked as I approached.

"My friend is locked in the dance room in the gym."

"What? Are you sure? We never lock any of those doors. They are open to guests 24/7."

"Ma'am stop asking questions. She is locked in there and she's been in there all night." The woman grabbed some keys off the hook and headed to the gym. I followed closely behind. When we got in there, she went over to where the ladies were standing and unlocked the door. Jess burst through the doors and out of the gym. We ran behind her as she flew up the stairs.

By the time we got to the suite, she was going through the door and straight to the bathroom, closing and locking it behind her.

"Jess!" I exclaimed, knocking rapidly on the door.

"Jess, open up," Tuesday called. There was no sound except for the shower she had just turned on.

"I think we should cut this trip short," Chey suggested. "We don't know what happened or how she got locked in there."

A knock came at the door. I went to answer it to find Khoralyn standing there, smiling.

"Hey, boo," she said, pecking me on the cheeks before inviting herself in. I closed the door and turned around to find her sitting on the couch.

"Where have you been?" I asked.

"I went to eat breakfast and then came up here."

"Why didn't you wake me?"

"You looked like you were sleeping peacefully."

"Where were you last night?"

"What is with all the questions?"

"We found Jessamyn this morning locked down in the gym."

"Are you trying to insinuate something?

"No, I'm sorry. We were all just worried something had happened to her. She locked herself in the bathroom and won't come out."

"Oh no," she said, hurrying to my side. "Is she okay?"

"I don't know." Chey came walking to the living room with an unreadable expression.

"Jess says she's ready to go home, so we're going to head out. Kahlani said she's going to ride with us." I nodded at her.

"I really hope she's okay," Khoralyn said. Chey eyed her and turned to go back to the others.

"I guess we better get packed then," I suggested, heading to the front door.

"Why do we have to leave just because they are?" Khoralyn asked as we headed to our room.

"Listen, Khoralyn, I've been meaning to talk to you." We got in the room and I started packing my bags. My phone beeped and it was a text from the chief asking if I had looked at the video footage yet. I had forgotten all about it. I opened the video and watched a woman run from an alley and jump into an awaiting car, which was extremely familiar.

I rewound it back so that I can see where she was and then it hit me. This was not too far from Jess's studio that was burned down. But my only question is, why was Khoralyn there. I looked up from my phone to look at her. She wore an irritated look.

"I've been talking this whole time," she snapped.

"Sorry, I just got some disturbing news. Where were you when Jess's studio was burned down?"

"Uh…uh…I was at work," she lied, stumbling over her words.

"You were off that day." Her eyes shifted as she took a step back. "You blew up her studio and tried to kill her. I'm calling the police." I went to dial the number, and before I could hit the call button, my phone and I were flying in opposite directions as Khoralyn pushed me over the back of the couch and ran.

My head hit the floor with a thud. Even though it was carpeted, it didn't make it hurt any less. I tried to stand up, but my head was throbbing. I heard the door slam shut and feet scuffling.

"What happened in here and why was Khoralyn running for her life?" Kahlani asked.

"She was the one who blew up Jess's studio," I groaned, pain shooting through my skull.

"She what?! And you let her go?"

"Do you not see that I'm hurt here?" Kahlani took off running before I could say anything. When the pain settled to a dull ache, I was able to get up and grab my phone. I shot the chief a message and told him where we were staying, and that she had run off.

He didn't respond, so I packed my things up and set my suitcases by the door. I left her clothes in the room. She had given them her card to hold for the room. Then I got an idea. I completely trashed the room. Getting out all that pent up anger, I broke everything that would shatter first. Each time pieces of glass went flying, I felt some of that anger slither away.

When there was nothing left to destroy, I got my suitcase and headed down to the lobby where Kahlani was waiting.

"Where's everyone else?" I asked.

"They left already. I figured since Khoralyn caught ghost, I would ride with you so you don't have to ride by yourself."

"Thanks." We got loaded into the car and hit the road. I knew Khoralyn would have to come back at some point.

After Kahlani had left my house, I unpacked and took a shower. I wondered where Khoralyn was and why she tried to kill Jess. She could've killed multiple people with that stunt. I knew one thing though. She and I were through. I had given her too many chances, but now that she was blowing up buildings and trying to commit homicide, we could not be together. She belongs in jail.

11

Jessamyn

I stayed in the bathroom for a while after running from the gym. I had to shower and wash the piss off of me. I don't know how I was locked into the gym, but the resort offered to delete our bill and have our stay on them. I didn't really care. I was ready to go at that point.

When we made it back to my house, the girls offered to stay with me, but I sent them home. I wanted to be alone. I unpacked and got something light to eat before heading to my in-home dance studio. I blasted *Surprise* by Chloe Bailey and made up a dance routine as the song continued. I had it on repeat for I don't know how long.

Exhaustion hit me and I turned the lights off in the studio. As I headed up the stairs, I heard a thud and a door slamming. I froze in place. The sound of glass shattering made me blood ice over. Somebody was in my house. I tiptoed up the stairs and looked around both corners. I heard some glass break again and went in the opposite direction of the sound.

I had almost made it to the garage when searing pain shot through my skull as I was pulled back by my hair and thrown on the ground. All the lights were off, so I couldn't see the face of the dark figure standing over me.

"What do you want? I can give you money!" I begged. They kneeled down over my body, straddling me as they pinned my arms down with their knees, wrapping their hands around my throat. My head was slammed against the floor a couple of times, stars dancing across my vision. I was losing oxygen and was sure to have a concussion if I lived. I heard scuffling and then there was no more pressure before I blacked out.

I wished that beeping would fucking stop. It was doing nothing but making this headache worse. It was a steady rhythm and then began to speed up the more irritated I got.

My eyes fluttered open and were instantly assaulted by the bright lights above my bed. Adjusting to the light, I realized I was in a hospital bed. Images of my attack came rushing back. I began to panic as Sydney's face came into my line of vision.

"Hey, Jess, I'm here. Calm down." She grabbed my hand and squeezed as the door flew open and in came Chey Tuesday, and Kahlani.

"She's alright!"

"She's awake!"

"What the hell happened?" They all spoke at once, and I smiled at their concern. I loved this group of women.

"She was attacked," Sydney said, not taking her eyes off of me. "I came to talk to her and her front door was wide open. I heard someone inside, and then a scream. I followed the sound and saw this figure on top of her, choking her. I tackled them to the ground and we fought. I got in a few licks, but as you can see, they bested me." She had some bandages on the right side of her forehead where it looks like she got stitches.

"Oh my gosh!" Tuesday gasped, grabbing my other hand.

"Did you talk to the police?" Chey asked Sydney.

"I did. I told them what I saw, but they should be back shortly, now that she's awake. They want a statement from her. But there's something else." We all looked at Sydney, questioningly. "I think it'll be better if I showed you."

She pulled out her phone and showed us a video of Khoralyn running to her car and driving off. The next screen was a video from inside of my studio, and Khoralyn was seen placing bombs in different locations. My heart rate sped up as anger bubbled up inside.

"I confronted her when we were at Great Wolf Lodge, we tousled and she fled. I don't know where she is, and I haven't heard from her. But I do think that she had something to do with this attack."

"Why would she do all of this?" Kahlani asked.

"Because she's a fucking psycho, and we told you to leave that bitch alone," Tuesday snapped. "Look at my fucking sister?" Tears brimmed her eyes as Sydney looked down towards the bed.

"Excuse me," a nurse said as she came in to check my vitals. "It seems like you are doing fine. You don't have a concussion, but I would take it easy for the next few days. I will get your discharge paperwork." She left the room and it was quiet. No one said a word. If this was Khoralyn's doing, she wouldn't stop until I was dead.

"So where are you going to stay?" Tuesday asked. "You can't go back home. You are more than welcome to stay with me."

"I would," I croaked, "but I'm not sleeping on a bunk bed." She had a two bedroom apartment with a small loveseat as the only other sleeping option.

"She's staying with me," Sydney said. The look on her face was serious as her eyes lit me on fire.

"Are you sure that's…" Kahlani started.

"I said what I said. She's staying with me." No one argued.

After I was discharged, Sydney drove me to her place in silence. I could feel the guilt radiating off of her. I wanted to say something, but what could I possibly say?

She put her car in park in her driveway and we got out. She led me to the guest bedroom and said she'd be back with some clothes so I could shower and go to bed. She gave me the clothes and then left back out, closing the door.

Clean, clothed, and in bed, I let out a deep sigh. I was exhausted. I took two of the pain relievers that the doctor had given me, and drifted off to sleep.

Around two in the morning, a storm had rolled in and the lightning and thunder jolted me out of my sleep. It was loud and bright outside. My heart began to race each time lightning struck and I could see so many shadows, some that looked like someone was in the room with me. The next clap of thunder had me springing out the bed and down the hall to Sydney's room. I closed her bedroom door behind me and slid in the bed next to her. She was sound asleep as I wrapped my hand around her waist and snuggled up to her back.

I felt her shift and turn towards me. The light from the moon shone through the bedroom, illuminating her face along with several more strikes of lightning. She smiled at me before her lips met mine. Another sound of thunder caused me to jump and her to chuckle as she pulled me closer to her.

The kiss deepened as she made her way between my legs. Our hips bucked and pelvises ground against each other. Our tongues wrestled for dominance, neither giving in. Her hands went under the thin tank she gave me and grazed my skin, moving up towards my breasts. She pinched both nipples as she swallowed my gasps and moans.

She moved her lips down to my right nipple, rolling her tongue across it before sucking it in her mouth. My back arched off the mattress as she rolled my left nipple between her fingers, then she switched sides, giving both breasts equal attention.

Sydney made her way down my body until she was face to face with my pussy, a thin piece of fabric the only boundary between them. She tugged at the waistband as I lifted my hips for her to pull the boy shorts off. Taking great care to lick and kiss my inner thighs, she left me in great anticipation of feeling her tongue. But I didn't have to wait long. She laid her tongue flat and flush against my clit and swiped it up. A chill went up my spin.

My legs fell open even wider to give her more access to me. Gripping her head, I moved my hips in rhythm with her tongue as she gave my clit lash after lash of pleasurable attacks. She gripped my thighs and flipped us over so that I was riding her face. I squealed at being thrown around like a rag doll at my size, but Sydney was strong as fuck.

She feasted beneath me as my moans were drowned out by the thunder and heavy rain outside. I hit my peak as another slap of thunder shook the house. It was really coming down outside and it was coaxing my orgasm on.

Sydney flipped me around so that my pussy was still in her mouth, but hers was now in my face. I smiled as I realized that she didn't have any bottoms on, and instantly stuck two fingers inside her, her hips rising at the feeling. I slid my tongue between her slick folds as she sucked my sensitive clit into her mouth. My legs were shaking and hers flexed as I snaked my tongue against her slit.

Before long, we were gripping each other's ass as we came hard, a white light shooting across my vision, though it could've also been lightning. Something shattered and we both stilled. I noticed the bedroom door was open and I was certain that I had closed it. I moved to sit next to Sydney.

"That door was closed," I whispered.

"I know," she whispered back, pulling a gun from underneath her bed. "Stay here."

"Like hell," I said, feeling around for my boy shorts and putting them on. She grabbed some leggings out of her dresser and put them on, holding the gun out in front of her. She peeked out the door looking both ways before she nodded for me to follow.

12

Sydney

The sound of glass shattering had me on high alert. I know there was a bad storm outside, but it sounded more like something inside the house. We made it to the stairs and slowly descended, our backs against the wall. I could see all sorts of shadows moving, but I knew they were the trees blowing in the wind.

We got to the bottom and I looked around the banister towards the kitchen. I didn't see anyone. We headed to the kitchen where a window was broken.

"Must've been the strong winds flying things around," I said lowering the gun. I flipped the switch but nothing came on. Power was out.

"This storm is…" Her sentence was cut off as a scream pierced the air and I turned to see Jess getting hit with a cast iron skillet. The figure was clothed in black, and instincts had me shooting off rounds towards them. They retreated out of the kitchen as I went over to make sure Jess was okay. She was still breathing, so I went towards the living room and was hit from behind in the back by something hard.

The gun flew out of my hand as I hit the ground. It was too dark, so I couldn't see where it went. I tried standing but was hit in the back with a booted foot. I fell back to the floor as I was repeatedly kicked in the ribs. When the kicking stopped. I looked up to the figure standing above me. They pulled their ski mask off and it was Khoralyn. I gasped as she smiled something sinister.

"I tried my best to make you see that I was the only one for you, but you chose her over and over again," she spat. "She didn't die in that studio like she was supposed to. She didn't have a psychotic break in the dance studio at the lodge. And she didn't die in her house because you had to yet again, come to her fucking rescue. But that ends tonight. Neither of you will live."

She raised her foot and midway bringing it down to my face, she was tackled by someone. I looked up to see her and Jess fighting. Jess threw punch after punch at her face, and Khoralyn was swinging back.

Trying to feel for the gun, I winced as the pain in my back and ribs spread down to my toes. I cried out at the pain, but kept scooting until my fingers hit something cold, hard, and heavy. I picked the gun up and sat up in time to see that Khoralyn was now on top and about to bring something heavy down against Jessamyn's head. I let off four shots, each one puncturing her back.

Khoralyn's body froze and then slumped to the side as Jess pulled her off. Everything went black after that.

Two weeks later…

I woke up this morning feeling great. My ribs were healing well, and I was in physical therapy for my back. Although the four gunshot wounds to Khoralyn's back didn't kill her, one hit her spinal cord, and she was now paralyzed in jail. Her hearing was coming up soon where she would get her final sentencing, as well as the man she enlisted to kill Jessamyn.

Jess and I had been keeping our distance from each other, and I understood why. She had her reservations about everything that happened, and her new studio was almost done being renovated. She had found a building for sale and bought it. Kahlani was keeping me up to date about everything going on with her.

I had been out on leave and under investigation by internal affairs at the fire department since Khoralyn was my girlfriend. She tried to throw me under the bus, but there was just no evidence to prove it. She tried to say that she did it for me because I told her that I was obsessed with Jess and I wanted to get over my obsession, so I had her try to kill Jess so that I wouldn't have to be tempted anymore.

It was bullshit and no one believed her, but I still had to go through the process. Chey and Tuesday still came by when they weren't hanging with Jess. I hate having them feel like they had to divide their time to keep from choosing sides, but at the end of the day, I told them that they were her blood. They still came by.

I spent the day cleaning my house. After having the window replaced, I decided to have all of my windows replaced with double panels that were shatterproof. Khoralyn had thrown a brick through the backdoor window to get in. Showing up here was so fucking stupid of her if she wanted to get away with trying to kill Jess.

Being blinded by her beats me. It's like she had cast some sort of spell or enchantment on me and I kept crawling back. I jumped as my phone buzzed in my pocket. It was a text from Jess inviting us all over this upcoming weekend to watch the premiere of Milani Fae's new music video that she choreographed. I sent back my acceptance and continued cleaning the house.

The weekend rolled around, and I was standing at Jess's front door. My palms were sweating as I stood there with my midthigh length skirt, a crop top, some matching sandals, my crossbody, and a bottle of Jess's favorite wine. I knocked on the door, even though I had a key. We had been in a weird place and I didn't want to just walk in and she go off on me.

Jess answered the door in a sundress that hugged her hips and made her breasts sit up nicely, breasts that I had had in my hands and my mouth. My pussy aching with just the sight of her.

"Come in," she said, standing to the side. "Everyone else isn't here yet."

I came in and headed to the kitchen. I stood at the island with the bottle of wine, staring at her. Not sure how long we stood there, but she said and spoke first.

"I think that we should start over and give us a try, as more than friends."

"Really?" I frowned, taken aback.

"Yes. I needed these couple of weeks to not only heal, but to think about us and what that would look like moving from being friends to a real couple. I mean, Kayden would be thrilled. I talk to him everyday and he's always asking about you."

"I love the kid," I mumbled. I set the wine doena and walked over to her, pulling her into me. "Just know that if we do this, we will still always be friends. You are my best friend, and best friends tend to have the best relationships. I promise I won't hurt you, not intentionally."

222

"I know. I'm just glad we can give this a try, for real, and not have to worry about Khoralyn. I don't know what you ever saw in her." I laughed as she shook her head.

"She was cool once you got to know her, but her obsession with me and you was getting old. We would've broken up eventually even had she not tried to kill you."

"Yeah, and now I have nightmares and am in therapy." Kahlani had told me that Jess was now seeing a therapist for her PTSD. I got furious all over again thinking about the shit Khoralyn did and how it could've gone horribly wrong if she really had the chance.

Chey, Tuesday, and Kahlani finally arrived an hour later after I made Jess come three times. We watched the music video premiere and it was amazing. I couldn't keep my eyes off Jess the whole time in the music video.

13
Jessamyn

A month later…

My studio was finally finished being renovated and classes started back. Today, we were having a dance off. I had choreographed a short routine to the chorus of *Teenage Fever* by Drake. All of my students were there and gathered around the main dance room.

Kahlani and Sydney were able to join since it was their off day. We had dance battles a few times a week, but they were barely able to attend with people always causing fires around the city.

"Ayyy!" the dancers shouted as one group started off. I loved dance battles. They were the highlights of the week. It was almost my turn to go with Chey and Tuesday when Sydney came up behind me, wrapping her arms around my waist and whispering in my ear.

"Dance for me, Jess," she rasped, sending off fluttering butterflies in my stomach. I smiled, turned to kiss her, and then headed to the dance floor and did exactly what she had requested. I danced for her.

The end.

Bonus Epilogue
Two Years Later...

Sydney

I was nervous as hell. I had planned this big dinner for Jessamyn. Bigger than big. I even got Kayden in on it, and now that he was seven, he could hold a secret, well, for a short period of time.

Looking in the mirror, I admired the form fitting strapless dress. I went with black and was glad I did since I was sweating bullets. I chose some hot pink stilettos with matching hot pink jewelry. Kahlani had done my hair up into a tight bun that rested in the middle of my head, with two curls that spiraled down either side of my face.

"Damn!" Kahlani said as she came into my room. I smiled at her and turned around to give her the full fit. "You look so good, sis."

"Thank you, and so do you." Kahlani was the girliest of the two of us. She had on a bright orange skirt with an orange and green crop top. Her stilettos were black snake skin. Her box braids were braided into two going straight down her back.

"How are you feeling?" she asked.

"Nervous as hell. I feel like I need to shit. My stomach is in knots."

"Calm down, Syd. Relax. You're acting like this is someone new. You've known Jess since forever. It's going to be okay." I took a deep breath and nodded in agreement. She headed out of the room, and after one last glance in the mirror, I grabbed my purse and followed behind her.

Twenty minutes later, we arrived at the house: The House. I had bought a house in King Estates in Kingwood. I gave Kahlani the key card since she was the one driving because I was too nervous. The gates opened and we headed in turning to the right.

225

The house was located on Lake Houston, and it was gorgeous. I hadn't told Jess that I had bought us a house. We had just agreed to move in together, into a house so that Kayden would have a backyard, as well as any other children we decided to have. I prayed that she wouldn't be mad about it.

"I still can't believe you decided to buy this house with the insurance money," Kahlani groaned.

Khroalyn had miraculously survived me shooting her several times. She was arrested and sentenced to 20 years in jail for arson, property damage, and several counts of attempted murder. For whatever reason, she had named me as her beneficiary. Not only did I get her insurance money, I also got the insurance money her parents had on her, and their insurance policy since they had died and named her beneficiary. Needless to say, it was a lot of money.

I had enough to buy the house, set up Kayden's college fund, invest some, and then put some in savings. I know that Jess doesn't need my money, but I still wanted to do this for us.

Kahlani parked in the garage and we headed inside. Our parents and Jess's parents were there. Chey was there and brought Kayden with her. I got the idea for her to volunteer to babysit Kayden under the guise that I was taking Jess on a date. There was a theater room where everyone would stay until it was time.

I had it all planned out. I was going to give her a tour of the home and then end in the theater room Jess would have no idea what's coming. I went to the backyard to make sure everything was set up perfectly. I greeted our families and then looked at my phone to see that Tuesday texted saying that they were at the gate.

"Alright everyone," I announced. "They're at the gate. Head to the theater room."

Jessamyn

"I don't know why I have to wear this dress," I moaned to Tuesday. She was lying across the bed scrolling on her phone,

226

ignoring my complaints. "Hello? Earth to Tuesday." She looked up and smirked.

"Jess, you've been complaining since Chey came to get Kayden. Sydney bought the dress and wanted you to wear it."

"Okay, fine. But why are you so dressed up?"

"I have a date tonight."

"With who?"

"Don't worry about it. Are you ready?"

"Yes, let's go."

We got into Tuesday's car and headed towards Kingwood. I was confused because there weren't really any places we frequented there.

"Where are we going?"

"Jess, can you just shut up and go with the flow?"

I squinted my eyes at her. She only laughed at my expression. Letting out a huff, I looked out of the window.

Nothing was said until we pulled up to the gates at King's Estates. I was really confused now. Tuesday pulled out a white keycard and wiped it. The gates began to open, and I turned to look at her. She only smirked but kept her eyes on the road.

The house she parked in front of was massive. All the lights were on, and when I looked at the front door, Sydney was walking out, and when I say my clit began to throb like she ain't ever been strummed before. Syd looked good as fuck in that black dress and stilletos. The dress I wore was similar but flared out at the waist. My shoes had black and hot pink stripes.

She came to my door and opened it. I looked at Tuesday, and she had tears in her eyes. What the fuck was going on? Turning to look back at Sydney, she had a hand held out, and I took it. Getting out of the car, she closed it behind me and Tuesday backed out of the driveway.

Sydney led us into the house, and as soon as the door was closed, she pressed me against it and smashed her lips into mine. So this is why she said not lipstick. I let out a moan as her fingers feathered up my thighs underneath my dress. I squeezed her ass as she pressed into me, pelvis to pelvis.

227

"I wish I could fuck you right now," she whispered against my lips.

"I agree, but I have questions." Her tongue slipped back into my mouth and we kept at it for a while. I felt my panties being slid to the side and a finger sliding across my clit. Two fingers entered me and my knees buckled. That was the thing about Sydney: she made me so fucking horny.

Her thumb circled my clit in rhythm with her tongue in my mouth. I was already on edge, so when I came, I wasn't surprised at how fast it broke through the surface. She swallowed my screams as her thumb circled faster and her two fingers slid in and out of me.

"Syd," I whimpered, body shaking and convulsing.

"Let it go Jess. Give me the rest of it." She kept working me until my orgasm finally settled. In a daze, I looked at her as she leaned back a little. She pecked my lips a couple times and then I watched as she licked her fingers clean.

"You said you had some questions," she smirked, acting as if she didn't just give me a blinding orgasm.

"Whose house is this and why are we here?"

"Before I answer that, let me give you a tour."

She took me by the hand and led me through the entrance to the living room, dining room, kitchen, all six bedrooms, the garage and then to a door that was at the end of the hall downstairs. She opened it and led me into a room that was dark.

"This is the theater room," she said and flipped a switch.

"Surprise!" I screamed in shock as I saw everyone we loved standing in the room. Kayden ran up to me, and I scooped him into my arms. Tears sprang to my eyes as I turned to Sydney.

"What is this?" I croaked.

"It is our house warming party." My eyes widened and my heart beat so loud I was sure everyone could hear it. I placed Kayden down and threw my arms around Sydney's neck, pressing my lips to hers. There were cheers and hollers coming from everyone.

"Let's eat!" Chey called.

We all headed to the backyard which I can see why Sydney purposely did not show it to me. There were wicker tables and chairs with candles lit scattered across the yard. I saw the lake beyond the iron gate and the other houses in the neighborhood.

"You did all of this for me?" I asked.

"I did it for us." She pulled me to her and we placed our hands on each other's waists. "Jess, I love you so fucking much, and you know I've loved you since forever. I want to spend the rest of my life with you and Kayden and our future children."

"But babe, how can we afford this?"

"Khoralyn listed me as her beneficiary on her life insurance policy. Not only that, I inherited the money she was getting from her parents' life insurance policy as well as the policy they had on her. We are set for life. I even set up a college fund for Kayden." I was full on crying now and was glad I didn't have on makeup. This woman literally was filling my heart.

"I love you so fucking much, Sydney. You are everything that I could've ever hoped for. I don't know what I did to deserve you, but I thank God for creating us for each other."

"I'm glad you feel that way," she smiled, tears streaming down her face as she got down on one knee. I gasped and then let out a small cry as she pulled a small box from between her breasts. Opening it, she revealed a pink princess cut rose gold diamond ring. "Jessamyn, my best friend, my lover, my partner, my life, will you marry me?"

"Say yes, Mommy!" Kayden cheered. I pulled him to me and knelt down to throw my other arm around Sydney.

"Yes, yes, I will fucking marry you!"

"Whooooooo!" our families cheered. We stood and she put the ring on my finger. We kissed and then I pulled back.

"I guess we were meant for each other because..." I pulled a ring box out from between my breasts. "...I was going to ask you to marry me." I opened up the box and revealed a seafoam green princess cut white gold diamond ring. Green was her favorite color.

"I will marry you right now if you're up for it," she sobbed. I placed the ring on her finger.

"I don't suppose there's an ordained minister amongst you," I chuckled. Tuesday stepped forward, surprising me. :I thought you had a date?"

"That's what you were supposed to think. I got ordained a few weeks ago when Syd came to me with this idea in hopes that you would marry her right after she proposed."

"But you knew I was proposing to her," I tsked. She only shrugged.

"Am I marrying y'all or not?" she asked. I looked at Sydney, and saw all I needed to see.

"Yes," we said in unison.

The End.

M. L. Sexton

Old friends.
New beginnings.

Until We Meet Again

Prologue

(Shaleena)

"Fuck, Shaleena, shit!" Xavieon swore as he thrusted into me. "Damn this pussy good as fuck!" He hadn't even noticed that I wasn't moaning. Yeah, my pussy was wet, but that was only because he ate it first.

"Agh, I'm bout to bust!" His body went rigid and shook as he emptied into me. I was already seven months pregnant with our son, so it didn't matter.

He pumped a few more times to completely empty himself and then rolled off me. His breathing was annoying the fuck out of me. I just wanted him to get dressed and leave. I don't even know why I still let him fuck. I didn't even like him like that, and we weren't together. Never were. He was a sneaky link until I got pregnant.

"Have you thought anymore about us moving in together?" he asked for what felt like the hundredth time. Ever since we found out I was pregnant, he had been badgering me about us moving in together. Only thing was, I didn't want to live with him. I didn't want to be with him.

"We've talked about this, Xavieon," I mumbled, rolling to my side so I could sit up on the edge of the bed. This big ass belly prohibited me from doing a lot of small things, such as hopping out of the bed.

"Shaleena, why are you so against it? I mean, wouldn't you want to be a family?"

"Nigga, I don't even like you like that and you know that. We fuck, that's it, and even that is getting on my nerves."

"What you mean? You enjoyed it every time. I hear you scream and shit." He was on his feet now. Hands on my hips, I glared at him in disbelief.

"The only time I scream is when you eat my pussy. You never noticed I'm not screaming or moaning when you fuckin' me because nothing can be heard over your loud ass."

"Are you for real right now? We been fuckin' around for a year, and you're telling me not once has my dick made you come?" In the beginning it did, and it was great, but I'm not telling his ass that.

"Look, just because we are having a baby together, does not mean we need or have to be together. We can still coparent."

"And fuck?"

"No, Xavieon, we cannot continue to fuck. I don't enjoy it, and to be honest, I don't want you touching me anymore." He began to gather his clothes, finally. He got the picture.

"This is some bullshit. All I want to do is be there for my son, and I can't even do that."

"Hold up," I said, holding a hand up to make him stop talking. "Because I won't fuck you or be with you, you can't be there for your son? Tell me how that makes sense."

"How can I be there for him when we aren't together?"

"Nigga your parents divorced when you were four, and both of them were active in your life even though they weren't together. But

237

this is really about you no longer having access to me, so you'd rather be a deadbeat. That's fine. I'm pretty sure when I find him a stepmom, she'll be a better parental figure than you." He stopped at the door and slowly turned around.

"A stepmom? So what, you gay now?"

"I've always liked women," I responded, rolling my eyes. A smile crept across his face, and I immediately knew what I was thinking. "And the answer is no. I've been bisexual for a long time, and honestly, I don't want dick from a man anymore."

"So, you lesbian?"

"It doesn't matter what I am. What I am not, is a woman you can fuck anymore. We are done with that. The only time you need to call or text is about your son."

"If I walk out this door, and we don't agree to be together, I'm signing my rights over."

"Okay, bye." I could tell he was hurt, but I didn't give a fuck. I was prepared to raise my baby on my own, and if we were honest, I'd preferred it that way. I didn't want to have to deal with Xavieon anymore.

Two months later...

"Push!" Alaria shouted.

"I am pushing, bitch!" I screamed back. I gripped her hand with my left, and gripped the hand of Xavieon with my right. I bared down and pushed one more time and my baby boy came floating up into the hands of my midwife. After a few seconds of clearing his airways, he let out the shrillest scream as she placed him on my chest.

"He's so beautiful," Alaria said, choked up.

"I can't believe I have a son," Xavieon whispered, looking down at him.

"What's his name?" my midwife asked.

"Mikael Lee Shane."

The Set Up
(Shaleena)

Five Years Later...

"Hurry up Mikael. Your dad is on his way." I heard scurrying upstairs which meant Mikael would be down any minute. The doorbell rang at the same time I heard a loud thud. I whipped around at the foot of the stairs, ready to take them two at a time.

"I'm okay," came a little voice. I rolled my eyes. This boy damn near gave me a heart attack every day since he learned to walk and get into shit.

"Hey, Xa," I said as I opened the door and allowed him to come in.

"Damn, Shaleena," he whistled as he closed the door behind him. "You look good as fuck."

"Yeah, and those compliments are getting old as fuck."

"You ain't even have to do me like that." I still couldn't believe that five years ago, Xavieon claimed he was giving up his rights as a father and here we are today, and he's taking Mikael for the summer. He's been such an amazing dad and stepped up when I have needed it the most. Co parenting wasn't easy in the beginning, but we are now in a better place.

"So what you got planned for the summer since you'll be kid free?"

"I'm about to be in these streets looking for Mikael a stepmom."

"Here we go with this shit again." I laughed as he shook his head.

"Naw, but I have a conference coming up at the George R. Brown Convention Center. I am speaking at a virtual assistants' event to talk about my business and hopefully bring on some more virtual assistants."

"Don't you have like fifty already?"

"And? I could always use more. With more people requesting a virtual assistant with how everything is damn near virtual, I could use quite a few more." Little footsteps could be heard bounding down the stairs.

"Daddy!" Mikael screamed, jumping in his dad's arms.

"What's up, lil man? You ready for our road trip?"

"Yep, and I can't wait to see Nana and Pop Pop."

"Alright, well tell your mom bye." He ran over and I scooped him up into a bear hug. I squeezed him as he giggled, wrapping his arms around my neck. I placed kisses all over his face as he squealed.

"Hey, tell ya mama that's enough. Big boys don't like kisses."

"Boy, hush." I set him down as he grabbed Xavieon's hand and headed out the door.

I watched from the front steps as they drove off, a piece of my heart going with them. This was the second summer that Mikael spent with his dad up in San Antonio. It was extremely difficult last summer with it being the first time. I cried for two weeks straight, calling him everyday.

It got easier as Xavieon and I discussed trading off for holidays throughout the school year. Whenever he had a break from school, Xavieon would drive down to get him and go back. Mikael loved spending time with his cousins and grandparents. This time away also gave me a break to do things I needed to for not only my business, but myself.

When Xavieon and I first started talking almost seven years ago, we made it clear that it was just going to be a physical relationship as long as we were single. A baby didn't factor into that arrangement, but he came anyway, and Mikael was the best thing to ever happen to me.

I walked back inside to my home office to check some emails and make sure that everything was set for the conference that was in two days. I put on a Virtual Assistants' conference annually for other businesses to employ those looking to be a virtual assistant. However, this would be the first year that I am looking to add more virtual assistants to my business, so my company would be one of the vendors there.

I started Shane VA, LLC four years ago and it boomed quickly. I never expected so many companies from across the globe would find my little business and hire out services. With the panorama that began in 2020, many businesses went virtual, therefore, the need for virtual assistants skyrocketed.

In my first year, we became a multimillion dollar company, and as of yesterday, we are now a multibillion dollar company, as well as a Fortune 500, and I am the only Black and woman owned virtual assistant business in the country.

As I was clicking send on an email, I heard my front door open.

"Bitch, they gone!" my best friend shouted. I chuckled and shook my head.

"I'm in the office."

"Well, come out of there and come take some shots with me. The twins' grandparents came and got them for the summer. They triflin' convict daddy requested to finally see them since they'll be with his parents." Alaria's ex-husband was convicted on several murder charges and got two life sentences in prison with no possibility of parole. I tried my damnedest to get her to steer clear of him, but she loved the bad boy type.

As I walked in the kitchen, she had already pulled out my shot glasses and was filling six of them with Patron. I hopped up on a barstool along the island and waited for her to finish.

"Mikael gone already?" she asked.

"Yep," I nodded. "His daddy came and got him about an hour ago."

"Welp, let's toast," she announced as she screwed the lid back on the bottle. We each picked up a shot glass.

"What are we toasting to?"

"Let's first toast to a hot girl summer!" We clinked glasses and knocked the first shot back. It burned in the best way possible. We picked up the next shot.

"A toast to being a couple of fine ass MILFs with a snapback that's hella strong."

"Bitch, that's stupid," I grumbled.

"Take that damn shot," she fussed. We knocked the second one back, and I could feel my body heating up.

"This last shot, on the count of three, fuck them kids. One...two...three..."

"Fuck them kids!" we screamed, as we took the shot and then fell out laughing.

"We ain't shit," I wheezed.

"Maybe so, but shit, we need a break. Being a single parent is hard as fuck, especially when the father ain't around. Between you, my parents, and his parents, it makes it easier. I don't know what I would do without y'all."

"Awww, look at you being all mushy."

"I ain't mushy. I'm a whole G out here."

"Bitch, whatever. Are you ready for Saturday?"

"Been ready. The VAs are all prepped and ready. Resumes have been vetted. Our table is being delivered to the convention center as we speak."

Alaria became my assistant a couple years after I started my business. She was working as a nurse practitioner, but due to being around viral patients, she didn't want to continue to put the health of her kids at risk who have immune disorders. I offered her a job as my assistant which paid more than what she was making. Also, she's a damn good assistant. A little ratchet, but good.

"I can't wait for this event. I've been thinking about this all year. There are going to be some huge companies there. More than we've had in the past." She nodded as she began making margaritas and I grabbed a slice of pizza from the box she had brought. "But enough about that. We are off the clock, the kids are gone, and tomorrow is Friday, an off day. Let's talk about getting you some pussy." I choked on a piece of pizza that got stuck in my

244

throat. She ran to pat me on the back as the chunk finally made its way down.

"You can't just be saying shit like that when I'm eating or drinking."

"My bad." She went back over to the blender to shut it off and bring the pitcher to the island, pouring it into the two glasses she pulled out. I took a sip and shimmed as it went down. She made the best margaritas. The kind that'll sneak up on you and you won't know what hit you until you wake up naked in the fountain in the middle of campus. Don't ask.

"But seriously though. The last time you dated someone was over two years ago, and I'm sure that's the last time you let someone play with your coochie. I'm sure it's all sorts of cobwebs and shit down there." I glared at her as I took another bite of my pizza and she laughed. She sat down next to me and grabbed a slice.

"I'll have you know that Cirilla was not the last woman I slept with. Remember Charlie?"

"The bitch who flattened all your tires and then mine because she came over here unannounced and thought we were fucking?"

"Yes, her."

"That was a year ago, Leena."

"Okay, but my point is, it hasn't been that long."

"I can't believe you gon sit there and fix your mouth to say some dumbass shit like that. It hadn't been that long. Trick, we are going to find someone for you to pop coochies with this summer. We have three months, which is plenty of time. Plus, we going to

Mexico for the Pride International Fiesta next month. You will definitely get some there."

"Why is this so important to you?"

"Because you're my bestie and I want you to be happy."

"Who says I'm not happy? What makes you think having a woman in my life is going to make me happy?"

"Okay, let me rephrase Miss I Can Do Bad All By Myself. I want you to be happier. I want you to have someone who adds happiness to your life."

"That's cool and all, but I'm really not pressed."

"And that's the problem." My phone vibrated with an email notification. I pulled it out of my pocket and noticed it was from Watts Suites. I frowned at it.

"Watts Suites?" I asked aloud.

"What?"

"I got an email from Watts Suites. They want to be added to the list of vendors on Saturday."

"Well, the deadline isn't until tomorrow. Did they send payment?"

"Yeah, but that's not why I'm confused. Why does that sound so familiar?"

"It's the new luxury hotel that opened up last month downtown. I stayed there one weekend with my sneaky link. It's pretty fancy. Oh, and Lyn Watts and her sister Kaniece own it."

"That's why it sounds familiar."

"And they want in? Oh, I have to see how this goes on Saturday."

"What do you mean?"

"You had the biggest crush on Lyn in college. We were all friends, but you were trying to be more than friends. I remember you wanted to ask her out. Y'all had been study buddies for two years, and then junior year, she started dating Kyshelle Williams, and she had a problem with y'all being so close. That hoe damn near tore the friend group apart."

"She actually did. Everyone had to choose between me and Lyn."

"And since no one wanted to choose, everyone went their separate ways. I think they got married after graduation."

"Wonder if she still is."

"Nope." I looked over at Alaria who was scrolling on her phone. "According to public records, they divorced seven years ago, right before she opened the first hotel in Bali." I raised an eyebrow. Damn, she really was doing well for herself. "And according to this, she now lives here in Houston."

She raised two eyebrows at me and smirked. I only knew what that meant. Saturday was going to be very interesting.

The Meet Cute
(Lyn)

"Tomorrow is the virtual assistant convention. I got an email confirmation from Shane VA that we are a go and we will have a table set up." I listened as my sister ran down the upcoming events. Since we had gotten into the hotel business together, we had become closer. We didn't grow up together since we had the same dad and different moms, but my dad did try to allow us to spend as much time together as possible.

"What time do we need to be there tomorrow?" I interrupted.

"Set up time is at seven thirty, and the event starts at eight thirty. Are you nervous?"

"Nervous about what?"

"Seeing Shaleena, duh."

"Why would I be nervous about that?"

"Because you haven't seen her since college when that scamming ass bitch Kyshelle made you unfriend her."

"Damn, why she gotta be all that?"

"Lyn, she literally was only with you because of the hotel business you were going to start. She wanted your money."

"Okay, but I divorced her before we got the first hotel off the ground."

"Barely! She almost was going to get half of what *we* own. Everybody tried to warn you about her."

"I'm sensing some residual animosity over this past situation."

"Keep playing with me and you're going to sense my foot so far up your ass you'll only be able to smell toenail polish."

"No wonder your violent ass is still single."

"Whatever. We need to find you something presentable to wear."

"I'm a big girl. I can dress myself."

"Lyn, you come in here daily with sweatpants, a white tee, some expensive ass sneakers and your locs in a high bun. This is a professional event, and I be damned if you ruin this for me." I raised an eyebrow. "Us. Ruin this for us."

"Niecy, I guarantee you that what I wear will have no bearing on any of the applicants we get tomorrow."

"Umhm. I'll be over at six thirty in the morning to approve your choice of clothing."

And she wasn't lying. At 6:15, I awoke to rummaging in my closet. I knew it wasn't a burglar because my alarm wasn't going off.

"I fucking hate you," I moaned.

"Good morning to you too. Now get up, shower, brush your teeth and put this one on." She threw some clothes on the bed and walked out, closing the door behind her. I didn't even look at the clothes until after I took care of my morning routine. I grabbed some boxers and a sport's bra and then looked at the clothes on the bed, and I'll admit, I wasn't mad at what she chose for me to wear: skinny jeans, a black tee, a white blazer and some white Sperry's.

"Not bad. Not bad at all." One thing about Kaniece, she talks a good game, but she knows how much of a fight I will put up. Once I was dressed, I made it downstairs to Kaniece whipping up some bacon, egg, and cheese croissants. The coffee was already in two insulated coffee cups. I took a sip and instantly felt awake.

"So, just some stats. Shaleena is single, one kid, owns Shane VA, favorite restaurant is Creole Kid in Humble, and her favorite place to go is Kindred Stories."

"You sound like a stalker, and it's creepy as fuck. Also, why are you telling me this?"

"So, when you see her, you can cut the shit and ask her out."

"Wouldn't that look suspicious that I asked her out after last minute wanting to be a part of the convention?"

"When she sees you in that outfit, it won't matter. I did good, didn't I?"

"Yes, Niecy." She smiled as she handed me my container with my breakfast and headed towards the door. I grabbed my coffee and satchel, following behind her.

"How many assistants do you think we'll need?" I asked in between bites as she drove.

"Well, each of us will need one as well as our hotel managers and HR departments. So, maybe ten at the least." I nodded as I took another bite and she exited 59 to downtown.

Once we parked underground across from GRB, we headed in to set up our area. The table was already there as well as our signs. It took about thirty minutes to get set up as three of our recruiters were walking in. They would be handling the interviews while Kaniece and I caught up on inventory.

Two hours into the event, I was ready for it to be done. It was tiring looking over the resumes and notes from the interviews from our recruiters. There were several good candidates. I separated the resumes into piles of second interviews and backups.

"Hey," Kaniece nudged me. "There's your girl." I looked to where she nodded and saw Shaleena stepping up to the stage. She looked fine as hell with her huge afro and tailored fitted suit. Her stilettos gave her legs more definition in her tan tapered slacks. And from the side, I can tell her ass was just as plump as it was back in college.

"Greetings, ladies and gentlemen," she announced. "I want to welcome you all to the annual Virtual Assistant's Conference." She was rewarded with a loud round of applause and a few shouts and whistles. "I hope that each company and each virtual assistant has found the perfect match or matches for their needs. We are about to start our panel discussion in about ten minutes. There are refreshments out in the hall. Again, the panel will be starting in ten minutes."

I watched as she descended the stage. My first thought was to go up to her, but my stomach had me walking out to the hall to grab something quick to eat. Once I was back inside, I made my way to my seat next to Kaniece as the panelists were taking their seats on the stage.

After the panelists introduced themselves and there were several rounds of questions, I stood up to ask a question when Shaleena said there was room for one more. When her eyes landed on me, she froze, her mouth agape. I gave her a toothy smile.

"Uh, yes, you in the middle row," she managed to get out, acknowledging me. "What question do you have for our panel?"

"It isn't a question for the panel, per se. It's a question for you."

"I'm not on the panel," she chuckled.

"Yeah, but you are a business woman and one of the businesses here. So my question is, with owning your own business, being a mom, and putting on events, do you have time to go on dates?" There was chatter and a few "oooo's." I watched as she shifted from one hip to the other, visibly uncomfortable.

"Well, you know how they say, people make time for things that are important to them," she responded.

"Is dating important to you?" I shot back, applying pressure.

"Well, uh, it's not something that I have thought about. Also, I don't have any suitors so…"

"What if you did have a suitor, would you make the time?" Heads turned from me to her and back.

"Depends. What would this suitor have in mind for a date?"

"Drinks at the bar in the hotel they own, tonight at six o'clock." Heads turned to her for an answer. She smirked and cocked her head.

"I would say that I have the time, and I will be there." I sat back down and Kaniece clapped quietly next to me as Shaleena went on with the conference.

"Okay, the table is packed," Kaniece said. "The recruiters said to send them the list of candidates for second interviews." I nodded as I picked up my bag. We headed out into the hall and were stopped by Shaleena.

"I'll see you in the car," Kaniece said. "Hey, Shaleena, nice to see you again."

"Likewise," Shaleena responded to her retreating back. Her gaze turned to me and my heart stuttered. This woman was breathtaking in college, and the years have been good to her. "Lyn." My name rolling off the tip of her tongue curved my lips up into a smile.

"Shaleena."

"It's been a while."

"It has. You still look as good as you did back in college."

"Oh don't try to flatter me. I've had a kid and put on weight."

"In all the right places from where I'm standing." She rolled her eyes as she shook her head, her cheeks reddening.

"You were bold back there, and you are now. I see nothing has changed."

"Oh, you know me. *Bold* is my middle name."

"Suits you."

"So, we have a couple hours before our date, and…"

"Wait, our date?"

"Yeah, the one I asked you on in the conference room."

"I thought that was hypothetical."

"Seriously?"

"I mean yeah. You never said the suitor was you. You just asked what if there was a suitor, which means your question was

253

hypothetical." I looked her up and down, taking in her stance and the curves of her hips, swell of her breasts, and the plump red lips that were scrunched to the side. She was fucking with me.

"Shaleena, I would like to take you on a date to the bar of my hotel, Watts Suites, that's a few blocks from here."

"Oh, I don't know. I have to check my schedule and see if I have time." I stared at her, not blinking. She stared back, running her tongue along her bottom lip. Her eyes were filled with lust as the wheels turned in her head.

"I'll see you at six, Shaleena. And wear something short and tight." I turned and walked off, leaving her standing there, stunned.

The Date

(Shaleena)

"So tell me again what she said," Alaria said.

"She said she would see me at six and to wear something short and tight. She didn't even give me a chance to respond or agree to the date."

"Is that why you have tried on the fifth dress in the last ten minutes?" she asked as I walked out of my closet to the full length mirror in my bedroom.

"I mean her demand didn't seem negotiable."

"Everything is negotiable. Everything."

I looked at myself in the mirror at this hot pink strapless dress I had on. It came to midthigh and looked as if it were painted on. I paired it with some strappy heels, black hoop earrings, a hot pink flower clip in my fluffed out fro, and a hot pink and black crossbody purse with a gold strap.

"How do I look?"

"Like my bestie who is about to get her pussy licked!" she squealed with her tongue hanging out her mouth. "Now, go throw that coochie in her face, hell sit on her face and make her swim."

"You do the absolute most."

"Don't come back if you ain't let her make you come!" she shouted at my back as I walked out the front door.

Wyatt Suites was magnificent. It was a five story building that spans two blocks. It is made of off white stone and the windows are lined in brown. I pulled up to the front and handed my keys to the valet. Taking a deep breath, I headed up the steps and through automatic doors that opened up to a brightly lit lobby.

There were several seating areas with wine colored carpet with matching chairs and a coffee table. The receptionist desk was made of mahogany wood with a sleek finish. The woman behind it gave me a wide smile.

"Hi, how may I help you?" she asked.

"I am here to meet someone at the bar."

"Yes, the bar is around this corner and to the left," she responded, pointing to her right.

"Thanks." I followed her directions and walked into this dimly lit restaurant. The atmosphere was sensual and romantic. There was a small stage where a jazz band was softly playing. I had to hand it to Lyn and her sister. They did the damn thing.

I took my seat at the bar and ordered a glass of red wine. The place wasn't packed, but I could tell that it sees its share of customers. I looked at my phone to see that it was a few minutes past six. This was not a good first date impression. I went to take another sip of my wine when I felt someone sit down next to me. I turned to see Lyn sitting there undressing me with her eyes.

"Shaleena Shane," she whispered, as if in disbelief. "Still can't believe I ran into you after all these years."

"Believe me, the sentiment is mutual."

"I know you've been doing well business wise, but outside of that, how are you?"

"I'm actually really good. Business is booming, my son is smart and excelling in school. I'm happy. How about yourself?"

"Well, after Kyshelle and I divorced, things started to look up and has progressively gotten better since then."

"I'm sorry to hear about you and Kyshelle."

"Bullshit. You couldn't stand her."

"You right," I laughed. I hated that hoe. "I mean no one liked her. We tried to tell you that."

"I know, and I should've listened. I just wish someone had told me back then how they really felt about me."

"Not sure what you mean," I whisper, taking a large gulp of my wine. How the hell did she know I had a crush on her?

"So, you're going to sit there and act like you wasn't feeling me?" I refused to look in her eyes. She already had me squirming in my seat with the feel of her eyes on the side of my face. "I see how it is. A rum and coke, please."

The bartender moved around behind the bar and made her drink. Once he gave it to her, she stood up. I looked at her and she nodded her head for me to follow, her hand held out. Grabbing my wine, took her hand, and walked alongside her to a table that had two covered dishes on it.

"I thought we were just getting drinks," I said as we took our seats.

"That was the problem in college. You think too much, always psyching yourself out. I wonder if that's why you never told me you had feelings for me." Her eyes bored into me, leaving me feeling exposed and open. I shifted my gaze down and lifted the cover off the plate that was in front of me.

257

"Lobster?" I asked, looking back up at her. She nodded and lifted her cover. There was lobster, pasta, broccoli, and garlic bread. My stomach grumbling had my face feeling like it was on fire from embarrassment. A noise coming from across the table had me glaring at Lyn as she tried to hold back her laughter.

"Go ahead and let it out," I grumbled. She giggled as I lifted my fork to wrap some pasta around it. As soon as the flavors danced across my tongue, I let out an involuntary moan that had Lyn's eyes low and smoldering.

"Aren't you going to eat your food?" I asked once I had swallowed the pasta.

"I'd much rather watch you eat," she answered, rubbing her thumb along her bottom lip.

"Suit yourself." I went on to continue eating, and eventually, she broke out of her trance and began eating. We fell into catching up on each other's life since college. It was literally like talking to a friend I've known forever.

Once we had finished dinner and dessert, she invited me to the rooftop lounge for dancing and more drinks. *When We* by Tank came on, Lyn pulled me close to her. Even in my heels, she was a couple inches taller. Her cologne was intoxicating, waking my dormant libido up and setting it ablaze.

She buried her head in the crook of my neck as we danced pelvis to pelvis, breasts to breasts. Her hands moved to my ass, giving it a tight squeeze.

Despite the song fading into another, she didn't let up on her hold. We danced through countless more songs. I lost track.

258

"Hey, you want to go to Mexico for the Pride International Fiesta?" she asked abruptly, lifting her head to look at me.

"What? You're asking me to go on vacation on a first date?"

"It's not like we're strangers, Leena." I used to love it when she called me Leena. It was a nickname I always had, but it just hit different when she said it. It was smooth like rolling across silk sheets.

"Yeah but we haven't known each other as adults. It's been so long."

"Well, how about we get to know each other on this trip then?"

"I would like that." Her eyes held my gaze, a force pulling every bit of my attention towards her and how close we were, the heat that radiated between us, the way my pussy throbbed as it leaked, soaking my panties.

This feeling was sensory overdrive and I could barely breathe. As our bodies swayed to the music, my head fell forward to her shoulder, my cheek against her chest, her heartbeat in rhythm to the music, a lullaby tugging my eyes closed.

The next morning when I woke up, I thought I had dreamt last night until I looked at my phone at the "good morning' text from Lyn. My lips curved up into a wide, toothy smile, my stomach fluttering. I responded to her text and then got up to take care of my morning routine. Once, I was clad in yoga pants and an oversized shirt, I made my way to the kitchen and turned on the coffee to brew, then headed to my home office to answer some emails.

I noticed an email from Watts Suites and clicked on it immediately. It was an email from Lyn's sister, thanking me for

259

allowing them to attend at the last minute and the success of hiring a team of virtual assistants. I quickly keyed my reply and headed back to the kitchen to grab my coffee and close myself in my office for a few hours.

Around noon came and Alaria came through my front door. Her shoes clicked and clacked as she made her way towards me. I knew it was her because she and my parents were the only ones that had keys, and my parents lived six hours away.

"Okay, how was the date last night?" She plopped on the couch and gave me all her attention.

"Hi, Alaria, how are you today? I am fine, thanks for asking."

"Yeah, all that, now spill." I gave her a quick rundown about how things went with Lyn, including how she gave me a peck on the forehead after walking me to my front door. I even told her about inviting me on the trip.

"Wait," she said. "Didn't you tell her that we were already going to Mexico for the festival?"

"No."

"And why not?"

"I don't know. I just didn't."

"You are a weird ass bitch. Her inviting you means she's going to pay for you to go. We already paid."

"Shit," I swore. "I didn't even think about that."

"Duh, bitch. You need to call her and let her know. We leave in less than a week." We talked a little more and then got to work, combing through another set of online applicants that we got in the past few days. I was still in shock at how well the conference went. At this rate, we were set to make another million this quarter.

I don't know how long we had been working, but it was around two when my phone rang. It was Lyn.

"Hey," I answered.

"Hey, Leena," she responded, drawing my name out. "I was calling to get your info for the trip." Alaria side-eyed me as I rolled my eyes.

"Actually, Lyn, Alaria and I had already booked for the festival."

"Oh, word? Where are y'all staying?"

"At the Amánsala Yoga Resort and Spa."

"That's where me and my sister are staying. Maybe our rooms are next to each other."

"Maybe."

"Hopefully," she said, her tone sending chills down my spine. "I'll see you in a couple days."

"See you then," I said, and then hung up the phone. "Don't say shit."

"I didn't even say anything," Alaria rebutted, holding her hands up as if to surrender. She was about to get a kick out of this vacation.

When we landed in Cancun, we took a shuttle to the Amansala Yoga Resort. It was about a two hour drive through the cities of Cancun and Tulum. I love sightseeing and seeing the locals go about their everyday lives. We pulled up and checked in, one of the men taking our bags to room 4.

"Damn this is nice," Alaria squealed, "and we are right on the beach."

I smiled as I took in the view. Despite the beach being covered in seaweed, it was still a beautiful sight.

We followed the man up the stairs to our room. When we walked in, there were two queen sized beds surrounded by mosquito nets. There were two chairs facing a window on the right side of the room.

The bathroom was gorgeous and had a double vanity. Each side had its own bench where the man placed our luggage. Everyone knows not to drink the tap water in Mexico, so two gallon jugs of water were already on the counter waiting for us.

The shower only had a single transparent curtain. There was a small window that had a screen where someone on the balcony of their room could see in, but I didn't mind.

"Thank you so much," I said to the man and gave him a tip. Luckily it was after 9 and the AC was on because it was miserably hot.

"What do you want to do first?" Alaria asked.

"First, I need to empty my bladder." I walked into where the commode was, and there was a note that said to not flush the toilet paper, but to put it in the trash can next to it. I relayed the information to Alaria, and her crazy ass was outraged.

"You mean I have to wipe my coochie and my shitty ass and put it in the trash can for it to smell? I don't like that." I shook my head and giggled as I used the bathroom as instructed.

"Let's order room service, since it's late," I suggested, pulling out what I needed to shower and get dressed in bed clothes. We pulled up the menu and then called the front desk. By the time I got out of the shower, the food had arrived. We did little talking as we ate and then went to bed. I was exhausted from all the traveling.

The Balcony

(Lyn)

Kaniece and I arrived last night. We showered and hit the pillow hard. This morning, we woke up early for breakfast. I had texted Shaleena, but I guess she was still asleep.

After breakfast in the outside eating area, we headed to the rooftop to the yoga studio, and Shaleena and Alaria were already there. I saw her before she saw me, clad in yoga pants and a sports bra. I knew damn well I was not going to be able to focus on zoning out and aligning my chakras, when all I would be able to think about was aligning hers.

"Hey Lyn, hey Kaniece," Alaria greeted. Shaleena turned around and gave me a shy smile. She waved and I waved back. "Y'all should get a mat and come join us." Shaleena cut her eyes at Alaria and I just chucked and grabbed my mat, setting up directly behind Shaleena. I was trying to see all that ass in downward dog.

"I am so glad you all are here," the yoga instructor announced. "I am Arely, and I will be guiding you all through an intermediate flow since this is the intermediate class. We will play around with some inversions, but if that does not agree with your body, feel free to do what feels good instead. Since there aren't many of you, how about you move your mat here."

I moved to where she told me which was on the side of Shaleena. The windows in front of us held a magnificent view of the ocean. The waves could be heard continuously. She gave each of us a few drops of essential oils and instructed what to do with them and their purpose.

As she guided us through some sun salutations, I could see Shaleena's reflection in the windows, and she was definitely not new to yoga. When we got into the more flexible poses such as monkey pose and pigeon pose, I had visions of her doing those poses while sitting on my face.

We did some hand and forearm stands which were relaxing. I had been practicing yoga for years, so this was nothing that I wasn't used to.

"Now, as we lie in shavasana, or resting pose, I want you to think about what you are grateful for. Close your eyes and be mindful and still. I will come around and place a bean in each of your hands. Afterwards, I will tell you what they are for."

Not sure how long we had lain there, but it was the gentleness of Arely's voice that brought me out of my thoughts and back to the present.

"Now, gently wiggle your fingers and toes, waking up the body. Roll to one side and push yourself up to seated. Now, the beans are for you to make wishes and throw into the ocean to the goddess of the sea, who will grant your wishes. Thank you for coming to class today. Namaste." We chanted it back to her and then began to roll our mats up and place them in a pile to be cleaned.

"What are y'all about to get into?" Kaniece asked.

"Well, we were going to shower, then get in a taxi to see the ruins," Shaleena responded.

"Funny, so are we," Kaniece responded, not at all obvious. "Isn't that funny, Lyn?"

"Hilarious," I muttered.

"Why don't we share a ride then?" Shaleena asked.

"Good idea," I answered immediately, not taking my eyes off hers. She smiled as she turned to leave.

"We'll meet y'all out front," Kaniece called.

"Could you be more obvious?" I asked her.

"Just wait and see what I have planned tonight," she smirked, walking off.

"Hold on," I called. "What are you talking about?"

An hour later, we were meeting up in the lobby to load into the taxi. We had planned to bike, but because of the roads, it was best to get there by car. I made sure to sit next to Shaleena, her perfume intoxicating.

"It's so beautiful here," she said in awe.

"I agree," I responded, looking at her. Her cheeks reddened as she turned to look out the window.

Once we arrived, we got out and had to walk about a quarter of a mile to the ruins where we met our tour guides, Carlo and Sergio, who, if I were straight, I would definitely throw them some ass.

The tour itself was insightful and a learning experience. The history of the place was mesmerizing, making me realize even more that what I was taught in school about the Mayans was utter bullshit.

It took about an hour to go through all of the spots, and we took numerous pictures. However, I was drenched in sweat and needed a cold shower for many reasons. As we walked back to the taxi, I noticed Alaria and Kaniece walking ahead, thinking they're slick.

"I think our sisters are trying to push us together," Shaleena said, smirking at me.

"I believe they are. Is that a bad thing?"

"No, I guess not."

"You guess not? Shaleena, I don't need you guessing about anything. I want you. I wanted you in college, and I want you now." She was silent, but the expression on her face told me she was processing what I said, not sure if she believed me or not.

"If that's so, then why did you get with Kyshelle?"

"Because I thought you weren't interested."

"What gave you that idea?"

"Kyshelle. She said she had asked you if there was anything going on between us and you told her no."

"Kyshelle never asked me that. In fact, she and I never even held a conversation."

"I know that now. I'm pissed that I believed her. You and I could've been together."

"True, but I think things happened the way they were supposed to. I wouldn't have my child had she not done that."

"You're right."

We loaded into the taxi and everyone was quiet on the way back. When we got in the lobby, Alaria and Kaniece mentioned that they were going sightseeing. Shaleena said she was exhausted

267

and wanted to take a nap. As we walked to our rooms, we noticed that our room was right below theirs. We went our separate ways into our respective rooms.

When I got out of the shower, I had a text from Shaleena, inviting me up to her room. I dressed in a sports bra, tank, and shorts. I jogged up the steps and took a few breaths to regulate my breathing. I didn't want her to think that I was desperate, but in reality, in reality, I was. I double knocked and heard moving around inside. She had on a black romper adorned in flowers. There was lace that traced the swells of her breasts and the thickness of her thighs.

"Are you just going to stand there and stare, or are you going to come in?" I blinked and then smiled, heat rising to my neck and face.

I stepped in as she closed the door behind me. I followed her out to the small balcony. There was an off white oversized cushion chair to the right, and a bench with decorative pillows on the left. She took the bench, and I took the chair. We said nothing for a while, just taking in the beauty of the ocean and the serenity that the crashing of the waves elicited.

Down below, there were people at the cabanas eating and drinking, no one paying attention to us. Right below the balcony was a pool and a couple could be seen doing who knows what in the water. I turned to look at Shaleena, but she was already looking at me. The look in her eyes said it all.

I stood up and walked over to her, placing my hands on the side of her thighs. Gently, our lips pressed into each other. She moaned against my lips and I got wetter. In a rush, I didn't think to put on any boxers.

Her hands cupped my face and pulled me closer as she leaned back against the bamboo that lined the wall behind the bench. I brought my knees between her thighs on the couch, and I could smell how wet she was for me, which meant she wore no panties under her romper.

I moved my hand to run along the seam of the thin piece of fabric and it was soaked. A growl crept up my throat at the thought of how I made her feel. Moving the fabric to the side I slid a finger between her folds, trailing it along her clit, coating it in her juices.

Her head fell back as she gasped, breaking the hold our lips had on each other. With my free hand, I pulled her left breast out and licked her neck, making my way down to her areola, then sucking her taut nipple into my mouth. Her body shook as she moaned.

"I don't think you want those people down there to hear you," I whispered, her nipple still in my mouth. Her eyes were glossed over and filled with lust and urgent desire.

As I still played in her wetness and sucked her nipple, she took the straps of the material off her shoulders and pulled her arms out. I moved back as she shimmied it down her body, lifting her hips as I pulled it down her thighs. Her body was a piece of art, the kind that you have to handle with care because it was intricate, one of a kind, and fragile.

I pulled one of the pillows off the bench and put it on the floor and got on my knees, spreading her thighs and licking my lips at the sight of the meal in front of me. Starting with her right ankle, I

269

trailed kisses slowly down to her inner thigh, then over to her left thigh and up to her ankle. I looked up to find her watching me.

"Please," she rasped.

"Please what?"

"Make me come."

Bet." Holding the back of her thighs, I dipped my tongue in the depths of her pussy, circling her walls as she clenched it. She pushed her pussy against me to take my tongue deeper.

"Play with your clit," I demanded and then stuck my tongue back in. I watched her fingers work. She tried not to moan loud, but she was too wound up from both sensations.

Her legs shook and she convulsed, her orgasm moisturizing my mouth and chin. I pulled back and watched her work her clit faster as she rode her orgasm out. She smiled, looking satiated, but I wasn't nearly done with her.

"Extended child's pose," I said. Her eyes bulged.

"What?"

"I won't repeat myself."

"What if people see me?"

"That's why I said extended. Big toes together, knees spread wide, face in the pillow." I watched as she got into position, her ass glistening with her orgasm. Spreading her cheeks, I slid my tongue around the rim, and she jumped at the contact. Burying my face between her velvety soft ass, I ate like it was my last meal, moving my tongue from her clit, to her pussy, to her ass, and repeat. The muscles in her cheeks jumped as she got closer to her peak.

I moved my right between her thighs and used my index finger to hit that spot on her clit, and my thumb pushed into her pussy. Her shaking became violent as she screamed into the pillow and creamed my fingers. She sat up and turned to face me.

"Sit in the chair over there," she whispered, pointing behind me. "And remove your shorts." I did as I was told, slouching down into the chair, legs wide. She grabbed a pillow and came over to me.

What she did with her tongue against my clit should be fucking illegal and she needs to be arrested. I had never felt my orgasm rush out the way it did. My eyes crossed, and I saw stars as my scream got caught in my throat, my mouth stuck in an 'o'.

When she finally stopped committing that carnal crime against my clit, she straddled me, dipping her tongue into my mouth, tasting each other. She moved her hips against me slowly as I tweaked her nipples. Shaleena pulled back and looked me in my eyes, her gaze saying it all. This wasn't just going to be a fling.

I pulled her to me, kissing her hard, not nearly as passionate as before. We moved our hips against each other, chasing that release we both knew was going to be forceful. As I felt myself approaching, I whispered against her lips.

"Come with me."

As if my words could detonate a bomb, we both came holding each other close, moaning against each other's lips.

"Shiiiiiit, Leena," I groaned. "What are you doing to me?"

"The same thing you're doing to me," she whispered back. Our lips connected as I carried her inside her room, laying her on the bed.

We made each other come twice more before we fell asleep, wrapped in each other's arms.

Clay, Sis, Clay
Shaleena

"Wake y'all nasty asses up," Alaria yelled, laughing right along with Kaniece. I don't know how long we had been asleep, but it was not dark outside. We were also still very naked and not covered.

Lyn moaned next to me, giving them the finger. I went and got my romper from the balcony and Lyn's shorts. We dressed as Kaniece and Alaria talked they shit.

"Got it smelling like pussy in here," Kaniece chided playfully.

"Y'all washed y'all mouths, or y'all went to sleep with pussy juice on your lips?" Alaria added.

"And I know for a fact that Lyn likes to eat ass, so she probably got Shaleena's ass still on her face."

"Are y'all done?" Lyn asked.

"Yeah, for now," Kaniece answered. "Also, while y'all was sleeping, we moved rooms. Alaria moved into our room, and you are now in here with Shaleena."

"So that's what you had planned for tonight?" Lyn asked.

"We knew y'all would bump coochies eventually, so why not make it happen sooner?" Alaria asked. I shook my head as Shaleena rolled her eyes.

"Anyway, go take a shower and wash the pussy juice off so we can go," Kaniece said, heading towards the door.

"Go where?" I asked.

"Spicy Hookah Bar. Heard it's about to be gay and Black as fuck," Kaniece responded.

"I'm in," Lyn cheered, hopping up out of the bed to the bathroom.

"Be ready in an hour," Alaria called as she closed the door behind her. I made my way into the bathroom where Lyn was already in the shower. I sheathed my clothing and joined her, where she made me come three more times. I was going to sleep good tonight.

When we got to the hookah bar, it was packed and smelled of weed. Despite it being outside, there wasn't nearly enough room to move around, but we were lucky enough to find a table.

"What flavor y'all want?" Alaria shouted, barely audible over the music.

"Blue Melon," Kaniece answered. Both Lyn and I agreed. While we waited for the hookah, I ran out to the dance floor when my song came on with Alaria not too far behind. I felt hands on my hips and from the scent of the cologne, I knew it wasn't Lyn. I turned around to see this breathtaking stud smiling at me, her pearly whites gleaming in the strobe lights.

I rolled my hips against her as her hands settled back on my hips. She was a few inches taller than me with six long braids, skin the color of black coffee with a splash of cream, some taper legged jeans, a fresh white tee, a silver chain around her neck, and diamond studs in her ears. To say she was clean and fresh was an understatement.

"What's your name?" she asked.

"Shaleena."

"Damn, that's a sexy ass name for an even sexier ass woman. I'm Britt."

"Nice to meet you Britt."

"Can I buy you a drink?"

"Absolutely."

"Tell your girl she can join us in my section over there." She pointed to the left side of the place where a group of about five people were turned all the way up. Britt went to find a bottle girl and order us drinks. I turned to find Alaria dancing with some chick. I whispered in her ear about the VIP and she asked about Kaniece and Lyn. I had almost forgotten about them.

I turned to see a woman sitting on Lyn's lap, smiling in her face. A pang of jealousy fluttered in my belly. She and I weren't together, and hadn't even discussed us having had sex, but these sudden feelings had me feeling some type of way. I watched as they talked and giggled at each other. I didn't see Kaniece, so I figured she met up with someone.

Lyn caught my eyes on her and smirked, then turned her attention back to the woman on her lap. I was about to walk over when there was a tap on my shoulder. I turned to see Britt smiling, holding out my drink. I followed her to her section where she introduced me to her crew. They were all here for the Pride International Festival. We talked about the upcoming events over the next two days, and Britt invited me back to her resort. I declined and said goodbye as she and her crew headed out.

Back over at our table, Kaniece and Alaria were puffing on the hookah and I joined in. I scanned the room and didn't see Lyn anywhere in sight.

"She's over there," Alaria said, reading my mind, pointing to a corner where she was huddled up with the same woman, kissing on her neck. "You going to go say something?"

I shook my head despite this incessant urge to stomp over there and whoop that woman's ass, but she didn't do anything wrong.

As the night progressed, and a few shots later, I was ready to head back to the resort. Alaria and I went and got a taxi while Kaniece waited for Lyn. I was definitely sharing a room with them tonight because it looked like Lyn was going to be bringing that chick back, and I didn't want to be there when she came back.

The taxi arrived and what was a six minute ride seemed like it dragged on forever. Those shots caught up to me quick. Alaria helped me up to the room and laid me on the bed. My eyes closed as soon as my head hit the pillow, but images of Lyn and that woman filled my dreams. Lyn touching her, kissing her, spreading her legs wide. No matter how hard I tried to wake up to make this nightmare end, I couldn't.

I woke up the next morning, naked and in bed next to Lyn. Shock didn't even describe how I felt. My head was also throbbing from the shots. The light from the sun was hella bright and made my headache worse.

"Good morning, sleepyhead," Lyn moaned. I pulled away from her and tried to stand up, but the room kept spinning and my stomach started turning. I stumbled to the bathroom as fast as I could, barely making it to the toilet before my stomach emptied its contents.

"I see somebody still can't handle their alcohol," Lyn chuckled, pulling my hair back. I up chucked a few more times until I started dry heaving. She handed me a glass of water and I took a long gulp, resting my back against the wall.

"You remember, junior year in college when we went to homecoming?" she asked. I nodded and smiled, knowing exactly where she was going. "We went to the Omega after party and you had half a cup of Omega oil and was drunk off your ass, taking your clothes off, skinny dipping in the pool, and confessing your love for titties and ass."

I laughed my ass off, reliving the memory in my head. I was so fucked up off that oil. I couldn't eat for days after that. Lyn took care of me and got my homework for those few days I couldn't get out of bed.

"Those were the best years of my life," I smiled, reminiscing. "I remember maybe a month after that, we went to some Halloween party. You met Kyshelle that night. We got to the party, and it was like y'all were drawn to each other. I remember you saying to me later that night that you had found the one. I was so heartbroken when you said that. Felt like you had punched me in the gut."

We sat in silence for a while, Lyn sporting this sobering expression. I had never told anyone about that night. Not even what happened after that.

"I remember that after you left with her, I got in my car and drove while I was heavily intoxicated. Luckily, I didn't crash, but I made it back to campus. You had called me several times, but I turned off my phone. I don't even know how I ended up there, but I was knocking on Matthew's door. I fucked him that night."

Matthew was one of Lyn's closest friends. They grew up together. He was fine as fuck, too. Tall, caramel skin, long locs, a thick beard, and the way his muscles rippled around his body when he was fucking me was a sight to see. We fucked around the rest of junior year, and then he graduated and moved away. I didn't tell Lyn this because she doesn't need to know.

"Wow," she said. She didn't look mad, which I felt was a good sign. I saw a flash of something else, but it was gone before I could tell what it was. "My boy Matthew. He's going to have a field day when I tell him."

"Why would you tell him?" I questioned.

"Because he and I still talk, and he's my boy."

"I don't see why you need to tell him that you know. What? Y'all going to compare notes?"

"Maybe." I scoffed and stood up, still a little lightheaded. I turned the shower on and went into the room to grab some clothes out of my suitcase.

"Are you mad?" Lyn asked.

"No."

"You seem like you're upset."

"Nope." I moved around her and put my clothes on the counter next to the sink. I stepped in the shower and was glad Lyn didn't follow me.

"Is this about last night?"

"What about last night?" I knew what she was talking about, but I wanted her to admit it.

"Me and Violet."

"Who's Violet?"

"The chick you saw sitting on my lap." I didn't say anything. "I know you saw us, Leena."

"I'm not mad about that," I lied.

"You didn't seem too bothered when you were in that stud's face."

"Oh, you talking about Britt?"

"Yeah, what was that about?"

"Nothing, just being friendly."

"Uh huh, okay." I heard her footsteps going into the bedroom. I finished getting cleaned, moisturized, and got dressed. I went into the room to see that Lyn wasn't in there. I grabbed a towel and my water bottle to head to yoga.

Later that afternoon, I met up with Alaria and Kaniece on the beach. We were getting ready to do a Mayan Clay meditation ceremony. I came wrapped in nothing but a towel. There were a few other women there and we paired off. I heard giggling behind me and turned to see Lyn and Violet coming down the steps.

I was instantly transported back to college when Lyn met Kyshelle. Those feelings came back in the worst way. Lyn winked at me and then took her towel off and Violet's. Violet's body was banging. Anyone could see that, and a twinge of envy made its way in and got comfortable. Her curves were dangerously thick, and she was the type of femme i would even fuck. I focused my

278

attention back on my partner as the woman guiding the meditation gave us instructions and explained the importance of the clay ceremony.

Once we were covered in clay, we made our way into the ocean and formed a circle. We were told to close our eyes and think of all the negative things, and cast them away into the sea. Afterwards, we went deeper into the ocean and cleansed the clay away with the seaweed, which felt like a body scrubbing.

"Damn this feels good," Alaria screamed, twirling in the water with her face to the sky and her arms stretched out. I shook my head as Kaniece joined in. I loved seeing my sister this happy. It's not often that she takes the time out to do things for herself.

"Hey, Leena," Lyn said from behind me. I turned to see her and Violet holding hands. I tried my hardest to plaster on a fake smile, but I failed. "This is Violet. Violet, this Shaleena, and old college friend. That's her sister Alaria with the braids, and that is my sister, Kaniece."

"You all are so fucking gorgeous," Violet quipped.

"Thanks, boo," Alaria cheesed.

"Violet is coming to the yacht party tonight," Lyn announced.

"Great," I said, walking back to the beach, not even bothering to stay and listen to them talk. I grabbed my bag and towel, and headed to the room. After showering, I lay on the unused bed and drifted off to sleep.

The Yacht Party
(Lyn)

By the time I got back to the room to shower and get ready, Shaleena was already gone. I know I was being an asshole, but I couldn't help it. It was my go-to when trying to guard my heart. Seeing her with that Britt chick, did something to me that I didn't too much like. I've never had that feeling before, not even when I was with and in love with Kyshelle.

I'll admit that bringing Violet to the clay ceremony was overdoing it, but I didn't like this feeling. It felt like it was better to hurt Shaleena than to sit with these feelings. Yeah, I know how fucked up that sounds, but my heart was broken once before, despite it being my own doing. I wasn't about to let it break again.

The taxi took me to Violet's resort once I was fresh in my all white linen fit. I heard that this yacht was one of the biggest ones in Mexico, so I knew it was going to be packed with a bunch of Black folk having a good time.

Violet came out in this all white two piece bikini set, with a crochet top and pants as her cover up. I had no plans of fucking her, but the way she was looking, I might give her a little finger action.

I hopped out and opened the door for her. She smelled amazing, like lemongrass and lavender, with a little bit of cedarwood. Once I got in, she was already looking at me and smiling.

"What are you smiling about?" I asked.

"I know what you're trying to do, and I'm cool with it." I frowned.

"What do you mean?"

"Shaleena. I know you're feeling her, and she's feeling you."

"What makes you think that she's feeling me?"

"The way she tried to smile when you introduced us earlier, and the way she stalked off in the water to the shore. She has feelings for you. Now I don't know why you're trying to make a woman as fine as she is jealous, but I wouldn't put up this farce too much longer. You might lose her for real."

She turned and looked at the window as I stared at the back of her head, letting her words sink in. I don't know how she pieced that together, but the fact that she did meant that Shaleena had probably guessed I was trying to make her jealous too.

The taxi pulled up the pier, and already the yacht was lively. Music could be heard as well as people laughing and having a good time. I paid the driver and helped Violet onto the yacht. It had three levels to it. Below were a couple of cabins that people could crash in incase they got too drunk. The main level was where the party was at. Inside was a large area with plenty of floor space. On the front and back decks were cushioned seats and a bar. The third deck was where the captain would be steering the yacht.

I texted Kaniece to see where she was since she, Alaria, and Shaleena left before I did. She texted back saying they were on the front deck. I walked with Violet to the front and the first thing I saw was Shaleena twerking against Britt. My blood boiled at the sight.

"Calm down before you burst a blood vessel in your head," Violet whispered.

"What?"

"You have this crazy ass vein popping out of the side of your head. I know you're upset, but chill. Let's have a good time and match her energy."

Violet pulled me by the hand to where everyone else was dancing. She stopped right next to Shaleena and Britt, and began rubbing her ass against me. I placed my hands on her hips and my cheek against hers. Out of the corner of my eye, I could see Shaleena wasn't even paying us any attention.

"Oh my," Shaleena rasped. "I'm thirsty. Let's go to the bar." Britt put her hand on Shaleena's lower back and led her to the bar. They took their seats on two stools, and ordered. Shaleena turned to look at me and smirked. So what did my dumbass do? I turned Violet around and tongued her down the same way I ate Shaleena' ass.

When Violet pulled back, I looked at the bar to see that Shaleena and Britt were gone.

"Oh, they saw, if you were wondering," Violet said as she looked in her compact mirror to fix her lipstick. We grabbed some drinks and headed to the inner part of the yacht as someone from the crew announced we were about to depart.

We found ourselves a cushioned bench as the yacht peeled away from the dock. Kaniece found us inside getting another round of shots and joined us.

"I cannot believe that I am on a yacht," Kaniece squealed. You'd swear we grew up poor or something. Granted, she has never been on a yacht, but that was by choice.

"Yachts are always the classiest ways to sail in the sea," Violet smiled. I saw movement out of the corner of my eye and it was Shaleena and Alaria approaching us.

"Hey, y'all," Alaria sang, giving me and Violet a tight hug. Shaleena ignored us both as she took a seat on the other side of Kaniece.

"I'm going to go find something to eat," Violet said, getting up. "I am also going to find someone to bring back to my room. It was really nice meeting you, Lyn." She gave me a kiss on the cheek before sauntering off.

"Welp, Kaniece and I are going to find someone to dance on. Bye." Alaria pulled a protesting Kaniece by the hand, leaving me and Shaleena alone.

"Can we talk?" I asked her. She turned towards me and shrugged. I took it as a yes and directed her to the back deck where people were jumping off to go deep sea diving and snorkeling. There were also paddle boats, hooked to the yacht.

"Talk," Shaleena demanded once we were outside and out of earshot of other people.

"I have a confession," I breathed, nervous about telling her the real reason behind me kicking it with Violet. She cocked her head to the side as if to tell me that she was listening. "I used her to make you jealous. I was pissed about seeing you and Britt, and I'll admit, inviting her to the clay ceremony was a fuckboy move, and so was bringing her here as my date."

"So, and correct me if I'm wrong which I know I won't be, instead of telling me that you have feelings for me like a fucking adult, you decide to play games?" I nodded and before I could blink, I was submerged in cool water. She had pushed me off the yacht. I swam up to the surface to see her standing there, glowering before she walked off.

To say I was pissed was an understatement. My phone was in my pocket as well as my room key and wallet. Once I was back on the yacht, I looked everywhere for her, but she was nowhere in sight, and since we were on the yacht in the middle of the ocean, I knew she was on her.

I stumbled across Alaria sitting on a cushioned bench tearing into some chicken wings. Walking over to her, she looked up at me and then rolled her eyes as she kept chewing.

"Do you know where your sister is?" She nodded. "Can you tell me where she is?" She shook her head.

"Why are you soaking wet?" Kaniece asked.

"I told Shaleena that I was using Violet to make her jealous and she pushed me into the water."

"That was stupid."

"I know that."

"I would've pushed you into the water, too," Alaria added, finally speaking to me. "She should've beat yo ass first and then kicked you in so you would be too hurt to swim."

"You trying to say she should've killed my sister?" Kaniece asked, feigning outrage and offense.

"I'm glad that both of you think this shit is funny," I mumbled. "I need to find her and apologize."

"She doesn't want to talk to you, and she told me to tell you that you need to move back into the room with Kaniece for the remainder of the trip." I stared at Alaria in disbelief. I knew I had fucked up.

Until We Meet Again
(Shaleena)

The last day was a party on the beach that started that morning and lasted well into the evening. Alaria and I sat around the bonfire talking about how amazing this week and festival have been. Even though I had a great time despite Lyn and her bullshit, I was ready to go home and get in my bed.

"I still can't get over how after all these years, you finally fucked Lyn, and she fumbled the play yet again," Alaria said.

"I literally felt like this was the shit with Kyshelle all over again. No one should make me relive such a terrible time in my past again. I don't think Lyn and I were ever meant to be anything more than friends."

"You don't know that. You never know what the future may hold."

"Well if it's this bullshit, the future better start lifting weights because it's going to be holding for eternity." Alaria chuckled and then abruptly stopped. I followed her gaze and saw Lyn walking over.

"Gotta go," Alaria whispered, jumping up from her seat.

"Wait, no," but she was already sprinting away. Lyn took her seat.

"I'm sorry, Shaleena. I didn't mean to hurt you, again. I talked with Kaniece, and well, she actually talked at me and then began shouting. I was freaked for a bit. She's scary when she's mad."

"Yeah, I remember when her boyfriend in college cheated and him pissing his pants when she went off the deep end on that ass." We shared a laugh and then settled into an awkward silence.

"Listen, having sex with you wasn't supposed to be a one time thing, to me anyway. I had every intention of working to make us official."

"But?" I asked.

"I chickened out. I realized that maybe we need to get to know each other in this stage of our lives before trying something."

"I agree, but Violet wasn't necessary."

"And again, I am sorry."

"So where do we go from here?"

"Well, that's the thing. I'm leaving for Bali tonight. I'll be gone for about six months to a year working at the hotel."

I nodded, the pain in my chest a sharp aching. She was leaving again, just like before. I swear this was a case of deja vu, except, there was no woman this time that she was leaving with. It was just her.

"Until we meet again," I said.

The end.

Working with the enemy ain't so bad.

M.L. Sexton

I Hate Loving You

Cheyenne

"That fucking bitch!" I screamed, slamming my fist against the desk. I woke up this morning feeling like something was going to be off, and this whole day has been shit. I looked at the clock to see that I only had an hour left for work and then I could go to happy hour and get a few drinks alone since my best friend, coworker, and sister-in-law was pregnant.

"Are you okay?" Speaking of the devil, Xena walked in with her round belly, closing the door behind her. She maneuvered her way down into the chair on the other side of my desk. Seeing her softened my anger, slightly. I was a lucky woman to not only have my best friend as my coworker, but my sister. Xena married my brother, Ace, six years ago, but they had been childhood sweethearts. She was pregnant with their first child, a boy.

I was so excited to finally become an auntie and not having the only grandchild my parents had. My daughter, Bianca, was 16 and would be going off to college soon. I didn't want anymore kids, so for Xena and Ace to be having a child I could spoil and give back, I was more than elated.

"Fucking Felicity," I sighed. "Torrence gave her the assignment for that new club, Inhibitions, that's opening this Friday. I am the sex columnist, not her."

"That's bullshit. Why would she give it to her?"

"To be honest, I don't even know. And she works for the newspaper side anyway."

BLVCK Co. was a newspaper and magazine. I had been working here for the past eight years, and ever since Felicity joined the newspaper side three years ago, she had been giving me hell. It was like she woke up and thought of new ways to get under my skin.

I had been after this story since the owner, Basil, messaged me a while back. Basil and I had been good friends for a few years, and when he mentioned opening a sex club near downtown Houston and wanted me to cover it, I brought the idea to Torrence.

The fact that she gave it to Felicity made my blood boil all over again.

"What is it with her anyway?" Xena asked. "Since her first day working here, she has gone out of her way to push every button. If I didn't know any better, I'd think she liked you."

"Xena, you are lucky you are pregnant, or I would kick your ass for even suggesting some shit like that. That woman hates me, and I don't even know why. I have been nothing but nice to her, but every time we are around each other, she makes noises and rolls her eyes. She's even made jabs and snide remarks. I don't know what her deal is, but I'm sick of her shit."

We talked a little while longer before Xena left for her prenatal appointment. Ace was picking her up and going to see the midwife they hired in Third Ward.

I packed my things up and headed towards the elevator to go down to the garage. Pushing the button, I felt another presence behind me. I could see Felicity's reflection in the doors of the elevator, so I didn't even bother to turn around.

"I know you can see my standing here," she said. I ignored her. I wasn't going to give her the satisfaction of entertaining whatever bullshit she was on.

"You might as well get used to talking to me since we are working on this assignment together." I slowly turned around and looked at her.

"What are you talking about?"

"Inhibitions. Torrence offered me the job, but the owner, Basil, refused to do the story unless you covered it. Torrence should've sent you an email." The elevator dinged and the doors opened. We walked inside standing at opposite sides of the elevator. I pushed the "G" and the doors closed. Pulling out my phone, Torrence had indeed sent me an email, citing the same thing Felicity had just said about Basil. I smirked and locked my phone, placing it in the back pocket of my pants.

I stared straight ahead, but I could feel Felicity burning a hole in the side of my face. My lips curved up in the corner as a smug look spread across my face.

293

"You have nothing to say?" she asked, annoyed.

"No. We can work on the assignment, but that doesn't mean we have to work together."

"But Torrence said…"

"I don't care what she said. Besides, Basil really just wants to work with me. I can cover the club and give you the details."

The doors opened and I stepped out first, heading to my car. I could hear footsteps behind me and knew she was following me. I hit the locks on my car and pushed the button to start it.

"Why are you being difficult?" she barked. I stopped in my tracks and whirled around on her.

"Difficult? You have been a bitch since you started working here. I have done nothing to you, yet you treat me like shit. I don't want to work with you, I don't want to talk to you, and I don't even want to see you. I will email you the details for your story, and then please act like I don't exist. Don't look at me, don't talk to me, and pretend that I do not exist."

Her mouth opened and closed as if she were going to say something, but then thought better of it. I got in my car and headed to my favorite happy hour spot.

Felicity

Pretend she didn't exist? She didn't know how hard that was going to be for me. Cheyenne was fine as hell, and she was even sexier when she was angry. If she only knew why I treated her the way I did. It was a defense mechanism. I knew she was a lesbian and so was I, but when I first started working here, she was married. She and her ex-wife divorced a year ago, and I heard that she had been dating, well, more so stalked her social media to see that she had.

The thing was, she didn't give me the time of day, but preferred wasting her time on these other women who didn't deserve to breathe the same air. Why did I think that I did? I just knew I could treat her better.

When I picked my jaw up off the ground, I sent a text to my sister, Zariah, to meet me at our usual Wednesday night spot. She responded instantly as I got in my car.

A few minutes later, I pulled up to Los Cucos and parked. I made my way inside when I stopped dead in my tracks as I saw Cheyenne sitting at the bar, enjoying a drink by herself. She had that same look on her face as she did when I saw her less than an hour ago.

"How many?" the hostess asked, drawing my attention away from Cheyenne.

"Two, and can I get that booth over there?" I pointed to a booth that was in the back of the restaurant where Cheyenne would still be in my line of sight. The hostess grabbed two menus and walked that way as I trailed behind her. I sat down on the side facing the bar.

The bartender brought Cheyenne another drink, taking her empty glass away. Zariah walked in less than 30 seconds later, and I waved her over.

"Hey boo," she greeted, bending down to give me a side hug.

"Hey," I responded.

"Uh uh," she said, sitting across from me. "What is with this negative aura? I did not come here to have my spirit tainted."

"Bitch, really?" I said, rolling my eyes.

"Bitch, really," she sassed back. "What's wrong with you?" The waitress came and took our drink and food orders after bringing us chips and salsa.

"I was assigned to cover the opening for Inhibitions."

"Ooooh, that new sex club?" she asked, bouncing in her seat.

"Yes."

"But that doesn't explain the sour puss mood."

"The owner of the club, Basil, is really good friends with Cheyenne and didn't want me to cover it despite Torrence giving me the story."

"Okay…"

"Cheyenne doesn't want to work with me."

"Bitch, I wouldn't either. Hell, as much as you have put her through over the last two years, I'm surprised she hasn't poisoned you."

"Really, Zariah?"

"Yes. I prayed everyday that God would allow her to spare your life and that you would finally tell her that you liked her."

"I don't like her like that, Zariah," I mumbled.

"I have known you all of my life and I am married to your guy best friend."

"You're my sister, of course you've known me all of your life."

"Which is why I know that you like her, and I would even go out so far on a limb as to think you may even love her." I didn't even entertain her outlandish claims. I was not in love with Cheyenne. Was she sexy? Yes. Did I fantasize about eating her pussy from the back? Also, yes. Did I masturbate to thoughts of her screaming my name? Again, yes, but that didn't mean I was in love with her. She was a beautiful woman, and I liked fucking beautiful women. Period.

"Here are your drinks, your food will be out shortly," the waitress said, setting our drinks on the table. Zariah changed the subject to talk about her day as I half listened and stole glances at the bar. I wondered if Cheyenne had meant to meet someone here and they stood her up, which made me ready to whoop someone's ass.

"Are you listening to me?" Zariah asked, making me jump as I averted my eyes back to her. She turned to look where I had been looking then turned around with a sly grin on her face. "No wonder you chose this spot. You wanted to sit there and stare at her without her noticing."

"Shut up," I groaned, noticing Cheyenne getting up from the bar as she placed money to cover her bill.

"Hey, Cheyenne," Zariah called. I kicked her hard under the table.

"Ow! Bitch, what was that for?"

'Why would you call her?" I hissed as Cheyenne made her way over with a scowl on her face.

"Are you following me?" she asked, more so demanded.

"You are not worth my time to follow, Cheyenne, so don't flatter yourself."

"Felicity!" Zariah scolded. I ignored her and took a sip of my drink.

"Ignore my sister. My parents raised us with manners, though I think sometimes she was influenced by wolves."

"She's your sister?" Cheyenne asked in disbelief. I narrowed my eyes at her trying to get what she was playing at. "Tuh. I'm sorry you had to grow up with...that." She looked at me in disgust as Zariah agreed.

"Thank you. Not enough therapy can help with the scars."

"I am sitting right here," I said.

"So you are," Cheyenne retorted. "It was nice seeing you, Zariah."

"Likewise." Cheyenne sauntered off as I glared at Zariah.

"I hate you so much right now." She shrugged her shoulders.

"You still love me though."

Back at home, I showered and got ready for bed. I got my laptop and worked some more on a story I was writing for a book. It was a lesbian office romance. The more I wrote it, the more I realized it was based on me and Cheyenne. Zariah was right about me being in love with Cheyenne, and that's what angered me most. I hated that I was in love with her.

These feelings made me feel like I was losing my damn mind. I first knew I was in love with her on my first day of work. I know, the cliched "love at first sight." She was wearing a zebra print pencil skirt that was so tight, I thought that if she bent over, it would rip, and I'd see that round ass bare. She had on a red cami top that was tucked into the skirt and a zebra print shawl.

Her skin was the color of oak wood and her hair was fire engine red, pulled into a high bun. We stood about the same height, 5'10. I had never seen any woman who looked like her. When she opened her mouth to speak, her sultry voice instantly made me pool between my legs. She was a knockout, and to have a 16-year-old daughter, you would never be able to tell.

At the time, she was married to Dakota Faire, a world renowned chef. A year after that, they got divorced, and I thought it was my time, but Cheyenne made ab post about being "Fuck Bitch Free," stating she was done dating and only wanted pussy. That shit pissed me the fuck off. I was a bitch to her before, but I was even more of a bitch after that. She was out here giving her pussy away to bitches that weren't worthy.

I hated that I still felt that way. So, to harness some of that anger, I got back into writing. This book was almost done, except I was stuck on the ending. Since our story was still going on in real life, I didn't know how to end it.

After a couple of hours, I put my laptop back on my desk, put my bonnet on, and went to sleep.

Cheyenne

"Mom, it's the first day of summer break. Do I really need to be up this early?" Bianca groaned as she rolled over in her bed.

"Any good entrepreneur would be up everyday at the ass crack of dawn no matter if it was summer break or not," I said, opening the curtains to let in the sunlight. She pulled her blanket over her head. Bianca had started a makeup line as a project her sophomore year in freshman year in high school, and it had blown up.

She had made enough money to hire some Black scientists to help with her new skincare line that included face wipes, moisturizers, cleansers, makeup removers, and a host of other things. I helped of course, but it was mostly her. She got some of her friends to work for her and was even able to pay them.

"Jennifer and Sade are already at the warehouse. Give me another hour." I yanked the comforter and sheet off of her.

"Get up."

"Mama wouldn't do me like this."

"Your mama ain't her," I responded. Dakota was my ex-wife and we had Bianca through IVF, Dakota's cousin being the donor. After I birthed her, Dakota wanted another kid, but I told her she would have to carry it. We then found out after numerous miscarriages, she couldn't carry a baby. I suggested a surrogate, but she wasn't having that.

Ultimately, that was one of the reasons we had divorced. The other was that she had been cheating. I was devastated when the bitch came to me "as a woman" and expressed her love for my then wife. I didn't even say anything to Dakota. I had her shit packed and the locks changed the same day. Divorce papers were served to her the next day. The part that hurt the most was she didn't even try to fight it. It was almost as if she didn't care.

Once the divorce was final, I couldn't get out of bed for over a month. Luckily, Torrence understood and allowed me to work from home. I had given Dakota 20 years of my life. We'd been together since we were 16.

When I finally got over it, I was fucking damn near every woman I came into contact with. I was on a downward spiral, and was then forced to go to therapy. I hadn't had sex in almost six months and my body was starving.

"Fine," Bianca said, getting out of the bed and walking into her bathroom, closing the door behind her. I headed downstairs, satisfied that she was now up. I was making coffee and packing my bag for work. Half an hour later, Bianca came down and was dressed to head to her warehouse.

"Thank you, Mom," she said, wrapping her arms around me and placing a kiss on my chest. "Also, Mama called a little while ago, and I'm going to go stay with her for a few weeks."

"I'm glad that you are going to spend time with her." And I was. Despite Dakota and I not communicating, she was very involved in every aspect of Bianca's life. I didn't put her on child support because when it came to financially contributing, Dakota never missed. To say Bianca was spoiled was an understatement.

She grabbed her juice and bagel I had prepared for her to take on the go, and she left the house. For her sixteenth birthday, Dakota and I went half on a car for her. Bianca was a good kid. She made straight A's, ran her own business, and volunteered in the community. She even had a boyfriend who was on the straight and narrow, helping her with her business as well. I met his parents, and they were some really stand up people.

After making sure I had everything, I went to the office to find Felicity sitting in the chair across from my desk.

"What are you doing in here?" I scolded, slamming my things on the desk. "My office door is always locked when I'm not here."

"I asked someone from the custodial staff to let me in. I told them I needed to get something for Torrence and that you'd said it was okay."

"You do know that since that is a lie, this constitutes breaking and entering?"

"Technicalities," she shrugged.

"What do you want?"

"I thought about what you said about just emailing me the details. It didn't sit right with me, so I'll be there at the grand opening."

My eyes saucered and she gave me a smug grin. The thing that irked me the most about Felicity besides how she treated me, is how attractive she was. Her skin was silky smooth and always glowing, inside or outside. I could tell she stayed in the gym. Her curves were always on display, and her almond shaped eyes were smoldering and piercing, the pools of brown so deep I drowned in them.

Today she was wearing slacks with a crop top that went into her pants which I then assumed was a leotard. Her slacks were fitted and tapered down to her ankles. Her breasts sat up nicely, the swell of them on full display. She was literally breathtaking, but her stank ass attitude overshadowed all of that.

"Basil doesn't want to work with you," I reminded.

"Correction, he doesn't want to solely work with me, which means he still wants to work with me, as long as you are working with him, which means you have to work with me." She leaned back and crossed her legs, clasping her manicured nails over her knee. She had on this gorgeous shade of purple lipstick that was perfect against her dark skin.

"Fine. We can meet at the club tomorrow night. The grand opening is at…"

"10, I know." She stood to her full height, her stare burning into me. "I'll see you then." She walked out, and I plopped into my desk chair. Not even a moment later, Torrence came walking in.

"Good morning, Cheyenne," she greeted.

"Good morning, Torrence," I responded, offering her a weak smile.

"I saw your email and ideas for the female masseuse that gives intimate massages. I think it is a great idea, and I want the story by the end of next week. I have booked an appointment for you on Saturday. She will come to your house."

"Oh wow, thanks Torrence," I genuinely smiled, my mood instantly turning around. She nodded and closed the door behind her as she exited. She had no idea how much she had just turned my day around.

Felicity

It was Friday night as Zariah and I were getting ready to head to Inhibitions for the grand opening. I was surprised her husband and my guy best friend, Courtney, allowed her to attend. To say he was possessive over her was an understatement. She explained to him that she wanted to check it out and report back to him to let him know if they should go together. They both were a couple of nasty freaks, and I loved that for them.

"Damn, Felicity, you look sexy as hell," my sister exclaimed. I had on a fire engine red dress that was razorback with spaghetti thin straps. I opted for a thong since it was so tight. I didn't own heels and never would, so I had on some cute open toed slides to show off my fresh pedicure. I chose a black crossbody purse and my jewelry was all black. I pulled my hair into a low bun.

Looking in the mirror once more, I had to agree with Zariah. I looked good as fuck. She wore a flowy black dress that was strapless and tight around the chest and waist. She was a sucker for heels, so she had on some gold, sky-high stilettos. After having my goddaughter and niece, Amariana, you couldn't tell her anything after her body snapped back. She was the definition of a MILF.

The club was only a fifteen minute drive from my condo, and the line was wrapped around the building. I had never in my 37 years of living seen a building built with black bricks, but here it was. The black brick made the club look sexy. It was a two story building that covered a whole city block. The windows were tinted so dark that you couldn't see inside. Out front above the door was a neon red sign with the club name in cursive. It definitely gave sex club vibes.

As we walked up, I noticed Cheyenne before she noticed me. My heart began to race as my eyes roamed up her long legs to where her dress barely covered her ass. I could tell she didn't have on a bra since it was backless. When she turned around, I could see that the top of the dress had a plunging neckline and tied around the back of her neck.

Her makeup and jewelry were minimal, and her hair was bone straight, stopping in the middle of her back. It looked like she had gotten a fresh trim and a blowout.

"If you keep staring at her like that she'll go up in flames," Zariah joked. I elbowed her as she giggled. We walked up the steps to where Cheyenne and Basil were talking.

"You must be Felicity," he said, extending his hand. I shook it and noticed Cheyenne had her eyes on me, checking me out. She didn't even try to be discreet. When our eyes met, I saw a flash of lust before it was replaced with annoyance.

"I would like to thank everyone for coming out," Basil announced, grabbing everyone's attention. "This club has been a dream of mine, and to now see this dream come true, the shit still feels unreal." His bottom set of teeth were shining with a silver grill encrusted with diamonds. If I were into men, he would definitely be my type. He was a looker. "Without further hold up, welcome to Inhibition, where anything goes. Let's have some orgasms!" The crowd went wild as he cut the ribbon. He beckoned for us to follow him inside to give us a quick tour before letting the crowd in.

The walls were lined with purple, velvet padding. LED lights were fastened into the padding to give the place a glow. As we walked and Basil showed us around, we came to the second floor where the private rooms were, which were for VIP guests only. The pricing for these rooms ranged from $1200-$2500 depending on the client and the services they wanted.

We then were shown the showrooms where guests could sit around and watch people fuck on the bed in the middle. The sheets were changed after every session, and there was a mattress pad that was sanitized as well.

Basil was big on sanitation and safe sex, and in order to have sex with a stranger, you had to show proof of a recent STD test taken within the last 14 days. There were bowls of condoms placed around the club, and Plan B's could be retrieved on the way out of the club, free of charge. He had a partnership with Plan B as well as several major condom companies.

I was impressed with all that he had going on here. As we made our way back downstairs, Basil left us to explore on our own. Cheyenne left immediately to do her own thing.

"I'm going to get us something to drink," Zariah shouted over the music. I nodded and walked around as the club became more packed. There was a couple who was already on one of the numerous loveseats, naked and fucking.

I saw two women dancing on the same pole, slobbing each other down every so often. Zariah came back with my drink and said she was going to go call Courtney to come down here. So, I was left by myself.

I took my phone out and jotted down some notes for the article. I would compare notes with Cheyenne later. I took a few sips of my drink and walked towards one of the showrooms where I saw Cheyenne making out with some woman. My stomach tightened as my chest felt like it was constricting.

The woman had her hands on Cheyenne's ass as she moved to sucking on her neck. Taking one of Cheyenne's breasts out, she sucked hard and Cheyenne gasped. A waiter came by with a tray and I set my empty cup on it, never taking my eyes off of Cheyenne. She seemed to really be enjoying herself.

The difference between the magazine side and the newspaper side of BLVCK Co. was that the magazine side was about experiences which Cheyenne was clearly doing. The newspaper side was just a story. That still didn't make me less angry.

I watched on as they pleasured each other, eliciting orgasms as another woman joined in. This woman ate Cheyenne's ass as the other continued her trieste on her pussy. Tears pricked my eyes as my anger roared.

No matter what they did, I couldn't look away. I felt like that love of my life was cheating on me in my face. One a fourth woman joined in, I left. I couldn't take it anymore.

Cheyenne

Friday night was soooo much fun. It was Saturday morning and I was getting ready for my sensual massage after a night of being thoroughly fucked into a coma. My six month abstinence journey was over and I was pleased with myself. After throwing on some boy shorts and a sport's bra, my doorbell rang. The masseuse wasn't due for another half hour, so I was surprised she was here. When I swung the door open, I was instantly pissed.

"What the fuck are oyu doing here?" I asked Felicity. She pushed past me, ignoring my question. I grabbed her wrist and pulled her back. "Bitch, this is my house. You can't just walk in here like you own the fucking place." She snorted a laugh as she yanked her wrist out of my hand. I held the door open expecting her to walk back to the other side of it.

"I'm here for the massage. Torrence should've emailed you." I looked at my phone and sure enough, she had. I was too excited about the club and the massage that I hadn't bothered to check my emails.

"Why did it have to be here though? Why couldn't she come to you?"

"Because we are supposed to be working on this together," she retorted. I slammed the door and walked past her to the kitchen. I grabbed a breakfast burrito and threw it in the microwave. "You have a nice house."

I ignored her as I poured a glass of fresh squeezed orange juice. I put the pitcher back in the fridge as the microwave went off.

"Did your mom not teach you about having manners and offering house guests something to at least drink?" I took a long gulp of my juice and bit into my burrito. It scorched my tongue, but I didn't even give a hint to that. The doorbell rang and I went to answer it.

"Hey, I'm Cecilia. You must be Cheyenne." The woman was hot as hell. She had long cornrows that ended at her waist. Her black biker shorts left nothing to the imagination, as well as her black sports bra.

"Yes, come in." As she walked in, her perfume wrapped me in a chokehold. She smelled so damn good. "You can keep straight to the kitchen."

"I was told it would be you and Felicity," she said.

"Yes, she's in the…" I stopped short as we entered the kitchen. Felicity had made herself comfortable as she was polishing off the rest of my burrito and orange juice.

"Are you fucking kidding me?" I growled, my fists balled tightly at my sides.

"Hey, I'm Felicity," she smiled, standing up and holding out her hand for Cecilia to shake.

"Where should I set up?" Cecilia asked.

"On the back patio is fine," I said through bared teeth. I escorted her to the back door for her to setup as I stormed back into the kitchen. "What the fuck?"

"What? I was hungry and thirsty."

"But you knew I was eating that burrito and drinking that juice."

"Well, I thought it would've been rude to go into the fridge and freezer to get it myself, so, I figured you could just get some more." She smiled and bounced past me to the backyard. I was fuming. I angrily tapped out a text to Xena about what just happened, and she sent me six crying laughing emojis. I sent her a middle finger emoji back and she sent 10 more laughing ones. I threw my phone on the couch and stalked to the backyard.

"Why is there only one bench?" I asked.

"This is a tantric massage session for couples," Cecilia explained.

"Whoa," I said, backing up and holding my hands up. "We aren't a couple. Nowhere close. We just work together."

"Your boss, Torrence, said that since you both were covering the story, that it would make sense to have you try it out and report back to her." The muscles in my jaw tensed and ticked. This was bullshit.

"Fine, whatever." Cecilia had us straddle the bench, facing each other. She said not to touch, but to stare into each other's eyes. Felicity wore a smirk as I glared at her.

"Soften the muscles in your face and sit up tall." Cecilia placed a hand on my chest and one on my back. My gaze didn't soften, but Felicity's did. There was something unreadable in her expression. "This only works if you try."

"We aren't a couple, so how would this work?" I asked, turning to Cecilia.

"Even if you aren't a couple, it can help with how you communicate towards one another. I sense that there is a lot of animosity between you two."

"If you only knew," I mumbled, focusing my attention back on Felicity.

"Now move closer, and Cheyenne, place your thighs on top of Felicity's," Cecilia instructed.

"Excuse me?"

"Stop arguing with her and just do it so we can get this over with," Felicity groaned, clearly annoyed. I sucked my teeth but did as told. The immediate eclectic surge that charged through my body on contact had me sitting up straighter.

"Felicity, press your fingertips into Cheyenne's thighs and apply pressure as you massage them. Cheyenne, you do the same to Felicity." As soon as her fingertips dug in, I was aroused. Not my own damn body betraying me. Bitch, what the fuck?

I did the same to hers and I could smell her arousal. What the fuck was going on? I thought she hated me. How the fuck is she attracted to me?

"Keep looking into each other's eyes," Cecilia guided. She put us in a few different positions and instructed on pressure points and sweet spots. I regretted not wearing any panties when Cecilia had my to lie back with one thigh on Felicity's and the other on her shoulder. Cecilia showed her how to work her hands into my thighs, giving her some oil.

"Uh uh, what is going on here?" We all turned to see Bianca standing in the doorway.

"What are you doing here?" I asked.

"I thought I lived here."

"You know what the hell I mean."

"I forgot my planner, and when I saw the extra cars in the driveway, I just came on back. What kind of freaky stuff are you doing back here, Mom?" She crossed her arms over her chest, sitting into her right hip and grinning.

"Girl, if you don't mind your business and gon on," I snapped.

"Okay," she sang, giving us one more glance over before heading back into the house.

"How old is she?" Cecilia asked.

"Sixteen. She's staying at my ex-wife's house for a few weeks since she's out for summer break."

"She looks just like you," Felicity said. I ignored her. We went back to the massage, and when Felicity was done, it was my turn.

The last position was for us to sit how we were in the beginning, except closer. Chest to chest, forehead to forehead, our lips millimeters apart. This was way too close for comfort. Our arms were wrapped around each other's waist as Cecilia gave us the significance behind this position. When it was over, I couldn't get off the bench fast enough. I walked them both out the front and went back in, letting out a long exhale.

The close proximity to Felicity was making me feel things that confused me, given the back and forth between us. Instead of dwelling on it, I went to the farmer's market.

Felicity

"So, how did the massage go?" Zariah asked as we sat on the patio at her and Courtney's house. It was Sunday evening and we always had dinner together. Our parents moved to Florida after they retired, so it was just me and her in Houston.

"It was oddly good. I got closer to Cheyenne, physically, but she resisted the entire time. I'm not sure how I'm going to write a piece about this when she didn't fully go all in."

"Maybe try talking to her," Courtney offered. "Start with an apology for treating her like shit the past couple years."

I scoffed at his suggestion. The day I apologized to her was the day I would sit on a dick, and that was never. We talked and drank for the next couple of hours, and then I headed home. I had a slight buzz, but I was okay enough to drive the few minutes to my place.

After showering and putting on some shorts and a fitted tank, I went to my home office to attempt to put this article together about the tantric massage.

An email notification popped up from Cheyenne. It was her notes from the club and the massage. The notes from the club did nothing but piss me off, until I read her notes from the massage, which made me madder. I slammed my laptop shut and then went to bed.

It was Friday, the deadline for the piece on the tantric massage. I still didn't have anything that would remotely make this story tantalizing. Cheyenne had been avoiding me all week, so I hadn't been able to ask her. Every time I went to find her, she was busy, or at least she acted like it.

"Do you have that story for me?" Torrence asked as she walked into my office.

"Not yet," I responded.

"It's already nine at night. I need that story by 11:59." Without another word, she walked out. Around this time, there was really no one left in the building.

310

"Fuck this," I said as I got up and stormed out of my office in search of Cheyenne. I was lucky to find her in her office, tapping away on her computer. "I'm over this shit."

She jumped up at my words, clearly not hearing me come in. Leaning back in her chair, she pulled her glasses off her face and laid them on the desk.

"What the hell, Felicity?" she sneered. "Who the fuck do you think you are coming into my office like that?"

"You are not about to fuck up my career because of whatever issue you have with me."

"Me? You've had it out for me since you started working here. I have tried being nice to you, but you act like I'm the bane of your existence. I don't know why you are so fucking miserable and taking it out on me, but fuck you, Felicity."

"Fuck me?" I raged.

"Yes, bitch, did I stutter?" I rushed to her desk as she stood up and came face-to-face with me. "Don't you ever run up on me like I won't dog walk your ass all up and through this building."

"You'd have to get up off the ground first after I knock your ass out." She took a step back and just looked at me.

"I don't get why you have to be such a bitch all the time? Like, who hurt you?"

"Come again?"

"You act like I did something to you like sleep with your best friend. You've been treating me like shit for two years. What the fuck do you want me to do? Kiss your ass?" Fuck this.

"What I want is for you to bend over and place your hands on the desk while I like your pussy from the back, and eat your ass. And I dare you to fucking move before I'm done."

Stunned, Cheyenne gasped at my harsh words. I was done with this shit. I was going to fuck, tonight.

"Are you serious right now?" she whispered.

Cheyenne

311

Instead of answering my question, she moved so fast my head began to spin. My hands found their way to my desk and my skirt was hiked up as she ripped my thong off, her tongue swiping feverishly along my clit.

"Shiiiit," I hissed as she relentlessly drew out two orgasms that had me seeing stars. I could barely stand, but Felicity didn't care.

"Get on the desk," she ordered. I did as I was told, moving some things out of the way. Once I was on all fours, she slid two fingers inside my gushing pussy, the sound of the remnants of my orgasm echoing in the room. Nipping at each ass cheek, she then removed her fingers, sliding them between my ass cheeks, lubricating me before sliding her thumb in.

I was quaking on the desk, feeling myself about to collapse, but I remembered her words, so I didn't dare move, when she buried her face in my ass, her tongue long and searching.

"Agh!" I cried out as she inserted her fingers in my pussy and ran a finger along my sensitive and swollen clit. My body felt like it was going to spontaneously combust with how the sensory overload.

"Felicity, fuck, shit!" I was on the verge of coming and I didn't know what kind of orgasm I was going to have.

"Don't you fucking move," she warned, as if she somehow knew I was about to implode.

"Oh God, I'm coming!" I knew at this point that I was fucked. Having an anal, vaginal, and clitoral orgasm at the same time was unheard of to me, but clearly not to Felicity.

I must've blacked out because when I opened my eyes, I was in her lap, straddling her. I don't know when she took her clothes off, or when mine came off. I looked in her eyes as she massaged my thighs.

Pulling a nipple into her mouth, my hips instantly moved against her. We were clit to clit and with the pressure from her massaging my thighs, this shit was so erotic. I let my head fall back as I applied more pressure grounding harder against her, wanting to increase the friction. I pinched both of her nipples as she swore with mine in her mouth.

312

"Fuck, Cheyenne, I'm about to…" Her hips bucked and her fingers dug into my thighs deeper. I pressed my lips against hers and swallowed her orgasmic screams. I met my release right behind her.

When our orgasms settled, all we could hear was our heavy breathing as she trailed her fingertips along my thighs. We stared at each other, not saying a word, because what we had just done, said it all.

"You were paying attention," she said, referring to the tantric massage. I nodded before cupping her face and biting her lower lip, then sliding my tongue inside her mouth. I pulled back and then got on my knees between her legs. I lifted one thigh and placed the back of that knee on my shoulder as I kneaded the back of her thigh, nibbling on the inside of it.

"Damn, Cheyenne," she whined. I nibbled her pussy lips before sucking her clit into my mouth. Her hips rose off the chair as her back arched. She gripped the sides of my head as if that were to help the impact of her orgasm, but the way my tongue expertly lapped her up, sucked, flicked, and teased, her orgasm came barreling out bringing screams, curses, and writhing hips. Lifting her other thigh, I used my arms to pin her in place until I was done. She gripped the edge of the chair as she pushed her pussy into my face to ride out her orgasm. She tasted like the clear skies on a sunny day.

What did this mean? She began to push my head away and I moved to give her some reprieve.

"How the fuck did you ex-wife let you go, I will never understand," she breathed. I stood up and leaned against my desk, crossing my arms over my chest. "What?"

"What the fuck was this, Felicity? I mean, you go from hating me to giving me a triple orgasm that I didn't even know was possible."

"I've been in love with you since the first time I laid eyes on you. The fact that you were married pissed me off. Then you got divorced and were dating all these women, and that pissed me off even more. I hated loving you. But now, I can't shake this feeling."

313

She stood up and walked towards me, pulling me towards her. "I love you, Cheyenne, and I hope one day, you will feel the same."

The End

Post-Note from the Author

I thank you so much for reading my Hot Stepmom Summer series. I wanted to take my own spin on stepdad season because there are plenty of stepmoms out there. If you enjoyed this book, I'm sure you'll enjoy my other lesbian romance series, Skin So Soft. Also, if you enjoyed this book, I would greatly appreciate it if you left a review on Amazon/Goodreads. That would help me out so much. If you haven't already, check out my entire catalog here: M. L. Sexton's Catalog

Xoxo

M. L. Sexton

Twitter, Instagram, and TikTok @itsjustmoniqua

Made in the USA
Coppell, TX
21 August 2023

20594675R00174